TWISTED TALES OF HALLOWEEN HORROR

THE SISTERHOOD OF THE BLACK PEN

Before you read...

In a time like this, we all want to escape into a world of fiction, but the ones filling these pages may never let you go. They will haunt you long after you've closed the book. Readers, beware.

This anthology contains a collection of truly horrific short stories featuring blood, gore, and explicit content. It is absolutely not intended for those under 18. Adults, please review the following triggers and put this book down or shut off your ereader if it's going to upset you. We're not out to traumatize anyone, just to scare the shit out of them. We're twisted, not terrible.

Trigger List:
Suicide
Drug Use
Mention of Elder Abuse
Mention of Child Abuse

Dedicated to you, our twisted reader. Yes, we see you excitedly rubbing your hands together as you get ready to tuck into some of the most depraved content you will ever find. We see you, and we love you for it.

Table of Contents

BETWIXT AND BETWEEN BILL

DANA MONAGHAN

The Thinning of the Veil

The dead are not always gone. Some of them live on in our memories. Some send us friendly reminders of their love from the other side—a bird, a rainbow, an object with special meaning—something that reminds us of them. Others find themselves stuck in the liminal space between the living and the dead, unable to reach either side. On Halloween, the veil between the two is thinner, allowing those stuck souls an opportunity... but an opportunity for what is the question. If someone left this world angry with you, what gifts would they leave? What message would they bring? It's time to get your jack-o-lanterns ready.

She was a lightning bolt of red-hot anger and hate, parting a sea of black as she pushed her way outside through the crowd of mourners. Nessa was in her kitchen across the street but recognized the storm headed her way from the slamming of the old screen door. It was now four o'clock, and even though the funeral ended at noon, the tiny house had been overrun with a line of visitors waiting to pay their respects and say something nice about the dearly departed, Pastor Bill Nickel, all afternoon. There was no sign of it letting up anytime soon, and it was more than Tempe could take.

"Here she comes," Nessa said to Omen, who padded to the door to greet her. Nessa followed him, grabbing the basket of turnips and two paring knives just in time to hear Tempe yell to a stunned crowd.

"I'm glad he's dead! Why don't you put something honest on his tombstone! Maybe 'Here lies Pastor Bill Steal-A-Nickel?'"

Nessa could not help but chuckle to herself a bit before gaining control of her face to properly address the seriousness of the moment.

"Well, that oughta give the neighbors something to gossip about," she whispered to Omen, as they walked out the front door and onto the old wooden porch.

Omen ignored her and headed down the steps to greet their disgruntled visitor. He liked exactly two people in this world, and now they were both together, on his porch. He wagged his tail.

Nessa settled into a rocking chair and began peeling a turnip, eyeing the purple, black, and red swirling around Tempe. The colors were bright enough to make the fall leaves jealous. Nessa's hands were rough and calloused from cooking and gardening. She'd peeled a number of turnips in her lifetime and made quick work of the task. Tempe plopped onto the top step with a huff, and Omen settled next to her, placing his giant, black head in her lap and sighing as she rubbed his ears.

"Lies, it's all lies. I've been listening to lies all day. He was a useless, good for nothing son of a bitch. If anybody deserves to be dead, it's him, and I'm not sad about it," Tempe raged.

"You're right. Dying don't make a man good, it just makes him dead," interrupted Nessa flatly, as she sat in her old rocking chair, slowly and carefully winding the knife around the first turnip.

Then, she added a bit more sternly, "No use embellishing and running on about him after he's gone but ain't no reason to provoke the dead, either,"

She raised one eyebrow and shot Tempe a warning look, nodding matter-of-factly toward the bright red dress Tempe was wearing. Her knife reached the bottom of the turnip; the peel spiraled and fell onto the planks of the front porch in one long, continuous curl. She looked down and smiled proudly at her good luck. She needed it now more than ever. She knew exactly what kind of man Pastor Bill was. What she had not seen with her own eyes, Tempe told her over the last few months. He was a swindler, pacing back and forth in front of the pulpit each week, whipping the congregation into the type of frenzy that filled collection plates—and his own pockets. He was also a cheater and brazen enough not to try too hard to conceal the sideways glances between him and several women in the congregation. His arrogance grew more insufferable each time he lied his way out of trouble and got away with it. Tempe tried to tell her mother several times, but her mother either did not or could not believe her. At home with Tempe, he was all fire and brimstone, laying down the law and judgment from the first day he started dating her mother. He was everything her father hadn't been when he was alive, and Tempe hated him for it. She learned to hide what she was—tarot cards and pendulums stuffed in a shoebox at the back of her closet. She tried to hide the bruises too, but Nessa saw them anyway.

"Now you sound like Mama!" said Tempe, closing her eyes and sighing loudly, then mimicking her mother, "'Don't speak ill of the dead, Tempe. Don't speak ill of the dead.' All there is to say about that man is ill."

She immediately felt a twinge of regret as she looked down at her red dress and ran her hands over it to smooth the wrinkles. She knew how embarrassed her mother would be, but she could not bear to wear the black one her mother laid on the bed for her this morning. She would not mourn this man. Her mother may have loved him, but she never did, and she could not sit and listen to the lies people were telling about him in her own house. As far as she was concerned, his death was something to celebrate, and she dressed for the occasion, not caring who was offended. She turned her head away from Nessa, hoping the tears in her eyes would go unnoticed. Nessa and Omen had been her refuge for the last year and a half when her mom married Pastor Bill and they moved in across the street. Nessa was the grandmother she did not otherwise have, and unlike her mother, Nessa saw what Bill really was. Of course, Nessa noticed the tears. She noticed everything, but she always chose carefully when to mention it, knowing Tempe viewed her tears as a weakness she needed to hide from the rest of the world. She hoped Tempe would one day see how strong she really was but for now she respected the boundary and changed the subject.

"How 'bout you don't just sit there doing nothing and put yourself to work? The little ones will be here soon enough asking for their candy," she said, handing Tempe a turnip and a knife as she began to remove a large chunk from the center of hers.

"Do you think anybody will come this year? Mama won't let me put up any decorations. She says it would be disrespectful, and besides, Bill said Halloween was the devil's holiday. We'll still probably have a line of mourners at our house even then."

"I expect the trick-or-treaters will leave your mama and your house alone out of respect, but the thing about the living is, once they've paid their respects, they go on living. So, yes, I think the rest of us will still have our fair share of little ghosts and goblins this evening, and I'd like to be ready for them."

Tempe snorted. "Yes, let's respect the no good, lying, stealing, cheating pastor, by all means."

Nessa allowed a few moments of silence to pass between them and then asked, "Do you know why I use turnips instead of pumpkins at Halloween, Tempe?"

"Cause you live on the poor side of the mountain," answered Tempe, grinning at the chance to throw one of Nessa's favorite phrases back at her.

"Too clever for your own good, girl," chuckled Nessa, feigning irritation at the jab. "But no, that's not it. Turnips were the original jack-o-lanterns, long before anyone ever carved a pumpkin," Nessa replied and held Tempe's gaze for a moment longer than comfortable, attempting to add importance to her words and hoping Tempe would hear the wisdom within them.

"I assume when your mama and Pastor Bill make you go up the street to church, you learn about Heaven and Hell?" she asked.

"Sure, that's kinda the point of going, isn't it?" Tempe nodded irritably, rolling her eyes. "Scare us all into being good so we don't go to Hell while the pastor cheats, lies, and robs you blind as he pretends to be a man of God."

"Well, the thing is, those aren't the only options. Some folks ain't good enough for Heaven and too bad even for Hell. It's the reason we don't need to go poking at the dead, Tempe. I'm not asking you to lie, and I agree it's ridiculous the way folks try to turn a bad person into a good one just because they died, but you don't need to go out of your way to anger 'em, either.

"What are you saying?" Tempe asked, swallowing hard as a chill began to creep slowly up her spine.

"I'm saying some folks end up stuck, more betwixt and between than in one place for eternity." Again, she stared at Tempe for a moment as if she was watching to see the words sink into the girl's brain. "They can come back, Tempe. Dead isn't always gone," she finished solemnly, seeing the startle that her words were beginning to cause.

"He's dead, though. He can't come back, right? Nessa, please tell me he can't come back. I'm finally free of him. Tell me, Nessa. What do you mean exactly? What are you saying?" she implored, her voice breaking slightly.

Nessa sighed and decided it was best to start at the beginning.

"As I said, the original jack-o-lanterns were turnips, and it all started with a man just like Pastor Bill, except he was called Stingy Jack, an absolutely useless human being, just like Bill."

"I thought we weren't supposed to speak ill of the dead," interrupted Tempe, fifteen-year-old snark dripping from every word.

"This is you and me talking. I'm not out there screaming insults to crowds of people at a man's funeral. There's a difference," Nessa snapped, losing her patience.

This time the anger was real enough to silence Tempe for a moment. Nessa continued her story, hoping the girl was going to understand. Nessa needed to make her understand if she was going to stand a chance at keeping her safe. While she appreciated Tempe's spirit, she knew it only put her in more danger than she already was.

"Everybody thinks if you don't get into Heaven, that automatically means you're going to Hell, but as I already told you, some folks are too messy, even for the devil."

Tempe paid attention this time.

"I learned about Stingy Jack from my Irish grandmother. He was one of 'em that the devil decided was just too much trouble for Hell, and I'm afraid Bill might be, too." She paused just a moment to assess how seriously Tempe was following along with her story. Satisfied, she continued. "Like Bill, Stingy Jack was a liar, cheat, and swindler, so much so he caught the devil's attention. But when the devil came to collect his soul, Stingy Jack tricked the devil into turning himself into a coin. Jack trapped him in the coin and made a deal with the devil that the Devil wouldn't collect his soul for ten years. Well, in ten years, the devil came calling again. This time, Jack trapped him in a tree and made the devil agree to never take his soul.

The devil kept the promise he made for his freedom, and Jack went to Heaven, only Heaven didn't want him, either, no surprise there. So, Jack was stuck and doomed to roam the earth. The devil gave him one ember of coal that he put in a turnip head to light his way. Folks started carving faces in turnips and putting them out on Halloween night to keep Jack and any other evil spirits away from their homes. Once the Irish moved to the U.S., they started using pumpkins."

Nessa ended her story and waited to see how Tempe would respond.

The girl looked like she had actually seen Bill's ghost as she began to fully understand the reason Nessa told her the story of Stingy Jack. She remembered how he flew into fits of rage every time she tried to show her mother what he really was. Everything he had came from his carefully crafted reputation as a man of God, and it dawned on Tempe that even in death, he may still be angry enough to want to keep her silent. "Oh my God, you think he's coming back for me, don't you?"

Nessa moved to the steps on the other side of Omen, placing her arm around Tempe, looking directly into her eyes. "I don't know for sure, Tempe, but I know what he was, and today of all days, when the veil is a bit thinner than normal, I think we should be prepared. I'm concerned you aren't safe and don't want you making yourself more of a target than you already are. You understand me now?"

Tempe took the knife, angrily jamming it into the center of a turnip, removing a large chunk from the middle to make room for a candle.

"He threatened me the day he died, right there in the front yard," she said, pointing across the street. "He said it didn't matter who saw, that they'd still believe him over me. I caught him stealing money at the church. I actually saw it this time and told him I was going to tell. You know he's been stealing from me and Mama, taking money out of her stash of savings and convincing her to buy him things while she does without. She never believes me and thinks his intentions are good, but this time, I told him I would tell everyone and I wouldn't stop telling until somebody believed me. But the worst part... the worst part was he wasn't scared. He walked right up to me, put his hand around my face, and squeezed as hard as he could, forcing me to look him in the eye. He said I would never tell a soul because the dead don't talk. He said he would kill me before I'd have a chance to say a word. He's been trying to convince Mama to send me away, but this time, he wanted me gone for good. It was the last time I saw him, alive anyway. It was the day we went looking for wild carrots, and you made a stew, do you remember?" she asked, searching Nessa's face.

Nessa did remember, but she was quiet for a moment, noticing how Tempe's hand rubbed a spot underneath her right eye where a thumb sized bruise had been just a few days before. Nessa knew men like Pastor Bill. She knew he was the kind of man that would kill Tempe just to keep her quiet. She'd watched the argument from the kitchen window and knew she was out of time. A man like Bill wouldn't allow a teenage girl to stand in his way for long.

"I do," Nessa eventually said, gently pulling Tempe closer and kissing the top of her head. "What a lovely dinner we had, just you and me," she finished.

"I still don't understand why you had me take some back to Bill," Tempe said, pulling away from Nessa, irritated by the memory.

"I promised your mama I'd take care of both of you, and that's what I did. You remember that, girl. I took care of both of you, just like I promised," she said, patting Tempe's back.

"It's me he'd want revenge on. I'm the reason he'd come back. I'm the one that knows what a liar he is, the one that could ruin his reputation, the one he'd want gone even now," said Tempe.

"Everything is going to be okay. We are going to make sure he stays gone, you understand me?" Nessa reached behind her and grabbed the basket of freshly peeled and carved turnips, adding Tempe's to the pile and handing the basket to her.

Tempe looked down at the pale flesh of the turnips with their grotesquely carved faces. They looked like shrunken heads. "Ew," she said, "I think I know the real reason everyone switched to pumpkins."

Nessa laughed. "Pretty's not their job. Keeping you safe is. Take these back home, finish carving a face in yours. Place two on the stoop outside the front door, one in each of the windows of your room and one somewhere else in your room. Put them in a place where they can burn without setting the whole house on fire. You can light them around midnight, long after your mama's gone to bed, and leave them burning until first light, got it?"

"Don't you want to keep some?" asked Tempe "He wasn't too fond of you, either, you know. Said you were a woman of the devil," she finished, kissing Omen on the head before standing to leave.

"Nope, won't be needing them. Besides, if he's right, I got nothing to worry about then, right? It's you I'm worried about. And don't go 'round saying bad things about him right now, even if he deserves it. I'm not asking you to lie, just keep quiet for now, you hear me?"

"Okay," Tempe said and hugged Nessa goodbye for the evening. She gave Omen one last pat on the head, and the dog stood from his nap to watch her walk away.

"It's okay, O," Nessa said, patting the dog on the head. "I'm going to make sure she's okay tonight. Then, it'll be your job after that." Nessa gathered her knives and went inside to get the bones ready.

She stoked the fire and chose three bones from the small black bag in her pantry, lining them up on the mantle above the fireplace. She made herself a cup of tea and slid a sprig of yarrow in her pocket as she took out a pen and wrote one last note. She spent the rest of the evening gleefully doling out candy to the neighborhood children. At midnight, she turned off the porch light, left the envelope on the top step, smiling when she saw the jack-o-lanterns glowing across the street. She turned to Omen, letting out a sigh of relief.

"We'll sleep down here by the fire tonight. Not much time left." She kissed him on the head. "Until next time, my dear friend. You two take care of each other. Now, we should get some rest before our work really begins."

Omen barked and settled by the fire at Nessa's feet as she sank into her favorite and comfiest chair. Before long, they were both sleeping deeply.

Tap... Tap... Tap.

Nessa heard the noise, even in her dream, and had the sensation she was floating toward the wall, believing the sound was coming from inside it, though she could not find it.

Tap... Tap... Tap.

Again, it sounded as if there was something *in* the wall, something that wanted out. She ran her hand over it thinking she'd find a hole, a way to find what was making the noise and stop it.

Tap... Tap... Tap.

"NESSA!" a man's voice said loudly, like an explosion inside her head.

Omen barked, and Nessa startled awake, wondering what was making the sound and who—or what—had said her name. Still groggy enough to be uncertain whether it was all a dream or if the sound and voice were real and had just found their way into her head, she turned to look toward the front door and saw the shadow of a tiny bird pecking at the window next to it.

"You have a message for me?" she asked. "I'm not surprised. You tell him I'm not scared. Now go! Shoo!"

The bird flew away, and the porch light flickered on while the rest of the lights inside the house went dark. The house was eerily silent with the exception of the low flame still burning and crackling in the fireplace, casting odd shadows that danced along the walls and ceiling. Nessa knew enough to recognize an invitation from the other side when she encountered it.

As she stood and carefully walked toward the door, Omen followed close at her heels. Nessa opened the door slowly and stepped out onto the porch. There was a rumble of thunder in the distance, and even in the night, she could see pitch black clouds rolling in as the wind picked up. She shuddered and pulled the wrap she'd been dozing in tighter around her shoulders, knowing it could protect her from the cold but little else. It was harder to breathe, as if a shadow was closing in around her, smothering her ever so slowly. Omen walked in front of Nessa and stood with his back to her, snout in the air, sniffing out what kind of trouble was headed their way.

A thunder clap rattled the foundations of the entire house and then the wind settled, and all was completely silent and still. Omen growled, and every rocking chair on the porch began to rock slowly, back and forth in unison, despite the lack of a breeze. Nessa looked out into the night, knowing Omen could see more than she ever would. She knew if he was concerned, there was something to fear. Without turning her eyes from the darkness she inched her hand behind her, slowly feeling for the doorknob, as if any sudden movement may startle whatever was there, but it didn't budge. It was locked. She turned to face the door, her breath even more staggered than before, and pulled the key from her pocket. She put it in the lock, expecting it to open, but it held firm. She jingled the key around in the lock a few times, thinking maybe it was stuck, pushing with all of her might and glancing around her nervously. Omen's low growl turned into a defiant bark, and he kept his back turned to her, facing whatever danger was in front of them. As she glanced over her shoulder, she noticed the hackles standing up on the back of his neck and took note of the prickly sensation on hers as well.

After a few moments, Nessa gave up on the door, turned slowly toward Omen and the darkness again. She spoke calmly into it, "Pastor Bill Nickel, is that you?"

Behind her she heard the deadbolt on the door unlock on its own with a click that made her heart skip a beat. She turned and pushed the door open cautiously, her pulse racing, not sure what was waiting for her on the other side. The old farmhouse had always been her refuge, but tonight, something beyond her world seemed to be in charge of it. Omen whined, his big eyes imploring her not to go in, but he followed her when she did. All of the lights were out except for the fire that was beginning to lose its rage. She walked toward it, grabbed the iron stoker, and gave the log a poke. The flame leaped higher and cast a bit more light across the room. On her left side, Nessa thought she saw a slight flicker—a twitch, a shift, maybe nothing, yet something in the darkness. She kept her eyes on the fire.

"I know you are here," she said, trying to steady her voice, "but I won't let you stay. I can't. You have to leave that girl alone."

A chair from the kitchen table scraped across the hardwood floor and banged into the wall. Nessa turned her back to the fire and faced the noise.

"It's time for you to go," she said defiantly, sounding more confident than she was.

Suddenly, a knife came flying from the kitchen counter, whooshed by her head, and stuck in the mantle, close enough she could feel the handle of it against her temple. She dared not move. Nessa gulped, truly terrified now but not willing to give Bill's ghost the satisfaction of hearing it in her voice.

"Nice try." She laughed, her voice breaking more obviously than she'd hoped. "But you will have to do better than that."

Without warning, the darkness plunged toward her, enveloping her in pitch black smoke as another dark cloud formed in front of her face. It began to take a familiar shape, an angular jaw, a long nose with a slight bump that somehow made him more handsome when he was alive, and a mouth that always twisted into a slight sneer—unmistakably Bill. Shadowy arms lunged out of the mantle behind her and wrapped themselves around her neck. It was the coldest cold she had ever felt, like falling into a void, an emptiness where humanity had once been but no longer was. It shifted and moved closer to her. She recognized even more of the outlines of Pastor Bill's face even though it was so distorted. It reminded her of one of the carved turnip heads without the light inside—a poor, deformed approximation of humanity long gone. The mouth opened, and a whoosh of air knocked Nessa back against the mantle hard enough to make her dizzy. Omen lunged at the shadow, fangs bared, and bit where Bill's leg used to be. After a moment of resistance, Omen stumbled back, swallowing some of the ethereal substance. The distorted face looked shocked, and the arms around Nessa's neck loosened slightly.

Nessa choked out a laugh. "Didn't expect that, did you? You see, Omen's not an ordinary dog. He's a hellhound, and this hellhound and I are going to send you back where you belong. You are my responsibility now, and I'm taking you back to Hell whether the devil likes it or not!"

The arms around her neck regained their grip and began to squeeze tighter than before. She felt the last gasps of breath leaving her body, and her eyes began to dim as she fumbled for the bones on the mantle. She knew it was now or never, but she struggled for the words.

"Now," she forced a hoarse whisper from the depths of her throat but didn't have enough oxygen to finish the rest. She twisted sideways, trying to free herself from the shadowy grasp.

Omen slung his massive head from side to side as he dug his teeth into the shadow once again, until it moved just enough for Nessa to take one long deep breath while she threw the three bones into the fire and finished the spell.

"Back to the devil with you! Push, Omen!" Omen did, and Nessa flung herself back toward the fire. Omen rammed his head into the shadow, and Nessa and Pastor Bill's ghost fell into the flames. The fire flared wildly, singeing the tip of Omen's snout and blackening the mantle's edges, before dying down to nothing. Then, it was gone, and with it, Pastor Bill and Nessa.

When Tempe woke the next morning, the candles in all of the turnips were burned completely down, and no flame was left. She walked outside to see Omen lying on the front steps across the street. The day seemed brighter, lighter somehow, as if a weight had been lifted. She was relieved to have made it through the night without any sign of Pastor Bill, glad Nessa had either been wrong or the jack-o-lanterns did their job. She ran over to Omen, calling for Nessa. She stopped when she reached him and saw the envelope Nessa left on the first step the night before. It had her name on it. She opened it and began to read.

Dear Tempe,

It's all yours now. You and Omen take care of each other. He's a special dog with special gifts that I'm sure you will learn about when the time is right. Bill's gone for good. You don't have to worry about him anymore. I told you I promised your mama I would take care of both of you, and that's what I did. There are secrets in every kitchen, Tempe, but more in mine than most. I expect you will learn all of them, but I've left a few extra things in the envelope to help you understand and in case you ever find yourself in need of them again. There always seems to be a Bill or a Jack along life's way, so it's good to be prepared, just in case. My land is marked off by five railroad stakes, one at each corner and one more in the middle. Do not pull them out. Leave the yarrow growing in the front yard and slip some in your pocket anytime you need a little extra protection. Put your jack-o-lanterns out every Halloween. He's gone now as I said, but you never know what else may be lurking in the darkness, neither here nor there, especially on Halloween night. Don't go provoking the dead. I hope you hear me this time, girl. I'm short on time now, so this will have to do.

To TEMPEST ABIGAIL BALLARD, I leave my old farmhouse, the land it sits on, all of its contents, and my very good dog Omen.

All my love forever,
Nessa Oleander Adler

Tempe poured out the rest of the contents of the envelope into her hand and studied each one individually. On a small scrap of paper in Nessa's handwriting, there was a recipe for Wild Carrot Stew and two small clear envelopes with white flowers inside. Inside each envelope was a small note listing the differences and properties for each flower. One envelope was labeled "Wild Carrot – Queen Anne's Lace" and the other was labeled "Hemlock (notice the purple-reddish splotches)." Tempe finally understood, and with tears now streaming down her face, she read through the recipe for Pastor Bill's last meal, folded it carefully, and placed it in her pocket for safekeeping.

About the Author

Dana Monaghan writes short stories while regularly editing and re-drafting her first full length novel which asks the question 'What happens when a witch returns from the dead to confront a criminal justice system founded on the Puritan principles that led to her murder?' Dana favors ghost stories and supernatural themes wrapped in family history and sprinkled with herbalism. If you enjoy her writing, check out her short story, A Perfect Day at the Beach, from The Future of Us anthology by Moms Who Write. She's also currently working on a holiday romance with a dark, supernatural twist. She lives in Charlotte, NC with her eleven year old son, husband, two hellhounds, four hermit crabs, a few fish and a frog. She enjoys reading, gardening, cooking and being out in nature. For updates on her novel and short stories, follow her on Instagram and TikTok @danamonaghanwrites

MY DARLING GIRL

GLORIA LUCAS

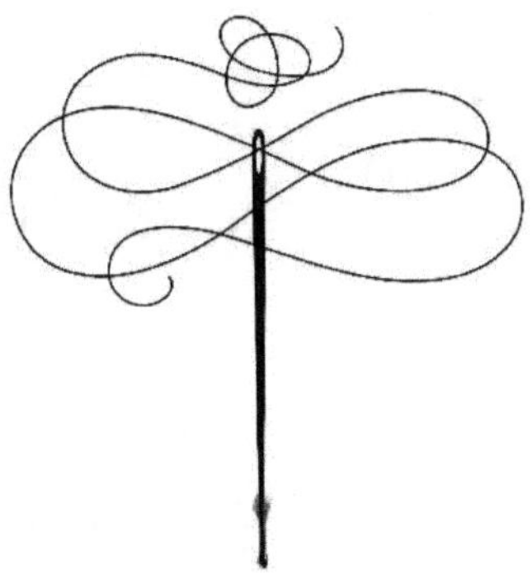

"Happy is the one who seizes your infants and dashes them against the rocks." - Psalm 137:9

The irony of it all is that I always wanted to be a mother. When I was a child, I had a collection of dolls, my little darlings made of cloth or wood or porcelain. Every night, I had to tuck them into their proper places before I was able to sleep myself.

My favorite was—is—a little raggedy thing I call Baba. Her construction is the plainest, simply cloth and stuffing. By the end of my childhood, she was thread-bare and stained. But even when womanhood arrived and softened the sharp lines of my body, when I knew I had grown too old for childish things, I held onto Baba.

When my end comes, I want her laid to rest with me. Maybe placed in my hand or tucked close to my side. I've heard some cultures bury their dead with the important artifacts of their lifetime, a way to send them into the afterlife with what they loved. I don't believe in such foolishness, but still, it would be nice to hold a familiar hand.

I'm sorry. I'm getting ahead of myself. Let me begin again...

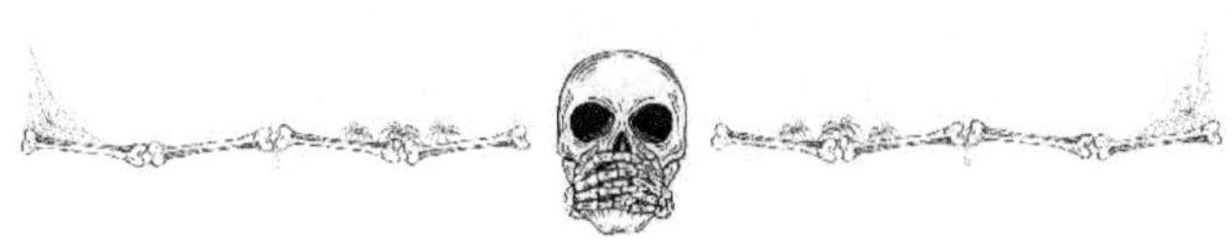

The woman awoke with a start. Her honey brown eyes darted across the ceiling as she listened to the sounds of the house. It groaned once, the natural sigh of a timeworn structure. Sometimes, she felt as if she understood the old building and all that frustrated it—the drafty windows, the persistent vines that loved creeping along its side, but most importantly, the solid foundation that would keep it upright for centuries to come. Sometimes, she would press her palm on one of the supportive walls and mutter her sympathies. Even as weary as it could look, the house was built to last.

What a burden.

The woman turned her attention to the window. A small gap between the pale yellow curtains revealed the prison gray hue of an overcast sky. Once again, she wondered who had chosen the décor. Someone had gone through the trouble of selecting the everyday items that littered its interior: blinds, side tables, curtains, pillows. She imagined there had been a day when that person had sorted through the variety of colors and styles, stopped, then triumphantly pointed to the set now hanging limply across from her. Had they been a warm cream once upon a time? Or had they always been the sad, piss color they were now?

Not that she'd had a choice in the matter. The house had been chosen for her and came mostly furnished, ready for its next inhabitants. Plus, the color of the curtains was inconsequential. They blocked the sun. And when one has a child with skin so fragile it blisters within minutes of sun exposure, color was irrelevant.

With a sigh, she slid the covers aside and sat up, testing the floorboards with her feet. The chill of the floor sent a shiver through her, as if Death had run its tongue up the length of her spine. She tilted her head, straining her hearing. Nothing stirred.

Maybe it could all end today...

Gabby looked herself over in the full-length mirror leaning against her bedroom wall. The mirror had been an impulse purchase during a visit to a traveling bazaar. The frame was a monster of a thing, a thick slab of wood carved into intricate scenes and, unfortunately, painted a gaudy, gold color. She had to beg a friend to help her pick it up and maneuver it up the unfriendly concrete stairs to her second-level apartment. It barely fit, and the pair was left panting and sweating afterwards, but she was thrilled. Eventually, she planned to remove the paint and stain the wood, then somehow mount it. But between work and caring for her aging parents, it was one more thing that kept getting bumped down her never-ending to-do list.

She smoothed her auburn hair back into a neat bun and gave her reflection a practiced smile. It was Monday morning, and she was meeting a new client. She worked as a home-health aide at Compassion HomeHealth. Most of her patients were elderly. She helped them with everything from daily living tasks to dispensing medications.

Less often, she helped with minor chores. Though, never in the beginning. Some adult children had a terrible habit of assuming they had hired a nurse, nanny, and maid all for the price of one. When the distinction wasn't clear, she was forced to set her foot down. Donald, her manager, had recently received a couple of tongue-lashes behind the young nurse with a smart mouth.

"I wasn't smart," she had replied. "I was blunt. I'm not washing windows and folding laundry. Especially since Mr. Edgar already likes to cross the line with his bath time requests. You know his daughter wanted me to fold some of *her* clothes since it was in the same load Mr. Edgar's were?"

Donald pressed his thin lips together, the act making it appear as if his mouth had disappeared. Mottled red coloring crept up his neck and cheeks like it always did when he was flustered. Gabby knew his job wasn't solely to manage the nurses and their schedules, it was to keep their clients happy. At the same time, he earned more than she did and wasn't the one at the other end of Mr. Edgar's grin when he needed help undressing. The silence ballooned between them. Finally, the redness dissipated and he sighed. "Fine. I'll swap you out with Paula. She has an opening in her schedule."

Gabby flashed him a grateful smile, but he saw the concern behind it.

"Don't worry. We have more families applying. You'll get a re-placement assignment soon."

Two weeks later, he called, his tone distracted and rushed. A single mother was seeking a home-health aide for her daughter, aged ten.

Gabby's eyes widened, and she fingered the coiled cord of her house phone. Compassion HomeHealth accepted both adult and pe-diatric patients. However, she had expressed an unwritten request to be assigned to adult patients only. This was adopted after her last pe-diatric assignment. She had grown extremely fond of the little boy. When the need for hospice arrived, she gave the transition profes-sionally and almost quit. With the support of her coworkers, she took a short vacation and came back, fresh faced and ready to continue her work... with adults.

As if sensing her rising anxiety, Donald reassured her that though the child needed medical support, her health conditions, al-beit chronic, would not prevent her from reaching old age. The little girl had a metabolic disorder and a rare skin condition. Her father was out of the picture, and therefore, her mother was reaching out for support in feeding her daughter and tending to any skin issues that arose. Being a full-time caregiver was a challenging role. Add the lack of a partner and no family in the area...

"I understand," Gabby said.

"Any questions?"

"Um, well, I'm curious as to why you're calling me on a Satur-day instead of just waiting until I come into the office on Monday."

"Because this Monday is your start day and it's quite a drive. Plus, the office is located in the opposite direction. Do you have a pen ready for the address?"

Gabby opened her mouth, ready to argue against accepting the family, but surprised herself by saying yes. She wrote down the address, then spent the rest of the weekend pretending she felt comfortable with the assignment.

On Monday, she woke up before her alarm, her nerves on fire. "I can't believe I'm doing this again."

After a shower and a simple breakfast of coffee and toast, she stared at her reflection in the bedroom mirror, wondering if she had made the right choice. However, the alternative was to decline an assignment right after requesting to be replaced from another. Even as good of a worker as she was, her work evaluation would look rough, and she was hoping for a raise after her annual review.

She sighed and squared her shoulders. *You can do this,* she thought. *Plus, if you don't do this, who else would be willing to drive that far?*

Her patient's home was located about an hour away in a rural area that could barely be called a town. With that in mind, she collected her work bag and made her way to the car. After sliding into the driver's seat, she pulled out the map with directions scribbled on the side, pushed her favorite cassette in to play, and put the car in reverse.

The woman made her way carefully down the wooden stairs, wrapping her nightgown around herself. Autumn was upon them, but the days were persistently hot and muggy, as if the season was protesting the advances of winter. Even so, the house felt impossibly cold, as if it knew what was housed within it.

She shivered as she descended to the first floor and subconsciously fingered the scar on her wrist. After peeking into the living room and then the dining room, she found the girl sleeping at the desk on the southeast corner of the library. *Her* little girl. The thought weighed on her chest like a stone.

The room was fully stocked with books and plenty of seating, belying the isolation of the house. The girl's head laid delicately on her arms, her raven black hair spilling over her arms and back. A few books were piled precariously around her.

The woman smiled gently, maybe even maternally. From this vantage point, the girl looked slight and fragile.

After a breath, the woman tiptoed to the kitchen. She bee-lined to the counter that held the kitchen knives and pulled one from its slot. This particular knife was used to pierce and slice through tough, sinewy pieces of meat. It was a delightful tool, and she enjoyed using it to prepare their meals.

She studied the blade a moment, then made her way back to the library, stopping when she stood directly behind the girl. In one swift motion, she swung her right arm above her head. If she was lucky, she'd bring it down hard and precisely, ensuring no suffering was caused to the dozing creature.

The little girl stirred, and the woman froze. The girl's eyes fluttered open, and she sat up, shifting her body to look at her mother. The woman's smile was a flash of teeth. She lowered the knife to her side. "We have company coming. Go get yourself ready. We want to make a good first impression, don't we, Antonia?"

The girl glanced at the knife before meeting her mother's eyes. The woman cocked her head toward the stairwell. "Go on."

Antonia nodded and left the library, her steps a whisper on the hardwood floor.

Gabby pulled onto the right shoulder of the county road and cursed the map. For a brief moment, she considered abandoning the attempt to find the house. She'd go home, call Donald, tell him she was unable to find the house with his worthless directions, and would try again tomorrow. Instead, she closed her eyes, uttered a quick prayer for patience, and noticed an aging gas station not far off in the distance.

"Oh, thank goodness," she breathed and placed her car back into drive. After topping off the gas tank, she entered the tiny shop, hoping the employee on duty would know the area well enough to help her with the directions.

A broken bell made a dull *tink* when she pushed the door open, but the thin, balding man standing behind the counter paid her no mind. He continued to leaf through a newspaper until she approached him to pay for a bottled drink and pack of peanuts.

She flashed him a smile. "Hi. Sorry to bother you, but I'm a bit lost. I have a map with directions, but I'm having trouble finding Booker Lane. I need to get to the Booker Estate."

"Yer lookin' t'see Ms. Harris, then?"

Gabby frowned. "Maybe. Yes? I can't remember her last name now. I have it written down somewhere, but I do know that I'm supposed to go to the Booker Estate."

"Yup. That's Ms. Harris. I think Booker is the name of her ex-husband or somethin'. I dunno. Don't really care for gossip, y'know?" He scratched the side of his neck. "Anyway, she comes in here e'ry now and ag'in. Buys a couple a' chocolate bars, then leaves. A bit of a recluse, that one."

"Oh," Gabby said. "I see. Well, I feel I must be passing the turn and not seeing it. Not sure if you can help me figure out where it is?"

"Aw, yup, pro'ly. You can hardly see Booker Lane from the road. But if yer payin' attention, you'll see it to yer right. I think there used to be a sign, but it was removed or knocked down." He keyed in her purchase. "That'll be $1.79."

Gabby let out a sigh of relief and fished a couple of dollars from her billfold. "Thanks so much. I almost gave up the search."

The attendant's smile revealed a missing tooth. "Maybe that's a sign."

She accepted the change and laughed awkwardly. "Yeah, maybe. Well, I'll be on my way, then."

His eyes followed her out of the store.

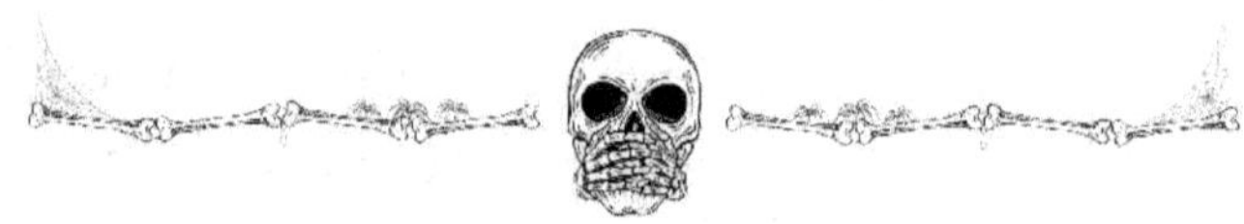

Motherhood is a gift. But it's also a yoke. Even after years dreaming of a child, I was woefully unprepared. In those dreams, my child was healthy. That's what everyone wishes for, right? That's what they say—I don't care if it's a boy or girl. So long as it's healthy.

Well, I can attest that that isn't quite correct. If your child is different, you'll still fall in love. You'll still care. You'll move mountains for them... Until the day those mountains become too heavy. It pains me to admit this, but sometimes, when the weight of them presses so heavily on my chest I can barely breathe, when they weigh me down so much I can barely move, I want nothing more than to let go and let them fall, regardless of the consequences.

I need help. I needed help. And like an angel... you came...

Gabby parked near the front of the house, uncertain of the best place to leave her vehicle. The dirt road had eventually made way to a paved one, and she followed it through an open iron gate. She stepped out of her car and whistled, impressed. The brick-faced house towered over her, cords of ivy creeping up the exterior.

A stiff breeze ruffled her hair, and she smiled, enjoying the feel of the moving air, even if it was thick with humidity. Winter couldn't arrive quickly enough. The trees surrounding the property waved their branches as if in agreement.

Beads of sweat began to form around her temple and on her back, but she continued to look around. She took in the lack of neighbors, the driveway that ambled its way to the solitary dirt road leading to the county highway. There was something odd about the place, though she couldn't put her finger on exactly what. The wind blew again, this time feeling cooler because of the perspiration on her skin and she shivered.

She walked to the front door, the porch stairs complaining under each step. She knocked, looking around again as she waited for someone to answer. Suddenly, she realized it was the silence that was out of place. There were no chittering squirrels bounding through the trees, no buzzing insects cutting through the air, no intermittent singing from the local birds. The porch hid her from the sun but also blocked the breeze, making it feel as if the entire world was holding its breath. She shivered again, but this time it wasn't from the feeling of the wind against her sweaty skin.

The front door swung open and broke her out of her thoughts. A pretty young woman stood at the entrance, smiling in greeting. Gabby imagined she was anywhere between sixteen and twenty. Her first thought was that the young woman was the oldest child of the single mother, even if Donald had implied that it was a family of two. Her second thought was surprise at how pale the young woman appeared, as if she rarely ventured out into the light of day.

Gabby opened her mouth to ask to speak with her mother, but the young woman spoke first. "You finally made it! You cannot imagine how pleased I am to see that your company was able to honor such a last-minute request. My daughter is still in her room getting dressed, but I can introduce you to her in a moment."

"Oh. Adelaide?" Gabby felt her face flush. The young woman looked more like a high school student than a mother with a ten-year-old. "I mean, Ms. Harris? I'm so, so sorry for being late. I got a little lost—"

"Call me Ada. Come in, come in." She opened the door wider and stepped aside.

"Thank you, Ms.—I mean, Ada. I'm Gabby." She looked around the entryway. "This is a beautiful home."

The interior was dim, illuminated only by the natural light spilling in through the gaps made by the curtains hung on the surrounding windows. Gabby felt as if it would be natural to assume cobwebs occupied the corners of the room, perhaps even stretched across the chandelier mounted in the middle of the hallway. However, when she looked around, she found everything was neat and tidy.

Ada cocked her head. "Hmm, eventually, it might be a home. We moved in not too long ago. Still unpacking."

"Ah, well, it's good you got the essentials in." Gabby gestured toward what looked like the living room.

"Actually, this house came fully furnished. Well, mostly."

"Oh, really! That's convenient."

Ada crinkled her nose. "Until you have to dust and disinfect everything yourself."

"Okay, maybe not as convenient as I thought." Gabby laughed.

"Do you want anything to eat or drink? I know it was quite a journey for you."

"Oh, no, I'm okay."

"It's no trouble at all. Let's take a quick tour of the house, then we can sit and talk over your work days while we eat. Afterwards, I can introduce you to Antonia."

The tour consisted of being introduced to the living room, the study, the library, the two bathrooms located on the first floor, the main upstairs bedroom, and the guest bedroom. When Gabby insisted she wouldn't need a room for herself, Ada shrugged and explained how muddy the dirt road could get when a storm came through.

Gabby smiled politely and made a mental note to check the weather prior to future work days.

The tour ended in the kitchen, and Ada set up the small, round table with the promised snacks. She went over the list of ailments that plagued Antonia and what tasks required extra support. Gabby nodded along, affirming her understanding.

A floorboard creaked. "Antonia, meet Gabby."

Antonia was even paler than her mother, her hair the color of a moonless night. Gabby had always heard of children being described as old souls and found they were simply quiet or less prone to laughter. But Antonia's piercing blue eyes brought the adage to the front of her mind.

"Hi, Antonia. It's so nice to meet you." She smiled brightly, hoping the little girl wasn't afraid of strangers. After a pause, she continued. "I hope you don't mind, but I'll be coming by every now and again, just to help out with a few things."

Antonia stood stoically at the threshold of the kitchen. Her blue eyes bored into Gabby's. She noted how dry Antonia's mouth appeared. She wondered if the metabolic disorder was paired with any sensory issues that made drinking enough water a challenge as well. She'd need to speak to Ada in more depth about her daughter's personality, likes, and dislikes. Now more than ever, she was extremely annoyed at Donald for sending her so ill-prepared for the first day.

Antonia glanced at her mother, then left abruptly.

Gabby looked at Ada for help.

Ada shook her head. "Wait just a moment. I bet she'll be right back." She sighed. "She's always back."

A grandfather clock chimed, and Gabby felt herself shiver. She was impressed with how well the central air cooled the house on such a hot day.

The electricity bill must be something else, she thought.

Ada cleared the table. When she finished, she withdrew a cutting board from one of the kitchen drawers. She placed it on a counter and explained she was going to prepare some of the items for the evening's meal. She pulled a slab of meat from the refrigerator. After setting it on the board, she retrieved a knife and began to slice it into sections.

"Ben, one of my neighbors..." Ada paused and laughed. "I guess living out here means anyone a couple miles down the road is a neighbor. Anyway, he butchers his own cows and sells them. Very convenient. Spares me the time needed to drive all the way into town just to purchase something that's been dead a really long time. It's always funny to me how certain people—not saying you—find this phrasing odd. But that's what it all is, right? You walk down the grocery aisle full of meat, and you're among the dead. I like my dead fresh."

Gabby barked out a laugh. "Yes, I guess it does sound weird when you say it like that. But I get it. I think we all like fresh food."

Ada grinned. "Exactly!"

The sharp knife found no resistance as she made quick work of the meat, ensuring each slice was evenly proportioned. When she was satisfied, she wrapped the leftover portion. She popped a small piece of meat into her mouth. "Yes. Much fresher than the store."

Gabby's mouth opened slightly in surprise.

"I have to marinate the meat first before I can start dinner, my pet."

"What? I..." Gabby realized Ada was looking past her and was surprised to find Antonia had made her way back to the kitchen. "Oh! Hi, again. What do you have there?"

Antonia had a small doll pressed to her chest. It was worn and well loved.

"Is that your doll?"

After a moment's hesitation, Antonia nodded once.

"Does she have a name?"

"She's not going to answer. Right, my love? At least not yet. Not until dinner. Do you want to show Ms. Gabby your room?"

"Is she not going to eat until dinner?"

Ada lifted her eyebrows at the question and glanced skyward. "Yes, I suppose it seems early but she is picky. Picky is the wrong word. Her food has to be just so. And it's so difficult to get things prepared so early in the day."

"I can help—"

"Of course, and you are by minding her while I prepare this."

Gabby turned and startled when she found Antonia had walked up next to her. "Oh, sorry, I..." The words died in her throat, and the room closed in around her as she finally got a close-up look at the little girl's face. Beneath vibrant blue eyes and a button nose was the unsmiling mouth of Antonia. The mouth that from a far enough distance appeared dry and chapped. The mouth that, instead, was delicately sewn together.

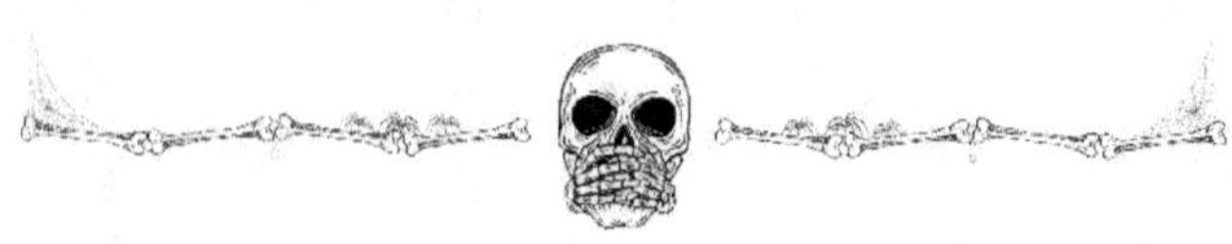

You probably think I'm a monster. I saw how scared you were when you first noticed her mouth. I saw your panic, how you wanted to grab hold of Antonia and run away from the house.

She's so beautiful, isn't she? Such a delicate little face. Big, blue eyes. Pure innocence.

You must understand that I didn't do that all the time. Just during times of desperation. I mean, what mother hasn't wanted to quiet her child? What mother hasn't snapped at her children to stop asking when food would be on the table? And that's mothers with normal children. Children who can run outside and eat whatever they'd like.

But I do not have a normal child...

"Oh, don't worry. That didn't hurt. At least, it didn't hurt me a bit when I did it." Ada laughed at her joke and then waved the knife in a shooing motion. "Anyway, Antonia, please go show Ms. Gabby your room. I've already asked you once and would prefer not to repeat myself."

Antonia placed a hand on Gabby's forearm, and the young nurse rocked as if unsteady. Ada smiled at the panicked look in her eyes. Even if she didn't understand, it was always nice to find those who were willing to do so much for her daughter. Hiring Gabby had been a good choice.

After the girls left, Ada continued to prepare the meat. She washed her hands and retrieved another knife to cut the herbs and roots that would go into the marinade. After adding them all to a container, she poured in small amounts of vinegar and water. The smell made her mouth water, and she cut herself another raw piece to sample before wrapping the container and placing it into the refrigerator.

She washed her hands one more time, wiped them dry, and pulled the butcher's knife from the wooden block. Humming, she walked to the back door. "Where are you two off to?"

Gabby froze, eyes wide, one hand on the doorknob, the other holding Antonia's. Her eyes darted to the knife Ada held, then back to her face.

Ada smiled wide.

"We..." Gabby cleared her throat. "I thought it would be nice to take a walk outside. See the grounds."

Ada frowned and shook her head. "I already told you Antonia is extremely sensitive to the sun. If you aren't careful, she can get severe blisters."

"Yes, but it's overcast, and I thought—"

"The UV index can still be very high on an overcast day."

Gabby swallowed hard. "That's true. I—well, maybe I can get her dressed a little more appropriately for the sun."

"Well," Ada said and tilted her head as if thinking hard. "Maybe a walk would be fine, but not until much later in the day. You'll have to wait until the sun's setting, then it'll be safer. I think you'd agree with waiting until it's safer, yes?"

"Of course." Gabby attempted a smile. "This evening sounds like a safer alternative. Um, I was going to ask if I could use the phone. I just want to report in to my supervisor. Let him know I got here without incident and—"

Ada shook her head. "No, sorry."

Gabby blinked.

"We don't have any phone lines in this place. It's in the plans to get one installed, but for now, we just have to do without."

"I understand." Slowly, Gabby turned, Antonia's hand still in hers, and the pair made their way back upstairs. The little girl stole a backwards glance at her mother.

Gabby flashed Antonia a quick smile and took a few deep breaths. The bit of food she'd had earlier threatened to come back up. She worried a fingernail against her teeth, then dropped her hand. Antonia's wide eyes searched her face, and she tried smiling again.

"Okay, it's okay. It's going to be okay." She didn't know if she was saying this to Antonia or herself. She dropped to her knees and gently probed the area around Antonia's mouth. The little girl's eyes widened, and her breath quickened.

Gabby winced. "I'm so sorry. That probably hurts so much."

The little girl blinked.

"We need to get you to a hospital." Antonia's brows furrowed, and Gabby rushed on. "No, it's okay. I know you love your mommy. But... we need a doctor to look at your mouth. That's all. It'll be okay."

Antonia gave a slight nod, then retreated to her dolls. Gabby watched her play, her heart thundering in her chest. How could she ever get out of here with Antonia in tow?

After an hour of playing in her room, Gabby realized they needed to be closer to the front door. The morning's tour replayed in her mind, and she turned to Antonia. "Hey, do you mind showing me your library? I saw it for a little bit this morning and would love to see what else is in there."

Even with the consternation surrounding the day's circumstances, Gabby couldn't help but feel impressed at the size of the house's library. She wondered who had chosen the books. More importantly, she wondered who had abandoned so many valuable items when they chose to move elsewhere.

Unless it wasn't a choice. The thought was involuntary, and the image of Ada with her butcher's knife made her chest feel tight. The floorboards behind her creaked, and she jumped, spinning quickly to face the person entering the room.

Ada smiled. "This is my favorite room." Her smile turned melancholy as she ran her hand down the spine of a book. "Sometimes, when I'm lonely or when this all feels like too much, I come down here and pick the ones that remind me of home."

Her expression held so much pain and grief, that despite the horror of what she had done to her child, Gabby almost felt pity for the young mother.

"I think this is Antonia's favorite place, too. Isn't it, dear?"

The little girl walked to a desk and sat, leafing through one of the books.

Ada walked to where her daughter sat and stroked her hair. A solitary tear ran down her face. "It's hard sometimes, you know.

Keeping her safe, keeping her strong. It can be a very daunting task." She turned to Gabby and wiped the tear with the back of her hand, then left the room.

Gabby waited until Ada's footsteps stopped before tiptoeing to the edge of the room and peeking out into the hallway. She half expected Ada to be waiting for her, butcher knife poised for an attack.

The coast was clear. Gabby rushed back to Antonia and coaxed her out of the chair. "Hey, sweetheart." Her voice was low. "Remember when I said it's important for us to get you looked at by a doctor? Well, I think now is a good time to go. We want to make sure we don't arrive after they close, okay?"

Antonia's steps grew heavier as they neared the front door. Gabby looked over her shoulder and confirmed the hallway was still empty. She palmed the keys in her pocket. They just needed to make it to the car.

Before they reached the door, Antonia stopped and began to pull away. Her eyes were wide and her breath ragged. Gabby followed her gaze and saw the sunlight spilling in from outside. She looked into the living room and spotted a thin throw blanket on the back of the couch.

"Stay right there," she whispered. "I'm going to cover you with that blanket until we get to the hospital. Okay?"

Antonia looked worried but did as she was told.

Gabby retrieved the blanket and draped it over the girl. She swore when she noted the door was locked from the inside. Quickly, she unfastened the locked on the doorknob and the larger deadbolt.

"No! You can't take her outside!"

Ice flooded her veins as Ada's screech echoed around her. Without looking back, Gabby threw open the door and scooped Antonia into her arms. She ran to her car and tossed the little girl into the back seat, praying she wasn't causing any more damage. She scrambled into the driver's seat and turned on the ignition. Ada threw herself at the driver's door, her face twisted with rage. Spittle formed at the corners of her mouth as she screamed and banged on the glass. Her eyes were wild, and to Gabby, the look transformed her into an old, ugly witch.

She heard a small moan from the back seat. The sound startled her into action. She put the car in gear and stomped on the accelerator. Her heart thundered in her ears.

Antonia moaned again.

"Oh, sweetie," she gasped. "It's okay. Don't try to talk. I'm sorry. I'm so sorry. I didn't mean to scare you. We're on our way to the hospital. You'll be okay. You'll be okay."

As she struggled to control her breathing, she made herself focus on the task at hand. There had been a county hospital along her route at some point. She figured it was a twenty-minute drive and prayed Ada didn't catch up with them before she could make it to safety.

"We'll be okay."

Ada calmed her breathing as she watched the dust kicked up by Gabby's speeding car begin to settle. The original plan was ruined—she saw that now. But a new plan began to form in her mind.

It had been so long since she had help for Antonia. Long stretches between support always wore her out. When she could reach Antonia's father, Ada explained the fatigue, the work required to keep their daughter safe and healthy.

"There's going to be a day when I'm not going to be able to do this anymore," she had warned.

I can't do this anymore, she thought. *And maybe now I don't have to.*

Gabby burst into the county hospital, Antonia in her arms, still wrapped in the blanket. The waiting room was partially filled. Most of the patients waiting to be admitted turned toward the commotion, but she barely registered them. She rushed to the front desk and gingerly set Antonia down. Halloween was in a few days, and the receptionist was wearing a halo and small angel wings. Her face blanched as Gabby relayed the situation and motioned at the girl's lips.

She picked up the telephone next to her and asked for assistance. "Wait right here. They're coming to get you."

A few minutes later, they were escorted to a private room. Antonia's eyes darted around at the personnel in her room. Her breathing increased until she was close to hyperventilating.

One of the nurses, a middle-aged woman with her gray-streaked blonde hair pulled back in a braid, smiled warmly at her. "It's okay, darlin'. You have such beautiful eyes. Did you know that?"

Antonia held the nurse's eyes until she straightened and took a step back.

"She's a little scared," Gabby said.

The nurse pressed her lips into a smile. "Understandable."

A doctor appeared amongst the commotion and began directing the nurses while peppering Gabby with questions about the incident. How had she met the family? How long had she worked with them? Where was the mother?

She answered the doctor as straight-forward as she could, some of the answers sounding ridiculous even to her own ears. It was bad practice not to go over a patient's records before accepting an assignment as a home-health nurse. But at this point, it didn't matter if her manager had been pushy or if she had made mistakes. All that mattered was ensuring that Antonia got proper medical care. The rest, discipline, audits, whatever, could wait until she was better.

The doctor probed Antonia's mouth with gloved hands. "I'd expect to see more redness. The sutures look like they were placed fairly recently. And well done. Does the mother have a medical background?"

Gabby shrugged, but the doctor wasn't looking at her.

He accepted sterile scissors from one of the nurses and, with a practiced hand, began to snip the interrupted sutures on Antonia's lips.

One of the nurse's shifted, crinkling her nose as she charted. With each released suture, a necrotic odor grew in intensity. Two nurses exchanged concerned looks. An involuntary shudder swept through Gabby's body as she imagined what else a mother might do to a daughter she felt talked too much or wouldn't eat what was provided. Fury also swept through her. How could she harm the very thing she was supposed to love and protect?

"Oh my God," the doctor's voice trembled, and he stepped back. "Her mouth…"

Gabby stepped forward, even as the stench in the room made the bottom of her tongue quiver. She took shallow breaths. Antonia shifted her dark eyes from the doctor's face to hers.

Commotion in the hallway stole Gabby's attention.

"Where is she? Where is my daughter?"

The blood drained from her face as she realized Ada had found them. The sound of thrown objects came from the hallway. A couple of people began to shout, their words inaudible due to the racket.

Ada burst into the room and looked at her daughter, then at the people in the room. Her eyes met Gabby's and her lips curled into a cruel, amused smile. "It looks like you've prepared a better dinner than I had planned."

A growling sound, almost the quality of a purr, made Gabby's skin erupt in gooseflesh. Slowly, she turned toward Antonia. She realized then why the little girl's eyes had seemed different. The pupils were dilated so that they only left a thin blue ring around their exterior. Antonia's mouth, now free of sutures, was stained with the sickly dark color of clotted blood. She inhaled deeply, as if savoring the scent of the air around her.

The room was silent, unmoving, as if everyone knew they were in the presence of a predator. No one wanted to be the one to trigger an attack.

Antonia grinned, her teeth sharp and menacing. The doctor stepped backward in response, and she pounced. His scream broke the spell, and the nurses began to run out of the room, some falling in the process.

The little girl sat up after a few moments, her face and neck covered in the rich, red blood of the now dead man before her. She smiled warmly at Gabby and burst out of the room, jumping onto one of the staff members closest to the entrance. Her scream transformed into a gurgle almost immediately, and Gabby stumbled from the room to find Antonia had severed the woman's aorta. Blood gushed from the woman's wound in pulses. The little girl frowned at the stream and ran to someone else.

Ada giggled and glanced at Gabby. "She hasn't had this much food to choose from in a long time."

Gabby felt herself grow faint. "What—what is happening? Donald knows where I am. My work is—"

A man crawled toward them, a thick streak of blood marking his trail. His hospital gown was torn and his left thigh was mutilated, small strips of muscle and tendons barely holding on to the lower part of his leg. "You brought the devil! You brought a demon to this hospital! God help us! God help us!"

Ada watched him, bored, until the blood loss was too much and he expired in front of them. She stepped over a body to reach him and pulled at a piece of his thigh. It gave with some resistance, and she placed it into her mouth. "Your work? Did you go in today?"

Gabby gagged.

"Who told you to come to us?"

"Donald—" Gabby tasted bile in the back of her throat.

"How do you know it was Donald? People can sound very similar over the phone. Especially when you're tired and need to fill a vacancy in your schedule. You were more concerned about dealing with a child again than the details, yeah?" Ada grinned as a look of horror blossomed over Gabby's face.

A woman screamed, and an infant wailed, then fell silent.

"I needed help. Her father called you so you could help feed her." Ada fingered the scar on her wrist. "I can't fill her entirely, only stretch out the time between good feedings. She needed *you*."

"Me," Gabby whispered.

"Except you surprised me. You wanted to protect her. Look at all you did, just to get her help. And it... gave me an idea." Ada's eyes were glassy. "I'm so tired, Gabby. More tired than you can imagine. It's been a few hundred years caring for her. Yes. I'm a little older than I look." She smiled sadly and sighed. "The irony of it all is that I always wanted to be a mother..."

Antonia returned to the hallway after Ada finished talking. The little girl's eyes were her normal blue again. A smile played on her lips. She walked to Ada and kissed her on the lips, then moved to Gabby and kissed her forearm, leaving bloody smears where her lips had been. Contented, she curled up next to a body and used the belly as a pillow.

"I really do love her, you know." Ada smiled as she watched her daughter doze. "I still do. I just—I'm tired. And Death hasn't wanted to visit me. I think, it was waiting until I found a replacement."

"Replacement..."

"Exactly! I wanted someone I knew would care for her. And this is the proof! You'll start doing anything to keep her well. Maybe even grow to enjoy it sometimes. I know exactly where to pierce someone so their blood flows quickly enough for Antonia but not so quickly it kills right away. But... I'm not like Antonia. Or her father. I am different from you, clearly. But I have enough humanity left that this existence drains me..." Ada's gaze shifted from the sleeping girl to Gabby. "But now you're here! I just hope he has mercy."

"He?"

As if in answer, the chorus of screams began again. Ada turned her head toward the sound. Gabby followed her gaze, unable to will her legs into action. Slowly, the screams died into moans.

The lights flickered, and a shadow seemed to grow at the other end of the hallway. Not a shadow... A man... Not a man... Something *other*.

"I found someone else for her. Someone she likes."

Gabby stood transfixed, her eyes locked on the man's pale face. It was a masculine interpretation of Antonia's—her father. When he reached them, he stroked Ada's cheek.

"Please," she whimpered. "I'm so tired." Her cheeks were wet with tears.

The man gripped her neck and squeezed.

Please, she mouthed. Her body sagged with relief when the man bit into her neck, only struggling at the very end. He let her body fall unceremoniously to the ground.

Antonia woke from her slumber and made a startled noise.

The man smiled at his daughter and picked her up. He held her tenderly and kissed her cheek. "It's okay. You have a new mother now."

Antonia wiggled in his arms and he set her down. She crawled over to Ada and closed her eyes, kissed her cheeks, then her mouth. She stood and pulled on her father's hand.

"Papa, we need to bury her with this." She pressed a small, cloth doll into his hand.

Gabby had expected Antonia's voice to sound otherworldly, like the buzzing of locusts or a collection of screams. Instead, her voice, though tinged with grief, was soft and sweet.

Her father nodded solemnly. "Of course, my darling."

Gabby's body trembled as Antonia walked toward her and took her hand. She watched as the little girl brought her wrist to her lips and winced when the girl bit down. The sting quickly dissipated into a warm sensation that washed over her body. She felt as if she were floating. Antonia looked expectantly at her father.

He caressed the top of his daughter's head, then took Gabby's hand from her.

Gabby choked out a sob. "No. Please, no."

She watched as he brought the cut wrist to his lips, felt the sharp bite of his teeth. Pain wracked through her body. She heard screaming and realized belatedly it was her own. Then, the world turned black, and the pain was gone.

Color began to seep in through the inky darkness until she found herself standing in a small room. As the scene grew sharper, she noticed a man weeping over a little girl. The girl's breath was quick and shallow. It was Antonia.

Memories of Antonia flashed through her mind's eye. She saw them in series, each tearing at her heart. Antonia, hours old, beautiful and perfect and healthy. Antonia, almost a year old, taking tentative steps at the market. Antonia, about three years old, squealing with laughter as her father tossed her into the air. Antonia, seven years old, helping her mother prepare supper.

Antonia. Ten years old. Dying.

Tears burned the back of Gabby's eyes.

"You cannot save her," a voice said.

The weeping man turned, and she recognized him as Antonia's father. "Then, what is the point of being what I am?" he roared. "Why am I cursed to walk this earth forever when my own daughter lies dying before me?"

A female figure walked into Gabby's view. "I'm sorry, Emil. This is why we advise to stay away from the family you had before. Especially children. There is a reason there are no young among our kind."

"If I am to be robbed of the ability to see her grow old, then I will use this curse to prevent her from dying young."

"You do not understand. The young are not turned because they do not hold the ability to control their impulses. We do not die from age alone, but that does not mean we cannot be killed. I am much older than you," the woman said. "Trust my wisdom."

"I was too late to save her mother. I will not be too late to save my daughter."

The woman's brow creased. "I have had to endure the death of many loved ones. It is part of the burden we bear as immortals."

"No!"

"You'd need to keep constant vigilance over her. It is impossible." She noted a shift in his look. "I will inform the council."

"So be it," he said. And the fight began.

Gabby desperately wanted to look away but found she was not in control. Emil had surprised the woman by pulling open the bedroom window. She hissed in response to the light, and he took the moment of distraction to strike at her face. He used his thumb to puncture an eye, and she screamed before throwing him from her. White and black fluid ran down her cheek and dripped onto her dress. She placed a hand over her injury and then Emil was on her again. This time, he used his teeth along with his hands. Nausea swept over Gabby's body as the room filled with the smell of spilled bowels and clotted blood. If the county hospital had been a nightmare, this scene was hell. Emil was a force of passionate fury, and the woman proved to be no match.

Gabby noticed burns and blisters across his face, neck, and hands as he tacked the curtain back up to block the sun. Somehow, she knew they'd slowly heal and his skin would return to its normal unblemished state. The woman, now pieces of flesh littered on the bedroom floor, no longer had the same opportunity.

Emil returned to his daughter's side. "My sweet Antonia. You will not die today. I will keep you safe. And if I alone cannot do this, I will find someone who will help us. This I promise you."

Gabby opened her eyes and found herself in the county hospital again. Emil's eyes pierced hers. He had wanted her to see what he would do for the sake of his daughter. Ada's death was his mercy. Her vision closed in around her, and she collapsed into his arms.

Time passed, though whether it was days or weeks, she had no idea. Compresses were applied to her forehead. Water, tea, and a coppery liquid was fed to her. The dreams that visited were flashes of teeth and blood and death.

After days or weeks of a blurred existence, she woke. She trained her eyes on the ceiling. A small hand grasped hers.

"Mama."

About the Author

Gloria Lucas is a Mexican-American author. She would describe herself as a chronic daydreamer and part-time karaoke singer. Her work generally explores mental health and trauma.

Her novel, How Deep the Ocean, *a work of literary fiction, received a starred review from Reader Views. Her short story,* My Darling Girl, *is her second to be published within an anthology.*

Follow her on Instagram @glorialucas_author. Or sign up for her newsletter to stay updated on new releases at glorialucas.com

Her novel, The Weight of Broken Memories, *is due for release Fall 2024.*

MIRROR, MIRROR

LAURAE KNIGHT

Bloody Mary

What really happens when someone summons Bloody Mary? Many people foolish enough to do the ritual say Bloody Mary is a myth. After all, they followed the instructions perfectly, but nothing appeared.
But what if they got lucky? What if she is constantly looking for her next victim, only to miss you by seconds? More importantly, what would happen if she got her hands on you?

The thump of my heart pounding against my ribs nearly drowned out the fits of laughter coming from the other side of the closed door. Those assholes were supposed to be my friends, but they found out the old folklore of the ghost in the mirror gave me nightmares, so they had the gall to shove me into the dark bathroom—*and lock the door.* With the power out due to the lightning storm beginning to settle outside, only two candles on either corner of the vanity provided light. Constantly, the flames flickered, casting dark shadows over my fair skin, which looked sickly pale each time white light flashed through the sheer curtains.

Every year for the annual Halloween party, my brother Donnie has to do some stupid prank. For the last couple years since we turned eighteen, that settled, but this year, he took it way over the line. In my intoxicated state, I stupidly mentioned still being scared of Bloody Mary. A few beers later, and the asshole scooped me up and locked me in the bathroom. Despite my pleas to be let out, he insisted I "just do it" and he'd let me out.

As soon as I was out, I had a few choice words for my "friends."

Bloody Mary. Bloody Mary. Bloody Mary.

All I needed to do was voice the words loud enough for them to hear, and they would let me out of this godforsaken bathroom. Okay, but saying that did nothing to stop my palms from sweating. I wiped them on the rough fabric of my jeans and gripped the edge of the bathroom counter. *Enough procrastinating.* The sooner I said it, the sooner I could leave and put an end to this childish Halloween prank.

Glancing at the giant seashells hanging on either side of the mirrored medicine cabinet, I tried to use the familiar sight to ground myself.

This was my bathroom. I grew up here, and despite moving out last year, it was still home. Which was exactly why we threw the annual party, even though Mom and Dad were off on a cruise.

Oh, how I'd hoped this would be bonding time with my brother and our friends. Oh, how this did not go as planned.

Swallowing, I licked my soft lips.

"Bloody Mary." Pathetically, my voice cracked, barely above a whisper. I would have to do better than that. Opening my mouth, I tried again. "Blood Mary! Bloody Mary! Bloody Mary!" I spat the name out quickly as loud as I could. Three times, just like the legend said.

An icy whip of wind cut through my hoodie, forcing goosebumps across my skin. Blood pounded in my ears as I realized the window was closed. As crazy as it seemed, I knew the wind came directly from the glass mirror itself.

The candles flickered violently, their fire morphing into two hands with long, thin fingers. They reached for me, singeing my sleeve as I jerked away.

In the pane of framed glass, movement caught my attention. The frail figure of a woman accompanied my own reflection, as though one overlaid the other. Dark hair hung in tangled ropes to her waist. A few strands shrouded a long, gaunt face marred with curved black lines. When she tilted her head, black droplets poured from her sunken eye sockets. Amid black-stained eyes, blood red irises met my eyes. The moment they did, ice crystallized every nerve in my body.

At the mercy of my terror, I stood frozen. In those eyes, a war of anger and sorrow raged on. Cracks formed at the corners of her mouth as she opened it, almost as though she were a porcelain doll shattering when its lips were forced apart.

My sluggish mind processed the words she mouthed flawlessly.

"Forgive me."

A scream tore from my throat in the same instant the candlelight snuffed out. Even as I spun on my heels to dash for the door, her fingers caught my chin-length hair and yanked me back toward the mirror. Roots tore from my scalp, the sound of it almost worse than the sting. Panic gripped my throat, cutting off my cries for help as she yanked me back. Fireworks erupted behind my eyelids as my back ricocheted off the sharp edge of the counter. A second hand buried itself in my hair, pulling my slender body up another inch.

Across the room, metal jiggled loud enough to be heard over the ringing in my ears.

They heard me. My friends heard me, and they were coming to save me. Knowing how close rescue was, hope sparked inside my chest, giving enough strength for me to cry out, "Help me!"

Desperately, my legs flailed, my cotton socks slipping easily on the linoleum. My hands closed around her bony wrists—cold and clammy, like an old corpse pulled from damp soil. Clawing at her did nothing as she hauled me onto the sink one agonizing inch at a time.

"Please!" I gripped the edge of the counter with my calves, the corners digging painfully into my muscles. "Leave me alone! I'm sorry, Bloody Mary! I'm so sorry!" The voice pleading for help wasn't my own. It was something born of primal terror and desperation, yet it came from my mouth, nonetheless.

One hand let go of my hair and snaked around my head. Jagged fingernails tore into my face as she tried to find purchase for her grip. The pain dulled with one agonizing thought.

The mirror. She wanted to pull me inside.

Torturous seconds passed as warm liquid began to drip down my face, tracing the outline of my lips. Copper coated my tongue as the cool surface of the mirror touched the top of my head. A guttural groan vibrated in my ears. Was she growling?

Blood dripped into my eyes. Clamping them shut, I begged for someone, anyone, to save me.

Hearing my terror, Bella and Sheila screamed for me to open the door. When I didn't, their pleas turned to Donnie.

"Rose, you're fine! Just open the door!" Donnie's alarmed voice called from the hallway.

Hearing the fear in his voice made my blood run cold.

He kicked the door open, his blurred form stumbling in as it splintered.

In slow motion, I watched helplessly as I pried at her fingers, but she ripped me through the mirror. It felt as though my body was submerged in a cold vat of slime.

A gargled voice penetrated my ears, so contorted I couldn't understand a word.

Once completely on the other side, my body unexpectedly dropped. Despite the thick feel of the air, I fell quickly. Bloody Mary's claw-like nails tore through my face. Then, she let go and jumped over me... out of the mirror.

The cold hard floor cracked against my elbow and hip, sending a jarring pain through my bones. For the first time since passing through the mirror, I gasped for breath. Oxygen. At least a little bit. Enough to stop the black spots from invading my vision. Not that it mattered. This realm, this *thing*, she pulled me into had no natural light. Despite that, I could see some shapes along the wall and silhouettes of furniture. Just enough to realize everything was a mirrored version of my bathroom.

Rolling to my knees, I found the edge of the counter and pulled myself up.

In the mirror, my reflection stared blankly ahead with my short blonde hair, bright blue eyes, and sun kissed skin. Behind me, Donnie, Bella, and Sheila spilled into the room as more footsteps hurried down the hall.

Relief flooded me as I spun on my heels, ready to grab hold of my family and friends and shake off the hallucination. But instead of comforting warmth, icy darkness surrounded me. White puffs filled the air with my gasping breath. Panicking, I whipped back around only to come face to face with myself again. This time, I knew it wasn't really me in the mirror.

Blue eyes I'd looked into my entire life no longer shimmered with life. They were soulless and dead. My usually glowing skin seemed dull and pale, even as the vanity lights flicked on.

Sheila grabbed my shoulder. "Are you okay?"

"What happened?" Bella looked around the bathroom.

My blank face only stared through the mirror into the abyss I stood in.

"Bloody Mary?" I whimpered, my voice echoing ominously around me.

A twisted grin cut through the face staring back at me as she raised her hands and flexed them slowly. She tilted her head and touched the strand of hair growing from it.

My hair.

"No!" Fear gave way to desperation for survival. When I tried to reach through the glass, my fingers hit its solid surface. The overextended joints bent and popped, sending jolts of pain up my arms. "No!" I cried again, slapping the surface repeatedly.

The smile on her face faded when she looked up with raised brows, as though seeing me for the first time.

"Why did you do this? Where am I? Let me out! Please, let me out!" Of course, she would never let me go. Why would she? The smile that twisted her mouth—*my mouth*—in an unfamiliar way showed the pleasure she felt from taking my body.

My friends seemed oblivious as they continued to try to talk to my possessed form. Their questions of concern quickly turned to annoyed complaints of my cowardice. After a few blinks, Bloody Mary took a deep breath. "One goes in. One comes out."

Shiela, Donnie, and Bella alternated worried looks. "We never agreed to do it after you."

Bloody Mary tilted her head slowly and began to turn around. Each one of them tensed, like prey becoming aware of the predator. Without another word, she stalked between them as they stood completely still with wide doe-like eyes.

The image shimmered, the looking glass becoming reflective long enough for me to see the lack of damage. Despite the pain I felt and the marks that should certainly show, there was nothing. It almost looked as though my physical body simply froze in a dazed state from the moment my attack began. As though completely unimpacted by the events that occurred.

Suddenly, the mirror turned completely black. So deep and dark that it almost felt like it would suck every drop of light from the bathroom. The weight of the darkness all around fell on my shoulders.

I was completely and utterly alone.

Why?

Where was I?

Too scared to move, I slid to the floor with my back against the sink counter. Tucking my knees against my chest, I curled into a ball and gave in to tears. I tried to keep as quiet as possible. After all, I didn't know what other creatures might be lurking in this world. All I knew was that I'd opened a gate, and Bloody Mary stole my body, leaving me to rot in this realm.

Surely, everyone would notice something was wrong with me in the real world, right? Could they figure out a way to save me? No, I couldn't lie to myself. Even if they noticed, they could never save me. How would they get me out? Where would they even begin to look? Even if they believed we switched places, how could they get me back?

They'd probably just throw my possessed body into a mental ward. Maybe they would, just to make sure she didn't hurt anybody. Maybe the facility would strap her to a bed and she would spend the rest of her stolen mortality subjected to hours of experiments. Did they do experiments in psych wards and mental hospitals anymore? Hopefully, they did. Thinking of her frolicking freely in my skin made me itch.

Long after the last tear dried up, I lay in the fetal position on the dingy floor. For an immeasurable amount of time, I remained there, my arms and legs growing numb as I tried to make sense of everything.

With my eyes pressed closed, I could at least pretend none of what just happened was real. No matter how much I attempted to will those thoughts into reality, the truth hit me like a brick when I finally pried my eyes open.

Seascape wallpaper lined the area around the clawfoot tub in the far corner. They should be bright blues and greens, but the colors looked faded and worn. It almost seemed like in this place, decay trailed its fingers over every surface, spreading the rot from one thing to the next. A layer of dust and debris covered the window panes, making it impossible to see beyond without working the courage to stand up.

Pain rippled through my head like a hammer striking it repeatedly. The adrenaline masked the pain for a while, but with it fading, I couldn't ignore the sting from the cuts on my face, the bruises from the fall, or the pressure in my head from sobbing profusely.

Concentrating, I worked to breathe in and out slowly as I strained to listen for any sounds from outside the room. Try as I might, I couldn't hear a thing past the echoes of my own mind. Eventually, I came to the conclusion that if there were any other spirits or monsters hoping to harm me, they probably would have by now.

Unless they wanted to hunt me? Nervously, I blinked back the white dots in my vision and used the edge of the sink to pull myself up. Seconds after, pins and needles began to prick my nerves up and down my arms and legs. Letting out an audible gasp, I doubled over and leaned heavily on the grungy countertop. A thick film of dust covered every surface, like many layers which built up over a long period of time, and I breathed it in, instantly hacking at the invasion of dust in my lungs. Every abrasive cough echoed through the air, and I was painfully aware of the attention such noise may draw from whatever monsters lurked in the shadows. Even knowing that, it took me far too long to stop and get control. All the while, I clung to the counter, entirely vulnerable.

Feeling returned to my legs slowly as I waited an impossibly long time for something—anything—to burst through the door and tear me to shreds. Yet, nothing came past the white fireworks exploding at the edges of my vision. I forced my eyes to focus.

Beneath the film of whatever dust particles filled this mirrored place, there was no longer a reflective surface, but a sheet of black stared back at me. It absorbed any trace of light. Tentatively, I touched the surface. I didn't know what to expect. To go through it? To be hit by some magical force? My fingertips almost burned at the feel of the icy cold panel. Sucking in a breath, I jerked back and tenderly kissed the wounds.

Looking around the room, I crossed to the window. The same matte black slate filled the window in place of glass. An attempt to open it proved futile. The wood cracked, the sharp sound cutting through the quiet space. I froze. Again, nothing came. Sidestepping, I leaned my back against the wall and faced the door.

Back home, it was bright coral, a true focal point. This one looked dark gray and rotted. Crumbled at the edges with rusted hinges, I wondered if it would even open. Gathering what little resolve remained, I took the eroded knob in my hands and turned.

Nothing.

I pushed.

Nothing.

Slamming my fist into the door, I called for help, flinching at the reverberation. Only once I was certain the door wouldn't open, I made the decision to crawl into the claw foot tub and curl up. Every time I tossed and turned, flakes of porcelain from the tub wall would fall away, clattering quietly on the ground. I worked to make myself as still as possible and closed my eyes tightly.

Sleep never came. My headache persisted to the point I feared it would turn my brain into molten matter. Each deep breath cooled the fire blazing in my skull. The room was freezing. No matter how tightly I held myself, I couldn't get warm.

Trickling in from somewhere beyond the room, whispers came to me, but I couldn't quite make out the words. They sounded close and far away all at once. The sound had been there all along, but I thought it was a symptom of the migraine, like a hive of wasps buzzing somewhere out of my line of sight.

Why did she do this to me? What was the point? I couldn't stop thinking about what she said.

Forgive me.

As if anyone could forgive someone for putting them in this hell. Why did she do this? What was she doing with my body? Thinking of some demented spirit walking around in my skin made my stomach churn, like hundreds of maggots were writhing all through my middle. My body. My blonde hair. My vibrant blue eyes.

No, not vibrant. Not anymore. The instant we switched places, Mary became the imposter whose demonic energy snuffed out the light in my eyes and the mortal flush of my skin.

A fresh wave of tears rolled down my cheeks to drip off my pointed chin. They splattered against the muck-filled tub, resembling black ink more than translucent bodily fluids. Wiping at my eye and examining my fingers confirmed the change. All at once, I jumped from my makeshift bed and rushed to the mirror, completely forgetting its uselessness. Sniffling, I wiped at my nose and looked at the snot. Black goop oozed from my palm.

"What the fuck?" I cringed at the grainy sound of my voice. How much time had passed since I last spoke a word? The inaudible chanting continued relentlessly, and it had been my only company.

For how long?

How long had I been there?

Hours? Weeks? Years?

There was no way for me to tell.

I longed for the warmth of the sun. Closing my eyes, I tried to remember what it felt like to stand in a pool of light. I tried to bring myself there, if even for a moment. Just a drop of those golden rays would make me feel something, anything, aside from this agonizing cold.

No matter how much I concentrated, I couldn't craft a tangible sensation. Was Bloody Mary basking in the bright sunlight? I didn't know what made me feel worse—the thought of her soaking up sunshine while I rotted away or the idea of her mistreating my body until it withered to nothing. I would give anything to be back in the real world.

The incessant cacophony of voices seemed to crescendo. They demanded my attention, driving the phantom sunlight away and forcing their way to the forefront of my mind. Fighting them only brought on more agonizing pressure. Almost like rubber bands were being wrapped around my head one after the other until my head would burst like a melon.

"Stop, please, stop," I begged. "I hear you. I just can't understand you. Please."

Acknowledging them seemed to lessen the pain. With each heartbeat, the metaphorical bands snapped off and the lyrics became a little more clear.

"*Bloody Mary. Bloody Mary. Bloody Mary.*"

Her name over and over again. Thousands and thousands of voices. They echoed all around, consuming my thoughts. All at once, it became too much. Clutching my head in my hands, I unleashed a blood curdling cry and fell to my knees.

"Stop it! Stop it! Stop, stop, stop!" My voice cracked, the words fading among the chorus taunting me.

Where could it be coming from? Could there be other people outside? Other victims? Other dark spirits? There was only one way to find out. Quiet as a cockroach, I tiptoed to the door. Just like everything else, corrosion ate it away. My house back home was designed and built by my parents a few years before I was born. With me being only twenty-two, it couldn't be more than twenty-five years old. Everything in this realm could have been aged for centuries. With no other options, I took a shaky breath and wrapped one hand around the cold knob.

The door swung open easily. Could this be a sign I was going the right way?

The voices became louder, but the headache eased slightly.

A long dark hallway stretched as far as I could see with dozens of matching black doors lining either side, all evenly spaced apart. It looked nothing like what was there back in the real world.

"Bloody Mary. Bloody Mary. Bloody Mary."

A dagger of fear pierced my chest, sending adrenaline through my veins. No. Why would I want to go toward something chanting the devil's name? Slamming the door shut, I retreated into the room again. Piercing pain split my skull, like nails being driven into each temple. Crying out, I fell to my knees and cradled my head in my hands. The more I fought against the calls, the worse the pain became. Like a strike from a hammer, my refusal to oblige drove the affliction deeper.

Soon enough, my long fingernails were digging into my scalp as I begged for something, anything, to make it stop. Pure exhaustion trickled into my muscles, working its way through every fiber from head to toe, forcing each one into a spasm.

The sweet escape of unconsciousness never embraced me. When the last of my resolve turned to shredded remains, I could only lay there in a catatonic state, hounded by the voices I didn't understand.

Why did the voices say her name but call to me? They demanded my presence, I could feel it. I needed to go to them. They wanted me. No, not me. Bloody Mary. My name wasn't Bloody Mary. It was something pretty. Something floral. Squeezing my eyes shut, I pushed for the memory. Images flashed on the back of my eyelids, and for a second, I heard Donnie calling my name through the bathroom door. *Rose.* My name was Rose.

"I am Rose," I whispered the words, hoping it would give them more power. What was my surname? Try as I might, the answer would never come, but flashbacks of the attack lived on.

For a long time, I lay there, repeating the name aloud. Trying to commit it to eternal memory.

Eventually, I scraped myself off the hard floor. All I wanted was to find a way out, and it became painfully obvious this room wouldn't offer me one. I needed to look for it. First, I tried the window, but it didn't budge and another check of the mirror only stung my palms. Digging my fingers into the gunk covering one of the giant scallop shells, I pried it off the wall. I lost count of how many times I hit the window and mirror with it, but I swung until my arms trembled and the makeshift tool fell from my hands with a bang that made me flinch. Collapsing to my knees, I held my head in my hands and tried to cry. Whatever oozed from my tear ducts wasn't warm saltwater, but something thick and cold.

"*Bloody Mary. Bloody Mary. Bloody Mary.*"

Where were the voices coming from? It sounded like they seeped in from beyond the door, teasing me with the thought of company while torturing me with the name of my murderer.

With no other options, I did the only thing I could think of—got up and tried the door again. Taking the corroded knob in my hand once more, I twisted it. This time, something clicked. My heart clenched. Unable to muster much more than a gentle push, I couldn't believe it when the door swung open freely. Easily, in fact. Again, a long dark hallway stretched before me with doors lining either side. Clenching my teeth, I took a half step out.

Rhythmically, the chant continued, just as it had every second from the moment I'd been pulled into this realm. The voices came through each door. It took a long time to muster the courage to slide my foot across the dirt-covered floor. That first step was the hardest, but the next came with less resistance.

Picking one at random, I leaned closer to the damaged wood, straining to hear a muffled young woman speaking. Could someone be on the other side? Struck with energy for the first time since crossing into this place, I ripped the door open without a second thought. I didn't know what I expected to find inside. It opened into a large bathroom with a massive arched vanity. The mirror shimmered, a figure appearing. Black shoulder-length hair, tattered clothes, pale skin stretched over bones that protruded from her elbows and knees.

I scrambled back, tripping over my own feet and falling to the floor. I lurched to the side, curling against the wooden panel to hide from the open doorway. Frozen in fear, I trembled.

"Say it again," a girl said.

"Bloody Mary. Bloody Mary. Bloody Mary."

"See, I told you it wasn't real, Becca. Nothing's there."

"Shut up, Annie. Can we just leave now?"

"Fine."

Two voices came from the room. Each one feminine and sweet, like warm honey soothing my raw ears. Overwhelmed with the temptation of an escape, I crawled back through the door. Two teenage girls filled the frame with candlelight dancing over their plump young features. The taller brunette spun around and took a few steps away while the shorter redhead continued to look toward me. Wrapping my fingers around the doorframe, I used it to pull myself back to my feet.

The girl's bright green eyes widened. They weren't just looking toward me, but directly at me.

"You see me." My epiphany came out gravely and broken.

Absolute terror drained the peachy color from her freckled face. The vanity scintillated.

"No!" Urgently, I sprinted toward it with my arms outstretched.

Defensively, she threw up her hands before transitioning into a familiar black panel.

"Come back! Please!"

Closing my eyes, I rested my forehead against the black slab. Would I have been able to pass through if I reached it? *"One goes in.*

One comes out." Her words came back to me. In a heartbeat, I understood the weight of it. Every time someone performed the ritual, a portal opened in their mirror, allowing me to pass through for a short time. That was how Bloody Mary switched places with me. I opened a window, and she crawled through. Who was she really? How long did she suffer in this place? How many souls suffered the same fate in this realm?

Who was I? The memories wouldn't come.

Hitting my head firmly against the cold, I let a fresh stream of inky tears splatter on the moldy floor tiles. "What's my name? Who am I?"

"*Bloody Mary. Bloody Mary. Bloody Mary.*"

Snapping to attention, I turned back to the open door and passed through it to the hall of infinite doors. Hundreds of voices. All of them called for Bloody Mary's appearance, and each and every one offered a means of escape for me. Only, to gain my freedom, I would have to strip someone of theirs.

Could I do that?

Numbly, I trudged out of the bathroom with hunched shoulders and a hanging head. Fingering my clumped hair, I examined the darkened color. Stiff from being unwashed, there was nothing I could do to keep it from hanging in front of my face. Not that it mattered. Nothing mattered.

For some time, I wandered from room to room, standing where I thought I wouldn't be seen and just... watching. I'd perch on the edge of a moldy bathtub or crouch on a cracked toilet and listen to siblings tease one another over their fear of me. Some would laugh while others wept from the relief of my absence. All the while, I hunkered in the shadows, longing for the life they lived. Did I have friends before? Did I have family? Did anyone care for me?

It didn't feel like it. If those luxuries were mine, I'd forgotten what they felt like long ago.

With a renewed purpose, I exited the decrepit room and moved to the next. This one contained a tiny circular mirror with a man practically whispering my name.

"Bloody Mary. Bloody Mary. Bloody Mary."

Crouching in front of the low thing, I tilted my head, and watched as it glistened. Crimson eyes framed within bony eye sockets. Somewhere in the back of my mind, something tugged. With bony fingers, I traced the deep pits in my cheeks.

The portal opened to reveal a young boy. Our eyes met. He opened his mouth to scream, but I reached through the portal to wrap my fingers around his throat. His shoulders caught on the edges of the mirror when I tried to rip him through. Unfortunately, the portal wavered, and I let him go reflexively. As he fell, the obsidian wall appeared.

Freedom was within reach. Clenching my fists hard enough to draw blood from my palms with my chipped nails, I turned to the hallway and moved to the next room. Then, the second, and the third. Door after door, I searched for a window big enough and a person slow enough. It became a hunt I loathed and craved all at the same time. A craft I sculpted over hundreds of failed attempts. Instead of loathing the insomnia seeping into my core, I started to appreciate it. Without having to rest, I could hunt relentlessly. Although for every one door I opened, there were hundreds more I couldn't get to before the time ran out and the reflective surface they were using turned back to matte black. Not every room was a bathroom. Some were bedrooms or living rooms or closets, but every single one had one specific portal—whichever one the person faced when they called to me. Thankfully, the tale of Bloody Mary was alive and well, and I had plenty of victims to choose from.

At one point, a specific door drew me down the hall a few yards. The splintered wood pricked my fingers, the slight pain spurring me on as I entered the room. A massive full length looking glass wrapped in fake plastic leaves stood perfectly against the wall. Large furniture adorned every part of this room. Old antique sets of drawers and a vanity lined one side while a clawfoot tub rested perfectly in the center of the room directly in front of the mirror. Trailing my fingers over the curved porcelain edge, I admired the icy burn that came with touching anything from this realm.

"Bloody Mary..." A dainty little voice dripping in fear emanated from the mirror which already began to shimmer like heat waves against pavement before becoming reflective. With a looking glass as large as that, I could easily pull them through. Before that became a possibility, though, they would need to complete the ritual. Until it was completed, the veil between our worlds would be thin, but not open. All they needed to do was say my name three times. One, two, three. "She's not real. She's not real."

Oh, but I am. Stepping into the tub, I crouched inside of it and propped my crossed arms on the ledge to rest my chin on. After all this time, I didn't mind waiting a few minutes for them to work up the courage to say my name again. In the mirror, piercing red eyes glowed within sunken sockets. Pieces of skin flaked off sharp cheekbones and cracked lips. Clumps of black hair hung from my head, so dirty they were sleek and dark like oil. Dust and dirt smeared across my face, arms, and clothes. Whatever color it all used to be was long gone. Nothing about who I used to be remained. Two things were burned into my memory. *One goes in and one comes out.*

And I wanted *out.*

Three times. Come on, you can do it. Call my name. Do it. I stared at my own reflection as I silently pushed them to try again.

"BloodyMaryBloodyMaryBloodyMary!" She said it all so fast, it blurred into one solid word.

But I heard it. And it worked. A plump young woman in a short plaid dress materialized before me. Her blonde hair shimmered in the flickering candlelight coming from the skull-shaped candle in her shaking hands. Thick eyeliner outlined big blue eyes which searched for anything out of place. Tilting my head to the opposite side, the smirk on my ghostly face grew until my chapped lips split open and thick fluid dripped down my chin. A blood curdling scream tore from her throat as she spun around to check the tub in the room behind her, which put her back to the mirror—to me. Without hesitation, I lunged at the portal, but my prey already made it to the door. She ripped it open and slammed it behind her. Flying through the air, I couldn't stop myself from hitting the cursed onyx slab as it appeared.

Black bodily fluid shot from my head as my skull cracked open. For a while, I lay on the subzero tiles, screaming in agony until my throat became so raw, I could hardly breathe.

Time passed. Voices came and went. All the while, I remained crumpled, my body slowly healing as I drew swirls in the filth with my fingers, each one more distorted than the last, until the loops lost all shape, and I swiped them away with the palm of my hand. Getting up and moving took more effort than I could muster. Eventually, though, I grabbed the edges of the leafy mirror, pulled myself up, and heaved one foot in front of the other until that room was nothing but a bad learning attempt.

One particular room caught my attention. This one wasn't a bathroom as most were. On this occasion, someone called me to their bedroom. Upon first entering the room, it took a few seconds to locate the mirror. A massive four-poster bed took up the entire middle while a dresser dripping in slime sat against the wall. Large windows lined two walls, but as always, the glass was replaced by black bricks which seemed to absorb what little light tried to exist in the room. An unexpected moan had me looking up. Directly above the four-poster bed, a series of small square mirrors were put together to make a massive portal. Through it, I could see a woman climbing on top of an attractive man with broad shoulders. Both were completely naked, as though they'd paused in the middle of their intimacy to call me forth.

The man let out a throaty laugh. "What are you trying to do, Ida? Give her a show?"

"Gabe, face it, if Mary's real, she'd probably appreciate it." The girl's response came with its own laugh. A lighthearted one fueled by ignorance. "It's probably been centuries since she got any, if the poor thing ever experienced it at all."

A flash of jealousy singed me, burning through the final string of morality holding me trapped in this place. *Oh, I'd experienced pleasure.* I couldn't pull forth a specific memory or face or even name, but the clench of my pussy assured me the feeling was a familiar one. *Experience?* I scoffed. *I'll show her experience.*

Who I was before no longer mattered. One single thing of importance remained: my escape. After that, I could become whoever I needed to be. Whatever it took to get the fuck out of this solitary confinement.

Warmth—I needed to feel its caress on my mottled skin. No, on my *smooth* skin. The woman moving up and down with practiced rhythm was blessed with smooth skin down her back and long red hair. She sat straighter, allowing her partner's head to appear over her shoulder.

Thankfully, his eyes were closed as his hands groped her bouncing breasts.

I didn't have much time. Only seconds maybe before the portal closed. Determined not to fuck up again, I spurred into action. Running across the room, I climbed up one of the strong wooden poles, the carvings on it giving me somewhere to grip despite the film covering it. Willing every ounce of strength from my bones, I coiled and sprang from the pole, stretching to get every precious inch as I reached for the edge of the portal.

Unbelievably, my fingers curled around the mirrors, and I managed to mantle up. Once my head poked through the veil, I no longer needed to look up at my victim, but down.

The dreaded shimmer began, tingling the skin of my neck.

Now or never.

With every ounce of strength, I held on to the edge of the portal and hung from the ceiling and wrapped my feet around the top of one pole. The landing wasn't perfect, but I managed to contort enough to crawl down the pole.

Enraptured by the moment, the man never opened his eyes, but the woman? She threw her head back with wide eyes to look up at their reflection. Just in time to see me reach for her hair. Having just moaned deeply, she couldn't quite scream. From the instant my grotesque bony fingers threaded through her silky locks, her physical body went slack while a translucent apparition tore from her. Using her wonderfully soft curls, I worked every muscle in my immortal body and launched her soul into the portal.

The moment she passed through completely, I blinked, and suddenly, I was in her body.

No.

My body.

The man below me smiled softly with his eyes closed. They'd been moving in perfect synchronization, but as soon as I took control, the rhythm stopped completely. I froze. He continued to thrust a few times before slowing. His eyes opened. Jade green. Absolutely stunning. The most beautiful and vivid color I'd ever seen.

His smile grew, and he lifted his arm, brushing his fingers against my cheek. I jerked away, snarling.

He pulled back, eyes growing wide. "Are you okay?"

I licked my lips. Soft. Warm.

Pressure filled my core. One I recognized.

I nodded.

Putting my hands on him for support, I moved back and forth, testing each direction to see what felt best.

Spurred by the movements, he resumed thrusting with a grin on his face.

I knew exactly what this moment meant. I was free from that hell. Whatever life I lived before was dead and gone, but this one offered a renewed promise of the future. But I wasn't ready to let go of the dark world I knew completely. It had become my only home for what felt like centuries. The place my soul rotted and shriveled and turned into black goop.

This was my chance to live all over again, and yet... something about that thought made my pulse quicken in panic. Looking up into the mirror, I swallowed.

His hands moved up and down slightly, fingering the curve of my hips and smallest point of my waist.

Nothing in the reflection looked familiar. The mishmash of colors made my eyes hurt. For a brief second, I wondered if the portal were still open, if I could climb back in.

Until he raised me up. The sensation of his shaft moving along my core sent ripples of unexpected pleasure through every nerve. I gasped as he thrusted, hitting something deep inside of my body. Something that hadn't been touched for far too long.

Slick and wet, he moved in and out easily. Enraptured by this new sensation, I cried out, digging my nails into his chest as I found my release far too quickly. His came a moment later, and when I collapsed against his chest, he wrapped his arms around me and snuggled closed. When I rolled off him, a distinct emptiness filled my center, but the idea of continuing the passionate moment felt like too much. Lying there beside him was exactly what I needed.

"Hopefully, she enjoyed the show," he said with a chuckle.

Guilt sliced my gut like a knife. I knew who he meant. Bloody Mary.

Only, I wasn't in the mirror anymore. Was the portal closed already? No. I could still feel the power emanating from it somehow. Like it tethered to part of my soul and constantly pulled on the string.

Comfortably in the silken sheets, I curled into the warmth of his body as I looked up at the mirror. Everything about this body was foreign. From the beautiful fiery red curls to the mint green eyes. A light dusting of freckles adorned my nose and cheeks. What a perfect body to have.

Anger emanated from the portal. *Ida.* That was her name. Although, she'd forget it soon. With only seconds left, I gave her the only advice that'd been given to me.

"One goes in. One comes out."

"What?" My newfound companion reached for my face again, and this time, I stilled completely, willing myself to let him. His fingertips touched as gently as a feather. A tingling sensation rolled down my shoulders to the small of my back. My asscheeks tensed.

"I love you, Ida."

I snuggled closer to place my ear on his chest, listening to his heartbeat.

Thump. Thump. Thump. Quick and steady as he recovered from our encounter. Such a beautiful sound.

When I closed my eyes, the darkness was almost welcoming after so long in the other realm. "My name is Mary."

The steady thumps faltered as the mirrors above us shimmered, signaling the closing of the portal.

"Mary?"

I smiled. "Bloody Mary."

About the Author

Laurae Knight is an exceptionally talented writer, dabbling in darkness and romances with fairytale vibes and plus size baddies. She strives to be an advocate for authors and is a proud co-founder of the Sisterhood of the Black Pen. Within her amazing fantasy stories, readers can expect dark humor, steamy romances, and relatable yet diverse characters surviving fantastical and chaotic worlds you won't want to leave behind. When she isn't writing, she can be found playing monsters with her children in the dense forest, chasing her dogs and cat, hunting seashells on the nearby beach with her husband and mom, or taking the chance to touch something questionable.

She can be found on Facebook (Laurae Knight) or on TikTok, Instagram, and Threads (LauraeKnightWrites). Follow her to keep up to date regarding her ongoing projects like Silent Sunflower, *a sapphic sleeping beauty retelling, or* Amethyst Stone, *a "why choose" erotica, which can be found on Kindle Vella.*

HUNGRY

A.C. SALAZAR

The Bogeyman

Snips and snails
Puppy-dog tails
The children are beasts and Wildlings

Sugar and spice
Everything nice
The Sweetlings are running and hiding

For here comes the Bogeyman
In cover of night
To show you a place most frightening

And they say when he grins
It's already too late
You haven't a chance worth fighting

Ava has waited years for this day—the day she would finally take revenge on the creature who stole away her first love. However, when things don't go as planned, she will learn just how quickly one can go from hunter to hunted. In a world where fear is the main dish, it will take everything she has to stay off the menu.

Out of seventeen major attempts to date, who could have guessed that the comments section on a how-to-video for banishing negative energy would have been the key to finally finding a real summoning circle?

As for following her newest lead, sneaking in after dark to spray paint strange symbols onto the floor of the girls' bathroom at Gibson High had been the easy part. After all, it wasn't like she had a family to worry about where she was this time of night. Ava only ever knew one person who would have noticed her absence, but Charlie had been gone for seven years already. So, even though her hopes were so low they were probably waving at the devil down in Hell, she pressed on. She had to keep trying. There was nothing left to lose anyway.

That being said, it was hard to tell which of them was more surprised—Ava or the man who had singlehandedly haunted her every nightmare since that terrible day.

She stood shell-shocked at her achievement. Even after all that hard work and years of fighting off the thought that maybe she was crazy, he was here. True to his inhuman nature, nothing about him had changed, like time itself feared coming any nearer. She even felt the same as she had back then—cold and nauseous. Blinking did nothing to make his horrible face any less real. The sharply angled pools of glossy black that gazed around lazily, mottled gray skin stretched too tightly around a mouth of needle-like teeth grinning at her, an oddly well-tailored black suit, and greasy hair that curled to give the garish impression of horns.

No, time had not affected him in the slightest. She was the one who had changed.

Ava let the thought roll over again in her head. She was not that same helpless, clueless seven-year-old trembling in bed. She had prepared for this. Taking a deep breath, she clutched the bat in her hand tightly.

"So, do you want me to put 'Bogeyman' on your tombstone, or is that just your stage name?" Her confident quip bounced awkwardly off the tiled walls, the words echoing for a moment before falling silent again.

Unimpressed eyes stopped roving the room and landed on her like an iron weight. That paper thin smile somehow growing. Ava thought in fascinated disgust that the corners of his mouth might split altogether.

"Hello, little sweetheart. What an unexpected delight to see you again."

She shuddered, terror and fury battling it out in her gut. Back then, she hadn't heard him speak. He had just watched from the shadows. It unsettled her that, if blindfolded, she might have found the rich baritone of his voice soothing.

"So, you do remember me." Ava tried to keep her voice firm.

"Yes, of course. Your Little Bird made quite the first impression. Even now, she's still one of my favorites. Though, I'll kindly ask you to keep that between us."

Wait, did that mean what she thought?

No.

No, it couldn't be, but strange as it was, there was only one person that "Little Bird" could possibly mean.

It was as if a flip had been switched in her mind. Fear she'd been trying to control finally lost its battle to teenage anger and impulsiveness. The effect was like throwing a thick blanket over a speaker. She could still hear the voice of reason screaming *danger*, but damn, if it wasn't easier to ignore. She raised the bat over her left shoulder, ready for a good swing.

"You have three seconds to explain, or I'm gonna figure out exactly how long it'll take to knock all those nasty teeth out of your head!"

"You make that sound so easy. I can't help but assume that means you found the sigil capable of harming me when you were looking for this containment spell?" He tilted his head to regard her, feigning curiosity. "How did you happen to come across such a thing, my sweetling? Knowledge like that is normally kept under lock and key by your mortal authorities."

"The internet is a magical place," she snapped. "Tell me what you did to Charlie before I rearrange that mess you call a face!"

"You don't know the sigil. Do you, my dear?" he continued, relaxed as ever.

"I'll improvise! Now talk!"

"Very well, then."

With an ease and grace that clearly was not human, he stood. The spell meant to bind the monster did nothing, neither slowing nor stopping his progress. A gasp caught at the back of her throat as he loomed above her. Symbols she had marked the linoleum with started to pop and fizzle loudly. In only seconds, they peeled themselves clean off the floor. The courage she had scraped together shattered like thin ice over an early spring lake. The fluorescent bulbs overhead flickered, and Ava stumbled back in a blind panic. That circle had been the only thing protecting her.

Bogeyman took his time, rolling his shoulders and straightening his tie, all while Ava whirled around in a frenzy, trying to yank open the door. Nothing. It was as unimpressed with her efforts as the creature behind her had been.

"Now, to business. I gather that your ill-conceived plan was originally to kill me in some fashion. Though, really, sweetie, if it were as simple as that, don't you think someone else would have managed it eons ago? Still an amazing display of ambition, but I'm afraid you lose points for execution."

The door could have been reinforced with steel for all the difference it made. Ava couldn't budge it an inch. Pivoting back to face him as he brushed dust off his lapel, she saw a window behind him, beckoning her. She didn't care if they were three stories up, hopelessness was setting in, and it was a chance she'd be willing to take—if only she could get around him.

"You are quite entertaining. In fact, it makes me think." He made a noise of contemplation. "Yes, that just might have some merit. Tell you what, sweetling, I'm going to offer you an opportunity."

She briefly considered the advantages of trying to hit him. The bat in her hand felt like a poor choice when what she really wanted at the moment was a shotgun. Both fight and flight required getting closer to the ancient figure.

"See, while it is true that the children I've taken are food to me in a way, it would be inaccurate to think I sustain myself the way humans do." Speaking as he stretched out his hands, he rolled his grotesquely long fingers until they curled back towards him, his eyes inspecting each individual oily black claw. "Slaughter and consumption... So messy. I don't require death to fill my gut, but *life*. That is why I focus my efforts on the youth. Human willpower grows so stale with age. Even you, my dear," he shakes his ever smiling head, "the taste of you has hardened. Certainly you cling to your childhood, that lingering sweetness has yet to entirely fade, but where once was a honeyed heart, it's now sharp and brittle. Facing the world alone as a young woman will do that, I'm afraid." A shiny wingtip shoe took its first step toward her.

There wasn't enough air to fill her lungs, and she began to hyperventilate. Was that high pitched ringing in her ears from the lights? She couldn't tell. Even as she thought it, he took another step closer.

"Pleasing though your flavor is, I've never been the type to overindulge. I find those who embody a more animalistic spirit to be most to my liking. Curious little brats who hunt and play and howl in the face of danger. Those are my lovely wildlings. They burst from the seams with life, and so I have my fill of it while they are with me."

He was nearly on her, so close now that the smell of his cologne was forcing its way into her nose.

"I care for them for as long as they last, but that doesn't come without a cost. Pets need to be fed just as much as their masters, after all."

A choked yelp escaped her as one of the bulbs overhead heated past its limits and shattered with a bang. Then, another and another.

"A sweetling like yourself makes for such a good treat, not to me, but for the beasts in my gut. You'll find they have terrible table manners, though. I do apologize for that. Discipline has never been my strong suit."

A desperate shriek tore from her as she finally lashed out with her bat. He caught it effortlessly, the dull *thwack* of it against his palm nearly lost as the lights continued to go out one by one. He chuckled.

"Survive the others. Find your childhood, darling, and if all goes to plan, you may just be able to save her. I'm sure you of all people would agree she's worth the effort."

"Wait, s-save her?" Ava was trembling. Her brain was such a terrified mess that she didn't even realize she'd begun loosening her grip on the only weapon at her disposal.

That smile stretched again. Only this time, it didn't stop. His image distorted, growing, as he seemed to fill the entire room. She wanted to scream, but the sound stuck in her lungs. Her bat clattered to the ground. A second later, her knees gave out, and she slid to the floor. When the last light went out, her vision was overtaken by darkness. It spared her the image of a gaping maw, as large as she was tall, encompassing her as he swallowed her whole.

Ava's voice returned to her just as the sensation of free falling took over. It tore from her while she twisted and rolled through the sickly humid air. The sound of her own blood curdling screams trailed behind, her descent too quick to properly register the echoes. Her arms and legs flailed around in an involuntary attempt at finding something, anything, to grab hold of. Yet, she plunged on.

Each moment was an agonizing second. Soon, the seconds drew out until she realized that she was slowing down. A weight wrapped around her. The fall felt more like sinking now. Almost as if she was passing through something thicker than air, even if she couldn't tell what new sensation had enveloped her. Without really meaning to, her eyes opened again. She regretted it immediately, seeing blackened fleshy walls, slick with fluids, surrounding her. The desire to gag violently was forced down by the pressure around her, and she struggled, unable to actually puke.

He had eaten her. She was as good as dead, no matter what flowery speech he'd given. The details of his explanation were, in an ironic way, finally digesting. All that talk about not needing to kill like humans. The nerve of him, when that rapidly growing ring of sulfuric yellow below was no doubt his stomach. Did he think boiling to death in acid wasn't as bad as being put out of her misery first? At least if he'd killed her outright she wouldn't have to watch as the end of the line was approaching. She had only a fraction of time left to make peace with that. Covering her face, the sting of tears made her feel pathetic, even while she started passing through clouds of noxious gas. This was it. The heat was almost unbearable, and the rush of wind was changing in pitch, like a glass of water reaching capacity. She really was going to die.

Charlie, I'm sorry. It was my fault you got mixed up in this to begin with. You were the only one who ever tried to protect me, and how did I repay you? I couldn't do anything to stop him. I couldn't do anything to hurt him. Now I'm just another missing nobody on the evening news. I wish we'd been able to grow up together. Even if you didn't feel the same way about me in the end, I loved you.

Suddenly, the pressure around her popped like a bubble. Was it just shock keeping her from feeling pain?

If I had just faced my fears, none of this would have happened in the first place. I'm so sorry.

Wasn't there supposed to be a bright light? Weren't her memories of life supposed to play in her head? It would have been nice to see her one last time.

"I'm sorry."

"—m sorry."

"—sorry."

"Whatcha sorry for, lady?" a high, unfamiliar voice chirped.

Ava wasn't sure exactly when or how she landed, only that she had. She pulled her hands away from her face with a jolt. The scene before her was so bizarre she could only stare.

It looked like she was on top of some enormous trash heap. One mounted so high it had a view over what seemed like a small town with a dirty green lake, all of it sitting in the basin of an impossibly large cavern. Directly above her here hung an ominous yellow moon. Vile clouds, the same color as the waters below, swirled around in odd patterns.

More pressing at the moment, though, was the set of glowing feline eyes staring at her from the dark inside of an old busted up locker sticking out of the rubble. If she didn't know better, she'd swear it was where the voice had come from. "H-hello?" she managed.

"Hello," the same voice replied. The hinges squeaked when the thing inside moved slightly to get a better look at her. "You're such a pretty lady. Can I have some? I'm real hungry."

"Some of what?" she asked, moving carefully to get to her feet. She felt so strange in her own skin, she had to look down despite not wanting to take her eyes away from the metal box.

The body she saw was not her own. She was covered head to foot in shimmering facets like the inside of a purple geode. She wiggled sharp fingers before her eyes. They worked, despite not looking remotely real. It reminded her of something the Bogeyman had said. *Sweetling.* Ava could only hope that she'd gone completely insane and that she definitely wasn't stranded in the stomach of an unknowable evil, somehow reincarnated to be made entirely of rock candy. Bogeyman's warning about his 'pets' floated up to the top, past her shock. It raised an alarm bell in her head.

The speaker chose that moment to finally poke out their head.

It might have once been a normal little girl, but she didn't know what to make of it now. Those big eyes had icy blue irises and slitted pupils, unblinking. Her hairline came right down her forehead and stopped at her cheeks. Fur, if Ava had to put a name on it, and mixed in with the hair atop her head were long, spiny quills, just like a porcupine.

Ava swallowed, hard. She'd only ever seen something so bizarre in movies, and CGI was a very far cry from just how detailed the image of the strange girl was. Her brain wanted to reject it. At least Bogeyman was well past the Uncanny Valley. He had never looked human to Ava, but this girl clearly had been at one point. It was almost as if she were wearing a costume that had melded into her. It distorted an otherwise precious face.

"Don't be silly," the creature said, her tone both darling and feral. "I meant you, of course."

The container burst open, and the girl came rushing out. She scuttled forward on eight enormous spider legs growing horrifically among the spikes that covered her back.

Ava shrieked, running blindly in the opposite direction. Where the hell she was going didn't matter just yet, trying not to stumble in the semi-dark, uneven terrain was more important. There was playground equipment to weave through. A toppled chain-link fence rattled loudly as she passed overhead. Whole sections of differing sidewalks and asphalt, looking like they had been ripped up in chunks and dumped around at random, cut valleys between teetering hills of garbage, creating spaces she could make use of. It was crystal clear that she was already wildly lost with nowhere to go. Clothes and toys of every conceivable variety were so trodden down and compact that they acted both as mortar keeping the larger landscape together and gravel, making the option of climbing an impossibility.

A messy, girlish giggle was closing in behind her, the child-like abomination gaining ground. Even running as fast as she could was not going to save her. She needed her bat. She needed to hide.

Anything but find out what those spindly legs were going to do when they caught her.

To the right and further ahead there was a preschool building, half collapsed by a fallen stack. Windows facing the outside were dimly lit. A classroom door between her and the girl sounded promising if she could get to it, but her legs were burning. Meanwhile, there was a rusted cop car sharply to the left in a narrow passage, and if she was very lucky, there might be a gun in there somewhere. Ava's luck was questionable at best, but she was rapidly losing steam in this labyrinth, and there wasn't much else to do but try. In a split second, she made her decision.

She nearly tripped choosing a direction, her foot having caught on some random litter she couldn't make out. Whatever it was, it started to wail. A high, thin note pierced the air, not unlike an anti-theft alarm. Ava ignored it, going to the left, but the girl swore up a storm.

It was followed by more sound, two loud bangs, then angry, overlapping shouts. There was no time to look. Ava quickly made it to the car, wrenched it open, and dove inside before slamming it shut.

Dusty leather seats smelling of mold caught her. She got to her knees in the cramped space, one hand hammering on the inside of the door, hoping to hit a button that would lock the vehicle, while the other groped around for something to defend herself with. She was temporarily relieved to hear a familiar set of clicks telling her she'd at least managed the locks. Her chest was heaving when another click turned on the headlights. It illuminated the scene outside the dirty windshields. She wished it hadn't.

Where before the spider-spined girl had been alone was now a gang of twisted animal children. Had they come from the preschool? It didn't matter much. Clearly, they weren't here to help.

They had the girl pinned, not by dog piling her, which would have put them in harm's way of those quills, but by pulling her eight extra limbs out in different directions all at once. She was left struggling in the middle, unable to move toward any of her attackers without ripping something off. Ava might have been grateful, if the headlights hadn't attracted their attention.

Their eyes reflected the light pointing at them, and Ava froze. Some had rodent-like features that pinched their faces. Others were covered in scales that smoothed over everything like a flat mask. One of the boys closest to the hood had wide, bulbous eyes, no nose, and a mouth drawn like a flat line from one side across to the other. The lumpy skin covering him made her think he must be part toad.

"I told you I almost had it! Look at her! There's enough for all of us!" the spider girl yelled, struggling anew. The spell on Ava broke. She yanked open the console, looking for anything to use as a weapon. It was stuffed with fast food wrappers and paperwork in faded ink.

"All of us? You wasn't gonna share, though, were you? That's why we don't let you go to school! You wanted all that candy to yourself! You're a meanie! And we don't have to share with meanies no more!" one of them responded, the others barking out agreements.

The girl wrenched this way and that as they all pulled hard on her already taut legs. Her frantic screams burned Ava's ears. She yanked down the sun shades while the screeching outside reached an inhuman pitch. The sound of wet branches snapping made her nearly miss the jingling of keys as they fell to the passenger's seat.

You can have a breakdown later! You can have a fucking nuclear episode later! Just get the hell out of here before those little demons get you!

Shaking purple hands fumbled with grabbing the keys and getting them in the ignition. The small figure of the girl fell down now that the others had no leverage on her anymore. She curled unceremoniously into a ball. Greenish goo poured from her now mangled back. Was it blood? The key turned the engine a little, but the chugging from the motor sputtered out just as fast as her hopes.

"What? No! No, no, no. Please!" She tried again, but it stalled once more.

"Where do you think you're going?" the toad boy burped at her.

Schug-schug-schug.

"You don't get to leave without sharing! That's the rules! If you don't share with the whole class—"

Schug-schug-schug.

"—you gonna be in trouble! Even worse than Kitty!"

Schug-rhug-rhug-room! Vroom!

She thanked whatever gods might be out there as the engine finally sprung to life, and throwing it into gear, she stomped on the gas. She expected the lurch of the car, just not in the right way. Somehow, it was in reverse, and Ava had the wind knocked out of her as the steering wheel jammed into her frame. Her foot didn't let off the pedal. Enraged animal kids gave chase, their war cries lost under the roar of the motor.

She clipped and banged into all manner of things while she regained her wits enough to actually use the steering. All she cared about was not hitting a dead end, but that brought her back to her original problem. Where the hell was she going?

Something landed heavily on the hood, forcing Ava to stop looking behind her. The squat face of the toad boy howled at her through the glass. She jerked the wheel at just the wrong moment. They both yanked up as the tail end went over a ledge, the toad boy flung away as fast as he came. Ava's sight beyond the glass was a jarred mess of color while gravity took over, and she was sent backwards down the stacks. All the way down. Down. Down.

CRASH.

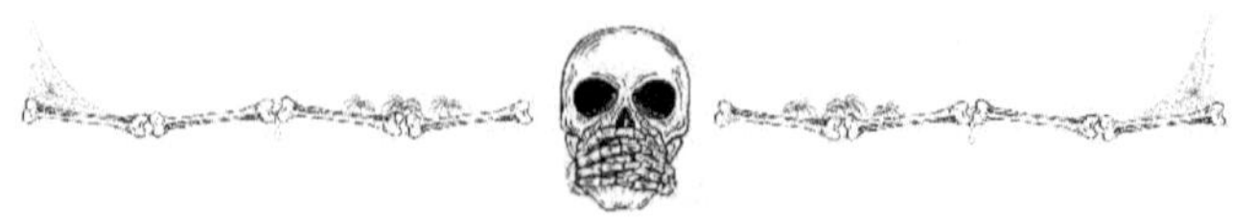

Ava had lived a difficult life despite being only sixteen. Most of it had been circumstantial though, at least at first. Her father hadn't stuck around, not unusual really. Her mother had ghosts she'd used pills and booze to smother. That had been unfortunate. Most of the rest of her family had been in no position to care for her, an understandable reality, even if it was disappointing. Those who could have didn't care, and that was where things started to spiral.

Ava had been put into the foster care system at the tender age of five. Not understanding anything, all of it had scared her. People with clipboards and tired faces had come for her one day, and after that nothing ever stayed the same for long. She learned to stay packed always, she learned the easiest way to say goodbye was to never say hello, and she learned that no one cared if there was a monster in the night.

Until she met Charlotte Bellamy.

They had been thrown into the same house when Ava was nine years old. Something about her shining pools of deepest brown eyes made her feel so seen. She couldn't ever remember someone making room for her in their lives the way Charlie had. All the baggage they both had, the walls they had built for others, just didn't seem to apply to one another. They talked for hours about all the weird stuff none of the other kids liked. They played pirates as if nothing had ever gone wrong in their lives. It had all been so liberating. Ava felt safe for the first time in her life.

That was when *he* started showing up.

Eyes like fresh tar started watching her from the shadows of the closet every night. She would have shut the door, except that it didn't have one. Most of the house was doorless. The lady who was watching them at the time insisted they didn't need them. That was a privilege, apparently, one that none of them had earned. After a few petrified nights of no sleep, she had begged on hands and knees for an exception. Mrs. Wilkner had laughed in her face.

"Scared of the Bogeyman at your age? Oh, that's rich. Wait till you learn about taxes," she gaffed.

Charlie hadn't thought it was funny. "That old bitch! Don't worry about it. You can swap rooms with me, Ava. I'm not scared of anyone!"

That had been the worst mistake of her life. At first, sleep had come easy, without the feeling of being watched. Yet as she started to drift off, something had occurred to her. She wasn't being watched anymore, sure, but now Charlie was. Ava had shot out of bed like it was a cannon and ran down the hallway back to her room as fast as she could. By then, it was too late. Charlie was nowhere to be found.

She was just gone, simple as that.

The fallout had been shockingly muted. The cops had, at first, taken her a bit more seriously when she told them a man had been in the closet that night. That had dried up like a sponge in the desert when everyone else in the house had told them about her "night terrors." Her description hadn't helped matters. She was young enough that it never occurred to her to keep the more supernatural elements of him to herself.

In the end, it was chalked up to Charlie being another runaway. The years that passed had been nothing but salt in the wound for Ava. She was labeled either crazy or attention starved by everyone from her caretakers to her schoolmates. No one could ever get her to open up the way Charlie had, and the fragile knowledge that something otherworldly was out there stole what little foundation she had left. She drifted through life.

She was still drifting, actually.

Blinking past the pain shooting through her whole body, Ava saw something she could only hope wasn't as bad as it looked. The car was still in one piece, more or less. The cracked windshield was bobbing along in what looked to be a huge, sickly colored body of water.

"Come ooooon..." she groaned to herself.

How in the hell she hadn't sunk yet was beyond her. Then again, everything that had happened up to this point was impossible, so she figured it was time to stop questioning things. Meanwhile, it felt for all the world like she had been rolling around on a bed of nails, the red hot prickly sensation being damn near more than she could stand.

A glance down told her why. Her legs were shattered. Not in the way of broken bones and split skin or bruises, but in the same way an ornament falling from a Christmas tree would. Jagged bits of shiny purple shards covered the floor. Her right foot was mostly intact, just not connected to anything. She was too tired to scream. It hurt, but it wasn't agony. Besides, barbs of colored crystals were growing from the stumps of her thighs already. Was that normal in this strange place? A sob bubbled up for a moment. She considered indulging in a good pity party, but that would be pointless.

She was still alive, so far as she could tell. Her damaged body was repairing rapidly, and the car was keeping her afloat, somehow.

There was still time. Even if the cards were stacked against her, she'd be damned if she stopped now.

There was an electric sounding squawk as the radio scanner on the dash came to life on its own. Dials turned themselves while static assaulted her ears. Ava reached out to try and switch it back off, but she couldn't, as it turned out most of her right hand was re-growing as well. The channel settled before she could worry about it much more.

"Congratulations are in order, it seems," came a familiar baritone voice.

"Oh, you son of a—" she bit out. Using her left hand was awkward, especially since she'd never seen a radio like this in person before, but after some fumbling, she managed to figure it out. "Hey, asshole, if you wanted to feed me to your minions, or whatever they are, why didn't you just kill me?" He wasn't so scary when he wasn't looking at her with that awful grin.

"Goodness, my dear, I would have thought the answer was obvious. I don't want you dead at all."

"Bullshit, you ate me!" she hollered back. "You dropped me into a horror movie! And after all that, do you wanna take a wild guess at how close I am to finding Charlie?"

"I certainly never told you the task at hand was meant to be taken lightly. You are free to give up any time, my sweet. I'm sure you would find a great many of the children would be happy to make use of you."

Ava scoffed. "Am I supposed to pretend that's an option?"

"Giving up is always an option. You have to know that. All your life you have been surrounded by people who gave up."

She was floored by his words. They were spoken with a little too much insight. How he knew was beyond her. She could hear the tiny waves in the water lapping gently at the sides of the car. He waited for her response patiently.

"Why are you doing this? Any of it, really?"

"Ah, that might take some time to explain, dear."

She looked around her, a thick fog keeping her from seeing much in detail beyond the mucky waters. "I've got a few minutes."

"Very well then, if you insist."

There was another pause, almost like he was trying to think of a good place to start.

"It is an odd relationship I have with my meals. Strange though it may be, try to imagine for a moment that you are alone in a small house. There is no way out of it, but it has large windows that let you see outside."

Given the situation she was in, that wasn't much of a stretch. For now, she kept the comments to herself. She had asked for him to spill, after all.

"Now, pretend that you find a dish left out for you one day. Naturally, you eat it. Outside the windows, every vegetable that passes your lips becomes a garden. A steak becomes a grazing cow. In some ways, it's rather pleasant. You are kept apart, yet it feels like company."

Static popped over the airwaves as he took another moment, seemingly to collect his thoughts.

"However, the reality is that life is always changing. That is one of the only things it can be counted on to do. Sometimes, the cows trample the garden, and other times, the garden overtakes the view. It's not perfect, but there is little that you can do about it. You are in the house, separated from everything outside."

She frowned at the radio. Was he trying to make a case for being misunderstood? She was not about to forget that he took the only good thing she ever found in life.

"After a very long time of all this, you eventually discover ways of making changes, here and there. You find that eating only one kind of food helps keep the weeds down or that having too many animals all at once leads to stampedes. Things settle down. Life is as good as it has ever been."

There was a loud bit of crackling. If she were paying attention, she'd have noticed that the fog behind her was darker than it was a second ago. She wasn't though, and she didn't.

"So, it comes as a shock when you eat something new and find that, rather than forming outside the window, one of your new pets is in your living room. Making itself at home."

A shadow slowly split the fog, like a curtain being parted. Ava still didn't notice. In spite of herself, she was trying to imagine the scenario he was painting. It was hard to put herself in the shoes of a creature so far removed from humanity.

"It is a better companion than all the rest. There's just one little problem. Being inside the house seems to make your new friend quite ill. You ignore that, hoping it will sort itself out, but it is a mistake. The pet dies. You are alone again."

Anxiety clawed at the back of her head. He wasn't talking about Charlie. If she were already dead, he wouldn't have started this whole charade, right?

"It becomes the first of depressingly few. Only every blue moon does anything ever inhabit the house with you, and always it passes away quickly. Well, my sweetling, that is now your dear Charlotte. She has the unique ability to understand my thoughts, to communicate directly without any need for me to strain myself, as I am now with you. Over the years, it has begun to drain her in a way I have never found a cure for. Until, possibly, today."

"What the hell is that supposed to mean?" Ava demanded. "If being here is making her sick, why not just let her go?"

"You of all people should know that the life I took her from could hardly be considered desirable. I have offered to let her go before. She was convinced that there was nothing for her in the human world. Unfortunately, I couldn't hide my agreement."

He may as well have slapped her.

"She only ever had one real regret. A pretty little thing, shy and delicate. A girl that surely had moved on without her."

"I NEVER—"

"Oh, but neither she nor I had any way of knowing that, now did we?"

Ava wondered about that. He seemed to know a lot more than he should. Outside, the shadow filled in the space where the fog had been, so utterly quiet that it continued to go unrecognized.

"So, can you picture my delight when you summoned me? That is why you are here, sweetling. Think of this as a medical trial. One where *you* are the medicine."

Without a single note of warning, the back window exploded in a shower of broken glass. Ava screamed as a hook caught the frame of the interior, the gentle drift she'd acquired lurched to a halt. Chains attached to the grapple started reeling her in quickly.

"There is little time left. I thought perhaps you, being the only thing in the mortal world that she craved, might just be the answer."

The car started lifting out of the waters, and Ava was tossed up against the battered windshield as it went vertical. With only half reformed limbs, there wasn't much she could do but holler in distress.

"I have done everything I can to help you get here. Now it's the moment of truth. You wanted to save her. So, here's your big chance. Best of luck."

The radio fizzled out, and Ava cursed him blue, even though she was ninety percent sure he couldn't hear her anymore.

Like a fish on a line, the car spun and swayed while it was brought in. She flopped around until she was in some semblance of sitting and could see outside. Not that she had much in the way of expectations, this definitely wouldn't have been it.

It was a pirate ship, just like the ones they used to be obsessed with in first grade. In fact, if memory served her, this one was a large Spanish Galleon. The name *Ava's Wrath* was painted in gold along the port side.

She'd be touched, if she wasn't in complete shock.

There were dozens of figures standing on the deck she seemed to be heading for. It was difficult to tell from a distance, and like the others, this place had altered her to an animal-like state, but she knew those eyes. Charlie stood with her crew of mutant children, their features a revolting exhibition of various sea creatures. A devastating smirk danced on her sapphire colored lips while shiny white shark teeth peek out from behind them. The dark luster of her skin was highlighted by patches here and there of silvery scales. Gone were the thick rows of box braids on her head, replaced with what looked like scorpion tails. Bogeyman called her "Little Bird," but there was nothing little about the huge magpie wings that flexed from the back of her shoulders.

It really was Charlie—at least, what was left of her. Seeing her standing head and shoulders above the rest, her dominating presence radiating power and command, Ava suddenly thought she might need all the luck she could get.

He said she was here as medicine, but what did that mean? As the car touched down on the deck, it was surrounded by wildlings. They looked at her with wicked joy, yet they cleared a path quickly for their captain. Ava told herself she had nothing to be afraid of, Charlie wouldn't eat her. She wouldn't.

Not her Charlie.

So then... why did she look so hungry?

About the Author

A.C. Salazar is a reclusive, social media-allergic asexual with a love for all things creepy and mysterious. Her passion for storytelling started at a young age and has long been an outlet for her chronic anxiety. Hungry marks not only Ms. Salazar's first fully completed project but also her first indie publication. Currently living in the lush and inspiring Pacific Northwest, she hopes that many more will follow. When she isn't writing, Ms. Salazar enjoys collecting vinyl records, spending time with her family, cuddling her dog, and looking for new inspiration for her stories. Although most future works can be expected to be supernatural romances, she also dabbles in high fantasy, horror, and YA stories.

DEVIL'S NIGHT

SARAH TRALA

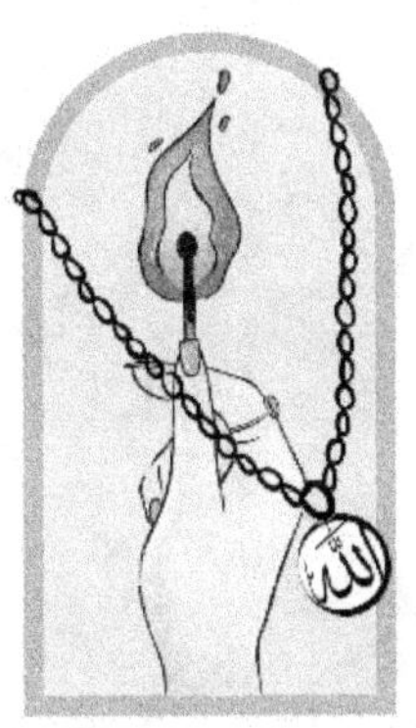

Devil's Night.

A time of harmless fun and pranks that slowly twisted into a night of horror for many in the Metro Detroit area. What began as a few soaped windows and egged cars became more than eight-hundred house fires with countless acts of vandalism...
just in 1984.

Many dismissed these events as expected rises in crime with the increased population, while others insisted something more sinister was afoot, and that, perhaps, what was once a night filled with laughter and youthful joy, had truly become one meant for devils.

Ever smell flesh cooking? The scent putrid, gagging? Hear eyeballs popping from the pressure as the fluids inside them boil? Feel the skin sliding from your bones? Your hair crinkling and curling up into your scalp, trying to flee the searing flames? A heat so severe your eardrums get tight and tear, the resulting itch driving you mad?

What about experiencing that, every night, for a week straight?

A month?

Waking to find you can't move, can't speak. Your breath stutters, your chest tightens, heart beats loudly enough the gods in heaven could hear it crystal clear. It's not the gods that are with you, no, that would make the moment bearable. The thing that watches you, only feet away, partially lit by the dim light from the scarf laden lamp on your bedside table, is anything but a god.

Skin scarlet red, darkened between thick muscles. Veins protruding down long arms crossed over a bare chest. It's the terror induced by the fire in his eyes, though, flames escaping to lick blackened eyebrows, that squeezes the breath from your lungs.

But this isn't you.

This is me.

I have a process for when this happens. It's not easy, it's not fast, but it works. The shadows around my room taunt me as I go, wordlessly creating new shapes, new horrors, reaching without touching. Twisting the words of encouragement on my handmade poster into horrifying, unreadable scripts.

First, toes. Picture them, because Lord knows I can't see them anymore. Imagine the muscles twitching, breaking free from their frozen nature. Wriggling and curving until the cool underside touches the ball of my foot.

Second, fingers. Mentally pushing each one into the mattress, until the mattress pushes back. Balling my hand into a fist, scrunching the comforter in a way that should be reserved for when I have a partner in my bed.

"Usually, by then, I've broken free enough that I can will away the visions." My voice cracks, the smallest of bits, as I tell Amara all my secrets. She's listened to me for years, following night terror after night terror, but her eyes are wide. The fake blood caked across her forehead will never recover. For the first time in a long time, I've shocked her. "This morning, I couldn't shake it until I got myself to roll out of bed. My brain jangled enough with the impact that I was finally able to wake up."

I laugh.

She doesn't.

The painted-on smile is enough for me to pretend, but I still hide the awkwardness behind a sip from my scalding coffee.

"That's, um..." Her toast is halfway to her mouth, a blob of egg precariously perched on the lightly browned ciabatta. "Quite the dream, Liz."

"It wasn't..." What's the point in arguing? We'd already bickered when I first sat down because I hadn't shown up in costume. While the great Amara dolled herself up in fake scars, dripping blood, and a splotchy green scarf, I'd stuffed myself into a pair of black skinny jeans and an orange sweater, the color clashing with the red undertones in my umber hair. Too much is on my mind. There's something about this last episode that stands out from the others. "What if this demon is trying to tell me something?"

"You've got the fire aspect, right? Have you seen anything else in the mornings? Scorpions, snakes, maybe a lizard?"

"Yes! Yes, all of that! Sometimes, they're crawling over my bed or curling around the bedposts. One time, a lizard was plopped on my chest, flicking its little tongue at my nose."

"Not a demon." As Amara takes a bite of her brunch, a bit of egg breaks loose and falls onto her hijab. I toss a couple napkins over, and she pats the stain lightly. "You've got yourself a jinn."

"A jinn? Like a genie?"

"Not exactly. Bit of a generic catch-all phrase for a spirit. Not good, not evil, just... is. At least, according to the Quran." She sets down the wad of paper and digs into her pocket, mumbling under her breath. "Could just be the run-of-the-mill sleep paralysis episode, but it might also be that the jinn has targeted you for some reason. Ah, there it is."

A silver chain wraps around her fingers, glittering brilliantly even in the dim light of Timmy's Diner. It's thin, delicate, holding a charm roughly the size of a dime. On the face is a curly symbol similar to a 'w' but with an extra loop, a few smaller etchings surrounding it.

I only reach out to admire the necklace, but as soon as my palm opens, Amara drops it, the light tinkling of a bell sounding as she does.

"The bell on the clasp has multiple uses." Just as small as the rest of the piece, the noise it makes is only loud enough for the two of us to hear. "It was added on to weigh down the necklace and keep it from spinning around, but the noise dispels demons while the iron keeps away fae."

Demons, fae, jinn? I came in hopes that I would be convinced all of this is in my head. While I had a small inkling there may be something more, I needed someone to tell me these are nightmares—and nothing more. Instead, I'm being given a protection necklace. This is all too much. Unnerving, even.

"Since when do you believe in all this?" Shoving the necklace toward her, she shakes her head. "Seriously, this is silly. It's just nightmares, and I'm waking up too fast. My imagination is getting the best of me, as is the lack of sleep."

"The silver will burn vampires." Without missing a beat, Amara continues to explain the benefits while loading up another piece of bread. This one, she makes sure to hold her hand under so it doesn't spill again. Chomping in, there's an ever so soft moan in delight. She's barely finished chewing before speaking once more. "It's the charm, though, that *you'll* get the most use out of. That script is

Allah's name. Wear it, and the magic from a jinn won't touch you. If you keep having sleep paralysis episodes, we'll know it's something of the *normal* variety."

"What's next? Holy water?"

"You could, but I've also got about a cup of Zamzam water left. My parents could send me more eventually." Leaning back in the seat, she rubs her chin in thought. "But it's probably easier to get a hold of holy water, to be honest."

"Oh my goodness. You're serious."

"One hundred percent. If you'd like, I can even write down a few prayers for you. English translation should work fine, it's all in the intent of the words. But I can always give you a phonetic version to memorize. I've heard reciting them in your head can help when you're trapped."

"Necklace, yes." To prove I mean the words, I undo the little clasp, being careful of the bell, and secure it around my neck. "Religious lines in another language, translated or not, no thanks. My luck, I'll be *summoning* something rather than getting rid of a jinn."

"Your faith in me is worse than your faith in God." She finishes off the last of her bread as I roll my eyes. "Now, what are you wearing for Devil's Night? Ah-hem, sorry, Angel's Night? Hot Mess is a great costume and all, but this zombie could use better prey."

"Ohhh, you're a zombie! That makes so much more sense."

"More sense than what exactly?" Amara glances down at her outfit, studying it with a distressed look. "Okay, yeah, my clothes could be a little muddier. But come on, I mossed up my hijab! Added fake scars! *And there's blood.* I can't be scaring people in public with a popped-out eyeball or exposed brain. How else could I have been more obvious?"

"I kinda just figured you grabbed from the dirty clothes pile." The devastation on her face made me drop my eyes and switch topics faster than trying to hand off a potato fresh off the grill. "As for *Angel's* Night, I'll be spending it at the cemetery."

"Oh, right. Sorry, I forgot." Cautiously, her fingers slide over mine. When I don't yank my hand away, she gives them a light squeeze. "Hey, you gotta be careful. We may have *thought* things were bad when we were teens. Compare that to these last couple years, though, and those were just appetizers for the real show. The angels are going to make a real difference doing these patrols."

"You know, that's likely what's causing these crazy dreams." I watch as the steam spirals over my coffee cup. "Just my mind realizing the anniversary was coming up."

"What's it been, eight years?"

"Ten." She knows this. Everyone knows. "Tonight marks *ten* years since I decided to sneak out to that Halloween party."

"It's a good thing you did because it means—"

"What? That they've gotten to rot while I continue living?" Throwing my walls up, I snatch my purse and toss ten bucks on the table. "Have fun with your patrols. Hope you keep some other kid from accidentally ruining their life."

"You were seventeen, Liz. People make mistakes. Wait, please come back! I'M SORRY!" she yells, loud enough that the patrons around us turn to see what's going on. I storm out of Timmy's Diner and into my rusted Jeep, refusing to acknowledge her shouts. There are a few hours left until dark, and I plan on getting in a few shots.

Maybe a nice nap.

Is it considered murder to completely smash your alarm clock until the little red light dies? What if you keep going, raging until the black plastic shatters, the wood splinters, and the tiny metal cogs fly under the bed?

I swear, my head hit the pillow and I was out like a light. Once the shrill beeping started, I sat straight up, nearly screaming along with it. No tall, beefy, mysterious red man hung out in the doorway, though. Nor a lizard wanting a French kiss.

Having that proper nap makes it that much easier to focus while I prep for the family picnic, load up the Jeep, and head out to cross the gates.

Now, it's just me, my blanket, my basket of treats, and my family waiting to start our dinner. They might be six feet below the leaves that crunch underneath me, but I'm sure they're rolling in their graves with my tardiness.

My fingernail slides under the cool metal, popping open a mostly warm can of Tab. My parents were never a fan of the calorie-free pop, but it's a favorite of mine. Just as the fizz dies out, laughter breaks the peace of the quiet space.

Faint at first, just a little bit of a high-pitched tinkle in the night—perhaps a young girl laughing at a not-so-funny joke. Then, it twists, darkens, matures. Becomes the thing of nightmares. A chorus cheer meant for the devil himself.

It's a cemetery—I don't know why I assumed I'd be safe within the fences. Hallowed ground means nothing to these assholes. These may not be the same punks who thought it funny to toss a couple Molotov cocktails into a random suburban home, leaving the occupants to struggle in the smoke, coughing, dragging burning pajama clad bodies to safety never reached, but they are no different. They aren't thinking about the victim, just their fun.

Cracks and splatters tell me at least one of them has a carton of eggs. What a waste of a dollar. Prices have nearly doubled in the last few weeks, might as well just set a wallet on fire. Maybe if I stay quiet, leave them alone to spray paint, toss their toilet paper, and feed the headstones uncooked yolks, they'll allow me the moment with my parents and brother.

"Looky-loo!"

But I could never be so lucky. From behind the old oak, a pale figure pops out. Black hair slicked up into spikes, jean jacket with the collar upturned, and a silver buckle that reflects my candle's light.

"Lorraine! Jerry! We've got ourselves a Clydesdale. How's it hanging, lady?"

"Leave me alone, and I'll leave you alone."

"Danny!" A few rows down, a woman calls to him. She's a few shades darker than *Danny*, with her midriff on full display. "Ugh, what a freak. Come on, let's bounce."

"Take a chill pill, Rainey-bird." He takes a lock of my hair and twists it around his finger. "Maybe she's hella warped and wants a choice stud for the night."

I slap his hand away and earn myself a laugh from the creep. Instead of retreating, he leans in closer, our noses almost touching. This is my spot, my night with my family, and I'm not backing down.

"What's your damage?" It takes grit to keep down my dinner as his eyes bounce up and down. "Is it something Dan-the-man can cure?"

"A wastoid like you couldn't cure his own boredom, let alone anything I'd need." My sandwiches get smushed under my extra drinks when I whip them into the basket, clearing the area as fast as I can. The blanket is my downfall. It isn't a soft tug, not in the slightest. But, like a toddler losing a game, the creep dramatically flings himself backwards and gives a cry.

"Danny!" Hair barely moving, the singular girl in their trio comes running to his side. Their third casually strolling up once the blanket has been successfully tucked into the woven wicker.

"You three sure are a piece of work." I turn away from them, basket on my forearm, ready to hustle to my Jeep. Prince is calling my name, and I have a fresh copy of *Purple Rain* in my case. "Get your kicks in while you can because I'm calling the cops as soon as I get out of here."

Wrong thing to say because a kick is exactly what I get.

Square to the back.

My basket goes sailing. Pieces of lettuce, chunks of turkey, chip crumbles, not even my soda is safe from acting as impromptu decorations on the nearby headstones.

"What in the fuck is happening over here!" A voice, deep, vibrating every bone in my body, turns me to jelly.

"Danny! It's the caretaker!" The girl's bracelets bounce against each other in her sudden shock. She tugs on the guy's jacket, hissing as he pulls away and leans into my ear.

"Gotta motor, darlin', but we'll be seeing you again real soon."

The seconds stretch out after I hear the gremlins scatter, but I don't move. It's hard to say exactly why. Perhaps the embarrassment of knowing my face is firmly planted in the damp, muddy leaves. Or it may even be that absolutely panty-melting reaction I had to hearing whoever made them run. Maybe the fact it might be a bit strange to be having a picnic in a graveyard, in the middle of the night, on Devil's Night.

"Miss?" Too caught up in my own mind, I'm not expecting the hand placed on my shoulder. Or to hear that same voice I was pondering in my ear. "I'm so sorry, I just wanted to make sure you were okay."

I can't help myself. Despite my self-consciousness, I raise my head and stare.

At first, all I see are legs. Legs that never end, clad in skin tight, darkened jeans, worn almost white at the seams and over the knees. Climbing higher, over a decently sized bulge and thick black leather belt, to a neatly tucked in work button-up. Blood red, with coal dark buttons that are left undone near the top to show off a full body golden tan.

"Do I know you?" Why do those have to be the first words out of my mouth? Of all the things I could say, I ignore the obvious, *Thank you, yes, I'm fine,* and instead, I have to know if he's the figure I see night after night. If it weren't for his large sunglasses, reflecting back how terrible I feel, he'd be a dead ringer for the demon who enjoys watching me from my bedroom door.

Minus the red skin.

"I don't believe we've ever been introduced." He reaches down as he speaks, offering me a hand in assistance. "But you've been coming here for the better part of a decade. Hard to not take notice of such care and heart." A pause. "And beauty."

Against my better judgment—because stranger danger and the fact a guy is hitting on me over my parents' literal dead bodies—a blush stains my face. In the off chance this turns into something real, at least we'll have a story to tell our kids.

"So, what's your name?" His hand is soft, warm, despite the fact he works the grounds. I wonder what else is soft, and what else is hard. "Miss? Your name?"

"Oh! Sorry! Elizabeth Ashe." I shake the hand I hold captive, unwilling to let go. "It's nice to meet you. I'm surprised we haven't run into each other out here before."

"Usually, people are too caught up in their mourning to notice the guy burying their loved ones." He doesn't let go, either, but instead, chuckles and pulls me closer. "My name's Levi."

Of course, I hadn't asked his name.

"Seems your picnic is a bit of a loss. I don't want to impose, but I've got some deli meat and cheese in the shop. And a couch, which could be seen as an upgrade from a blanket on the ground."

"You know what? That sounds like a great idea."

Does it, though? Would my parents approve that I'm leaving them behind on our day? Or would they be glad that I found someone living to spend my time with?

But none of those thoughts matter because I follow the man—mostly staring at the tobacco orange threads curving into a 'V' on his back pocket—that towers above most of the monuments in the older section of the cemetery. To me, they are huge, slightly crumbling, structures that are so old they aren't even original to this location. Years and years ago, they once rested where the McHattie Inn now sits. Halloween tradition involved going on a ghost hunt there, with Amara, hoping to catch orbs and ghostly figures in reflections with our Polaroid camera. But our adventure might be skipped this year. My heart just isn't in the holiday anymore, hasn't been in a long time if I'm honest.

"It's not much, but it's home."

Not much is an understatement. It's a shed. One side of the room is taken up by an oddly familiar smokey orange sofa, the buttons dangling from the strings, and the wood legs chewed by a long gone dog. A mismatched coffee table sits in front of it, the laminate peeling away to show the bubbling, compressed wood core. Jutting out from the left side, on the far wall, is a squared off room with a plain wooden door. I assume it's a restroom, but I can't say I'll use it. Beside the corner addition is an overturned milkcrate and atop that sits a tube tv with aluminum foil wrapped around the antenna ears.

"This is... where you live?"

"When I'm taking care of the cemetery, yes." He waves toward the couch and leans over to open a wood paneled mini fridge tucked under a pile of shovels and rakes. I take his silent invitation but hesitate before sitting. An alarm screams in the back of my head, but I push it down and settle down on the cushion, leaving a little space between myself and the armrest. "You could say this is more of a workshop than a home. We rotate out for each season. I'm here for fall."

"So, where do you spend the rest of the year?"

"A tiny community up north. Spiritus Villa. Do you mind lettuce wraps? It seems I'm fresh out of bread, but there's plenty of ham, cheese, mustard, and a whole head of lettuce."

Is it a mess? Yes. And yet, this is probably the most fun I've ever had on Devil's Night. *Three's a Crowd* just barely manages to play, static kicking in and out as Jack sees a psychologist, while we stuff our faces with far too much sodium-filled deli foods.

During one of my laughs over a joke that's not as funny as I make it seem, Levi reaches out to wipe mustard from the corner of my mouth. When he pulls away, I stop him, guiding his thumb between my lips instead.

Staring deep into the dark lenses, at my own heavily lidded eyes, I take my time and thoroughly clean the digit. Only letting go when I'm sure my point has been made.

Am I completely insane?

It doesn't matter. Nothing does at this moment.

I lean into him, and he seems willing as our lips touch and part, giving way to exploration. My hands push on his shoulders, and he follows my lead, carefully lying on his back while I awkwardly straddle his wide frame. Slowly, my fingers work their way from his shoulders, up his neck, along his jaw, to the thick black frames that hide his eyes. Wearing sunglasses at night is subjectively hot—thank you Corey Hart—but sunglasses during sex is a little bit strange.

Shock strikes me when his hand grabs my wrist.

Immediately, I pull away, halting all progression. The springs of the couch dig into my knees as I lift off him. I never should have thought he would be down for any of this. He invited me to his shop for food, not to be molested. What the hell am I thinking?

"They stay on." An equally tight grip graces my hip, dragging me down to him, forcing me to grind on the hardening spot in his jeans. "Feel free to remove anything else, but the glasses stay on."

"I've had guys want me to tie them up and spank them while they call me Mommy," I admit. A devastatingly satisfied smile spreads across his mouth as I pop the remaining buttons of his shirt. "Just make me cum, and your glasses are safe."

"That, I can do."

Before I know it, he flips us. Me underneath him, gazing up at my reflection, panting, the black lenses darkening my flushed cheeks, yet highlighting my blown pupils. I crave to see if he shares the same look. I wish I could bottle this moment forever.

He has my bottoms unbuttoned and off in one breath, and by the next, my reflection disappears with his tongue between my thighs. There's an inhumane quality to that skill, deftly swirling over my clit, bringing noises tumbling from my mouth I can't say I've ever uttered.

Like a mind reader, he knows I'm ready for more.

My knees dig into the cushion once again when I'm flipped to face the armrest. Bracing against the worn fabric, I listen for his zipper to fall.

Only, it doesn't.

Just as I start to turn my head for a check in, fingers knot into my hair, shoving my forehead into the cushion. Again, I wait for something, anything, but all I get is the smell of dust and grit.

I grunt my displeasure.

"You're good with freaky, right?"

Yeah, I'm good with freaky, but the only reply he'll get from me is muffled nonsense. So, I answer his question with a grunted laugh.

"Then, don't panic, just enjoy."

His fingers remain in my hair, locking my head at an awkward angle, while my mind wanders over what might possibly be coming. Perhaps, a little spanking, water sports, a toy or two. When the zipper finally falls, and I feel his warm head press against my opening, patience goes out the window.

I shove myself onto him and against him.

Somehow, he's both inside me and outside of me, teasing and pleasuring, hitting deep within and grinding my very soul to oblivion. It's a high different than any I've climbed before, and one I hope will last.

And last he does.

From the couch to the wall, the coffee table, even up against an old rusty push mower. He doesn't stop until I've lost track of how many times I've come and the television is giving a midnight sign off beneath us. His moans mix with mine as he finally pulls out, yanking my hair so I can't see more than my own reflection in his glasses. He finishes. White streaks paint my face, neck, and breasts, and I nearly spot his eyes when he tilts down to admire me like his own personal Mona Lisa.

Only then does he return me to the couch, sit me down, bring me an ice cold can of Tab, and wander off to the bathroom.

My eyes start to cross by the time he returns with a damp rag, motioning for me to lay back while he proceeds to clean the mess he's made. *We've* made.

"Sleep. I'll wake you in the morning."

The scent of something burning invades my nose, waking while not-waking me. Once more, I'm stiff as a board, unable to move. After a few agonizing moments, I manage to open my eyes, and instantly, I wish I hadn't.

Thin smoke fills the room, ash sticks to the sweat coating me. As much as I want to believe this is just another nightmare, I can clearly read the packaging from the wrappers that still sit on the coffee table. Pain is one thing, but reading is another.

On the other side of the wall, I hear giggles and hysterical laughter, liquid splashing against the thin wood. The click of a lighter. Crackling.

They've set fire to the fucking workshop.

And I'm trapped on an old, rotting couch.

Is this what my mother felt like as she held my baby brother? They said she was found on the poured cement floor, overtop William, so at least she was able to attempt an escape. Or perhaps, attempt protecting him when they truly never had a chance of getting out of the basement. The stairs had long burned by that time. Smoke inhalation caught my father in the hallway, just a few feet away from the door to my unoccupied bedroom. While I sat in a private room of the police station, I was told the devastating updates as the hours passed. There wasn't much else for my seventeen-year-old self to do.

In the few seconds it takes for me to pull myself out of my mental spiral, that thin gray smoke grows thicker, greedier, making each breath a little harder to take. My lungs burn, my skin begins to turn red, and I can't do anything about it. Those age old tricks of trying to move one body part at a time aren't working.

I search the room, looking for Levi. If anyone can help, he's the one to do it. Lord knows he has larger lungs, and he'd proved more than once that my frame isn't too much for him to handle. Red fabric catches my eye from near the television set, its static breaking through the smoke just enough to light up his face.

His sunglasses-free face.

He's not going to be helping me anytime soon. He won't be my savior. Beneath the sunglasses is pink skin, thin enough to see the crisscrossing of red veins lined with eyelashes. There had been nothing behind those lenses but empty sockets. And I'm fairly certain that despite everything happening, there's no possible way any of it is real. Yet, I have no way of waking up.

"Stay calm." I hear Levi's deep rumble, but the lips I'd spent hours memorizing aren't moving. His jaw hangs open, tongue rolling off to the side from the odd tilt of his head. A disposed puppet, and one that continues talking from somewhere else. "I can control the fire, keep it away from you. Just shallow your breaths until it fizzles out."

There is no calm for me, no way to keep my breaths level. Smoke tickles the back of my throat, but I can't cough to clear it. The discarded body is not the source of the voice. Standing at the end of the couch is the jinn, watching over me, holding the same pose as always, arms crossed over his chest. His scarlet skin a few shades darker, the shadows dancing over him as though alive. Shirtless, as typical, but he's managed to find enough time to slip back into his broken in jeans.

This whole time, Levi knew who I was, knew what would happen, and did nothing to stop it. How many times have I felt myself die? Felt myself cook on top of this ratty orange couch? That's why it looked familiar—I'd seen it before. Seen him. Watching, always present, but never speaking.

Only this time, he had.

What makes tonight different?

He acted like he didn't know me.

Is this just another dream... or reality?

I've never heard the jinn's voice before now.

How can I trust he's trying to save me from the fire?

If he's here, it means I have no chance at surviving the night.

I know exactly what's going to happen next.

My skin melts, along with my thoughts, my mind going empty.

Over the back of the sofa, the plywood wall turns black and flakes away, drifting embers onto my exposed flesh. Each lands with a soft sizzle, extinguishing once coming into contact with my increasingly dampening skin. A crack forms in the wall, quickly followed by a second and a third. The room becomes brighter, blinding, as the noise grows louder, muffling his words.

"Trust me, please trust me."

Flames flicker to life in the dark holes where his eyes should be, blazing, drawing the yellows and reds of the crackling heat from the wall, over me and toward him.

"I'm doing everything I can, just please trust me."

I want to trust him, but no relief comes. The heat around me increases, cooking me. My skin bubbles. Small pockets at first, across my stomach and down my legs, then my arms. It doesn't take long before the small amount of fluid, hoping to save my raw flesh, joins together and gets larger. Bursts. Exposing sensitive skin that repeats the process.

My ears go from a gentle muffle, barely hearing the jinn—*my jinn*—to only hearing my own heartbeat. Seconds pass, and that too is stolen from me as the membrane finally splits. Static would have been preferable to the unbearable itch that grows while my eardrums dry out in the heat and flap like a broken speaker.

As much as I wish the smoke inhalation would put me out of my misery, allow me to pass out and die in peace, I stay conscious as the fluids in my eyes begin to boil. A migraine has nothing on this pressure, and I'm helpless to stop it.

The last thing I see, before they split and my world goes black, is my jinn. Confusion and panic on his face as he reaches out to me, unable to touch me, screaming silent words while unsuccessfully trying to push back the flames.

"Then, I woke up. In my bedroom." Pausing, I watch Amara, waiting to see if she will be just as shocked as I'd dreamed her to be. I'm not disappointed. "My skin was clammy, my eyes burned, even my ears were ringing. Up until I walked through those doors, the smell of treated lumber was stuck in my nose. Now, thankfully, it's just burnt coffee."

To make the point, I hold up the plain white mug I'd ordered. This Amara isn't dressed as a zombie, much to my surprise. She'd chosen a thicker black hijab, layering a sheer orange scarf overtop. Her dress follows the color scheme but is also kept simple. Just like my last dream, though, she holds on to a slice of freshly baked ciabatta bread, a dollop of egg teetering on the crisp edge.

"Let's take this one step at a time because I'm freaking out." Amara holds up a finger, pausing our conversation, as she goes in for the bite. Knowing what would happen next, I pick up a napkin and lean forward to catch the egg that misses her mouth.

"Is that proof enough?" It wouldn't be, not for her. Not for me, either, if I were to be honest. The whole story is something right out of the *Twilight Zone*. Folding the napkin, I set it beside her plate.

"You mentioned I gave you a necklace." She drops the soiled brown paper and grabs a fresh napkin to clean up her face. "Here's the thing, I do have a necklace for you. Joann passed it along to me yesterday. *Yesterday.* There's no way you would have even known about it because I didn't know about it."

"Okay, so that's two points for this being some kind of warning."

With a sigh, she pulls the necklace out of her pocket and drops it on the table. It's identical to the one I'd seen before. Silver chain, iron bell, pendant with Allah's name.

"If I offer you scripture, will you turn me away again? The Al Kursi prayer would be a good one, and the English translation would work just fine."

"No, no prayers." Gently, I scoop up the jewelry. The metal is cold on my fingers despite having been kept in her pocket for who knows how long. "But I *am* going to take the necklace."

"Why? That's why your jinn couldn't help you."

Everything stops with that statement. Far away crackling fills my ears, the faint memory of a fire I hadn't actually lived through. Had he really been trying to help me? An intense stare from a pleading man not understanding why his attempts to protect me weren't working.

"Only while I wear it, right?" My question makes Amara's jaw drop. "This thing, when I wear it, will stop the sleep paralysis episodes and keep Levi's magic from affecting me. But if I were to take it off, and say, hang it somewhere, would that bar it's... fancy supernatural blocking abilities?"

"Correct." She loads up another piece of bread, but her brows remain furrowed in concern. "So, what are your plans for tonight? If you honestly think there is going to be a fire, how are you going to stop it?"

"Was he right in saying you're patrolling with the Angels?"

"Yes, but my area is closer to McHattie Township." She takes a bite of her breakfast, this time holding a hand underneath to catch any falling pieces. "We're not going to be inside the city."

"The township line picks up at Artindale Road, only a mile north of the cemetery. What if you ask your group to meet with you there? You could act as a kind of bodyguard to scare away the assholes before they even cross the tree line."

"And what are you going to do? Have a tea party with all of us?"

"Just a tea party for two, in a workshop straight from the sixties, with a man that's not really a man and some cold cuts."

"Don't forget to use your brain and grab a condom. Wouldn't want a bunch of fire-controlling jinn-human toddlers running about." She finishes off the last bite of her eggs and toast, giggling to herself. "'Mommy, Mommy! A kid called me a demon, so I lit his pants on fire. Now his parents want to talk to you!'"

"Fair point." I slam back the remainder of my coffee and grab my jacket. "Let's go pay the lady so we can get out of here."

We make our way to the break in beige capped bar stools, waiting for a waitress to come to the register. A few teens linger about, sipping on milkshakes. Our brunch started later than normal, landing as more of an early dinner. Better for me since I wasn't planning on eating tonight. No, that plan is meant for someone else.

"Oh, and that sensation you were talking about? How it felt like he was inside of you and outside of you?" Her face twists into a smirk as she whispers into my ear, "Another fun factoid about jinn, they have hemipenes. He's got an extra cock."

Well, scratch that. I might be sampling a bit of something.

"Well, you weren't wrong. Or should I say, your jinn wasn't wrong." Amara and I stand just outside the gates to the McHattie cemetery. "When I told everyone there might be some issues with vandalization, a motorcycle club said they'd stand watch."

"We have motorcycle clubs in McHattie?"

"They call themselves Blood Favors. The president said this one was on the house and to call on him if we needed anything else. Bit ominous if you ask me, but now you've got your guard."

"They sure make for nice eye candy." Two members position themselves stoically outside the gates, and a handful more are placed inside in various sections. Although she lacked a costume earlier, now with moss packed on, some carefully placed fake blood, and theater makeup, she's an even better undead version of Amara than the one from my dreams. "You liked the zombie idea too, I see. You look good."

"Thanks." Walking over to her car, she pauses and glances back at me over her shoulder. Only then does she give me a once over. "Go have fun with your jinn. *Bisalama*, Liz."

"A llama? Where?" I smile to show I'm messing around. "I'll see you tomorrow night at the McHattie Inn. Thanks for everything."

Her tires crunch over the dirt lot as she leaves. Nodding to the leather clad guards on either side of the gate, I make my way toward the workshop. A thin bit of light comes from under the door, but it's blocked when my hand reaches up to knock.

I hold my breath as the door opens.

"I'm sorry." He may be hidden behind dark sunglasses, but I know it's him. My jinn. Just as tall, this time in dark blue coveralls, the front buttons sloppily done. "Have we met?""

"Does every night for the last month count?"

"Nice to see you in the real world, Elizabeth Ashe."

Stepping back, he waves for me to enter the shop. There are a few more spider webs than I'd seen previously, as well as a pillow and blanket folded on the coffee table.

"Why?" The question spills from my lips before I can stop it. Levi walks past me into the shop, and sighs when he spots his mismatched buttons.

"Why what?" Starting from the top, where his collar lays lopsided, his fingers pop each button through their partnered hole. My mind goes blank, staring at the exposed wide chest, and I have to squeeze my thighs together as the previous night's dream runs through my mind. "You clearly figured things out, you know this is where you die. How about, *why* did you come here if you know what will happen? Despite feeling yourself burn alive, becoming nothing more than human bacon, I open that door to start my shift and find a stunning brunette, practically gift wrapped for her own funeral."

"I have questions, you have answers." A slight breeze blows under the door, chilling my bare ankles and causing goosebumps to blossom over my legs. "There will be no fire tonight, no chance of me dying, I've made sure of it."

"Those Blood Favors aren't exactly subtle, loud enough to wake the dead too, but you're right." He sits on the couch, making himself comfortable. "You'll be safe tonight."

Motioning for me to join him, I shake my head.

"First, tell me why."

"Because the future has changed. I've seen it."

One leg pops up to cross over the other. His hand raises to his sunglasses, grips the frames, and my heart beats against my ribcage in anticipation of what I'll see. To my relief, and a faint hint of disappointment, he pushes them further onto his face rather than taking them off.

"I'm allowed to be in McHattie for the fall season. For only four months I call this place home. Those other nine have been filled with visions of you. I watched you, unable to move, burning, *dying*, over and over and over." His head falls into his hands, shoulders slump as though he's a man defeated. "No matter what I did, you always found your way to this damn workshop. I couldn't fix the future, couldn't keep you alive. Even when I told you directly what fate had in store, you chose to run away from me and headfirst into the flames. I figured if I *showed* you what I'd seen, there might be a chance you'd save yourself."

"The dreams were meant as a warning."

"A warning you've clearly ignored."

There's more I want to say, but the night is only so long, and I'm already itching to move on. However, I need just one more point of clarity… "You never meant to hurt me or scare me."

"Of course not."

"You wanted to save the girl who lost everything."

"No." His denial is sharp. "I wanted to save the woman I knew I wouldn't be able to say goodbye to."

"Good because I don't want to say goodbye to you, either. Not yet." Turning my back to him, I reach under my hair to unclasp the gifted necklace. The silver shines against my palm as I study it. When I came here, I had the plan in my mind, but now I realize the gravity of what I'm about to do. By leaving my only means of protection to hang on a bent nail by the door, I accept that I'll be at Levi's mercy, and his magic. I'm putting complete and total trust in him and his word.

The sweater dress slips down my shoulders as I face him, neck bare of the jewelry, a smile on my face.

This is the man from my nightmares, a spirit who has forced me to live through the torture of burning alive, night after night, for weeks on end. Had me relive a memory of an event that never happened, but felt real all the same. But there's something more than fear, trapping my soul in a chokehold, that makes my heart race.

"You're the scorpion, the snake, the lizard. I've seen you—the human you and the real you, in my dreams and when I struggled to wake up. Always there. Always watching."

"Are you afraid?"

"Yes."

Without pausing, I take the few steps toward him to close the distance between us. Slowly, my hands lift to rest on the sides of his sunglasses, waiting for permission. Wide eyes, my own, reflect back at me. Underneath, in this reality, will they be empty sockets, an unearthly flame, or something beyond my imagination? Will he simply smile, allow me to reveal him, then set me ablaze? Could this be just another nightmare, a trick of a jinn? Is this my curse to forever feel my skin boil, blister, turn black and peel back? The fats separating from the retained moisture, steaming as it cooks away? My muscles contracting, shrinking, spasming? I'm trembling, nerve-endings raw as though already burning, eardrums thrumming with anticipation.

"But I'm not leaving, not now." Holding firm in my decision, I wish my body would get the memo. His plastic frames bounce against the bridge of his nose from my trembling hands, and even my voice shakes. A small part of me begs to run, to allow him a night to himself, but a larger piece demands his audience, my possible demise be damned. "So, am I allowed to see you this time? *All* of you?"

About the Author

Not only a horror writer, Sarah Trala also creates tales of mystery, trauma, and sometimes she even allows her characters to heal—unless she kills them off first. In Sarah's world, you never know who you'll run into or what to expect. The little old lady that knits blankets for the unhoused also keeps her dead husband's heart in the freezer. Our star quarterback spends his nights howling at the moon. While the waitress, who dropped off your meal, might just accept a tip in blood.

Writing takes up just a small portion of Sarah's time. During the day, and even afterhours for emergency cases, she's been a plumber since 2016. On top of that, she enjoys crocheting, building model kits, spending time with friends & family, collecting knickknacks, and reading anything she can get her hands on.

For more from Sarah, you can find her on TikTok (SarahTralaWrites) and Instagram (AuthorSarahTrala) as well as her full catalog at linktr.ee/SarahTrala

JACK

FAYE KNIGHTLY

Jack

Jack of the Jack 'o lantern was a drunk and a mischief maker. On a particularly loathsome night of his wicked existence, he called forth the devil and offered him his soul in exchange for a drink. Eager to claim Jack's twisted soul, the devil transformed himself into a coin to pay for Jack's ale and complete the contract, but the moment he transformed, Jack pressed a crucifix to the coin and trapped the devil within, forcing him to agree never to take Jack's soul before he would be released. The Jack of legend set the devil free once an agreement was struck, and, with nowhere to go upon his death, became a wandering spirit with an ember from hell inside a hollowed up turnip to light his way (the first Jack 'o Lantern).

But what if Jack had found a way to keep the devil within the coin? Trapped and at Jack's mercy, the devil's great power would be Jack's to wield through wicked extortion, perhaps granting him an unnaturally long life and twisting him into something much worse than the clever troublemaker he'd been- a once-man now struggling to maintain his own wretched self by sacrificing damned souls once bound for hell to the beast locked within his golden prison.

Look closely my dear, see my coin how it shines.
Let yourself go, for he knows all your crimes.
The ones you thought buried.
Forgotten!
Long lost!
All the bad, and the rotten.
Those friends you long crossed.
A good one?
Oh no...
My pet, you are ripe!
A fruit for the plucking and him just the sight
Don't fear him, my sweet...
NO, don't turn your head!
He just needs to eat- the devil must be kept fed.

Cheryl

The club was sticky—the kind of sticky that got under your skin and made you want to set the shower on scalding hot as soon as you got the chance to wash yourself. Not that it was particularly warm outdoors, but in the club with dozens of men huddling together and shouting their excitement at the semi circle of raised stages where mostly-naked women danced, it was uncomfortably steamy, and the scent of sweat from so many excited bodies hung in the air. It reeked of it, and all the sprays of perfume lingering in the air couldn't mask the stink underneath.

The smell reached all the way to my stage, though it was one of the furthest from the action, and practically empty, with just one disgustingly oversized John in a cheap gray suit, unbuttoned at the front to reveal an ill fitting white dress shirt underneath. His face was so red from screaming obscenities at me that someone really needed to call a doctor and keep them on standby. A beefy older man in a pair of overalls wandered over with a frothy beer and took a seat at one of my rickety stools. Fucking Tom had given me the shittiest fucking stage. Even the black painted floorboards were uneven and in danger of catching one of my toes on a turn.

Gripping the cheap aluminum pole, I leaped, using my weight to swing around and land neatly at the base, catching myself at the last minute to avoid an unflattering bounce against the hard unpolished floorboards. I stood slowly dragging my nearly bare pussy along the cold metal. Normally, I would be wearing a thong, making sure the goods were on full display—the Johns were always more ready with their wallets if they saws the promise of a fuck—but I was wearing more on the bottoms these days, a full short skirt in fact with a suggestive fringe hopefully hinting at the promise of what lay beneath.

The promise of what lay beneath, what a laugh. The image of Tom's face the day he'd told me there was too much cellulite on my aging ass and that I needed to cover 'that shit up' flared to life in my mind, pissing me off.

Fucker. If I had anywhere else to be, I would've spit in his face and kicked him in his tiny cock and shriveled nut sack. But you didn't bite the hand that feeds you, so I'd smiled real pretty and gotten the shortest skirt I could find to hide my 'distasteful' ass from sight.

At least my tits still had a bit of bounce, and I knew they looked fantastic in the string bikini I wore in place of a top. They were firm and round, if a bit average-sized, and I made sure to shake them at every opportunity. But as much as I put them on display, they could never be a match to Katie's. I side-eyed the new girl—fresh to the strip—now occupying the central stage that had once been mine. She danced around in a thin sparkly string top-thong combo with absolutely no rhythm, waving her big titties around and gathering a crowd in spite of her obvious lack of skill.

She couldn't dance, couldn't sing, and was, by all accounts, the worst stripper at the joint, but those titties were her ticket, and I watched with envy as a crisp, clean looking John in a tight black polo slipped a twenty into her sweaty cleavage.

A fucking *twenty*. I seethed, flinging my body around the pole, desperate to impress my own few attendees and spur them to action. But neither of the men at my piece of shit stage reached for their wallets. The man in overalls simply sipped his beer, avoiding my eyes, and the fat fucker kept up with his jeers. "Show me your pussy, show me your tits."

Yeah, yeah. I heard you. I might have to wear a fringe to cover my ass, but my pussy was on full display. What did he want me to do, rub it in his face? Something told me he wouldn't be willing to pay extra, and I smiled lustily at him, all the while fighting the urge to smack him on his big bald head.

Ignoring him the best I could, I got to work on the other fel-low—the newcomer in overalls, his head just as bald. He was definitely a 'sweetie,' my own term for those hard working men who liked to come to the club after putting in their hours and gawk at us for a while. He'd head on home afterward to bang his wife and carry on with his evening. If given the right kind of quality attention, sweeties could be great tippers.

A song with a deep bass came on, and I twisted in time to the music, falling to the floor and crawling forward until I was right in the sweetie's face. Pressing my tits together, I sucked on a finger, letting my ruby red lips wrap around it, my auburn hair falling across my face as I watched him suggestively, waiting for him to look up and meet my eyes.

At last, he did, so awkwardly, his eyes shifting and his face flushed. After an expectant moment, he reached into the pocket of his grimy overalls and fetched a couple of crumpled up dollar bills, holding them out to me in tribute in his meaty soot-stained hands. With a smile, I swiftly took them from him, turning in the same motion, and tucking the money into my waistband. A couple of dollars wasn't much, but it would count for something.

Fucking Katie. I looked over to see her waistband stuffed with bank notes. If this kept up, I would have to do something about her. No way was she going to replace me and take what was mine—what I'd earned from ten years in this old rat's nest.

It'd be a waste of drugs, but I could off her in the party room where I'd taken care of the last girl to fuck with my business. Katie was the dumb, trusting type. I'd bring her in there and offer her the trip of a lifetime... and it would be, of course. The last fucking trip. She'd fall to the ground, crushing those great big titties of hers, and I'd be back on center stage the next day, Katie written off as another useless druggie who had succumbed to her own poison.

Tom might gripe about my cellulite, but even he couldn't disagree that I was the best dancer The Crack in the Pavement had—the best fucking dancer on the strip. I side-eyed Katie again. The crowd around her had grown, and she wore a huge fucking smile on her fat face. Oh, she *had* to go. I would get the stuff tonight and offer to show her some tricks. Then, she'd come with me to the party room, and I'd convince her to try—

My chain of thought was broken by the appearance of a stranger at the center stool overlooking my stage. What a weird-looking fucker. Everything about him was strange. His face was gaunt, almost skeletal, with thin lips and a too-wide mouth. I couldn't see his eyes—lost in the shadow of a tall old fashioned hat, but I could somehow feel that he was watching me. Watching and waiting? Was he waiting? *What is he waiting for?*

I'd stopped dancing without even realizing it. Surprised at being so easily rattled- something that hadn't happened to me since my early days, I moved quickly to take up my position on the pole once more, but I was too late, and the red-faced fucker in his cheap suit huffed and stood up to leave, the buttons of his dress shirt nearly popping when he slid from the stool. *Shit.* I hadn't expected to get very much from the asshole, but I'd thought he was good for at least a dollar or two. With another twist and turn around the pole, I sized up the new John.

The light curved around the man, or maybe it was absorbed by him. Either way, he seemed to remain in the dark though he sat directly beneath one of my stage lights. What a strange getup. He wore a full plum-colored suit in what looked like stifling wool—entirely inappropriate for the humid club—and a black velvet fedora that had a tiny orange and green gourd where a feather might go. His age was impossible to determine. He was wrinkled, but the wrinkles were stretched out somehow, like cling wrap across a casserole, tight to keep the food fresh inside, only... something told me the food inside was rotten, and the covering was just barely keeping the rot in.

He smiled, as if knowing I was done with my assessment of him, and I caught a flash of gold from several teeth. The twisted smile he gave me consumed his face—so wide and his face so shrunken that it stretched ear-to-ear. His lower jaw was pushed forward so that all his teeth touched in an odd sort of snarling grimace pretending to be a smile. It looked as though he wasn't sure how to smile, and this was the best he could manage. Certainly, there was no warmth or merriment to it.

I hated Devil's Night. Halloween, I could stand, but the night before was unbearable. We always got at least a few weirdos wandering in, thinking they could play dress up a little early, and all of them looking to cause trouble. I was about to dismiss him as just another freak playing at mischief when, with one hand, he reached into his suit jacket and pulled out a wad of bills. He held up his other hand and gestured me to the edge of the stage with the crook of a thin, knobby finger.

Helplessly drawn to the bundle of cash in his hand, I creeped closer. He held a fuck ton of money. With it, I could get the good stuff, the shit that made my blood sing and made this stink hole seem like heaven. Fuck, I wanted it.

Forgetting how fucking creepy the man holding the money was, I dropped to my knees in front of him and reached for the bills, but he jerked his hand away at the last second, his too-wide smile growing ever wider. He looked up at me, and I met his eyes. Normal eyes, not creepy at all, a bit rheumy, making me think he was definitely older, but they humanized him in a way that was comforting. He wasn't that odd-looking, just a creepy old man with a ton of cheap makeup and effects to make him appear otherworldly.

He wanted a fuck for his money. I licked my lips, hungry for the cash. I was making shit out here tonight, and I had no problem with a man putting his hands on me. Especially if he was willing to pay me well for the privilege. With a curt nod, and a sultry smile, I returned to the pole, spinning around it and catching my knee to circle my way down to the ground and expertly kick out a tanned leg. I blew a kiss at the sweetie, noting his adorable blush in reply, and stood to exit down the stairs at the back.

Hands sweaty, I hurried to the rooms to find him already waiting for me at the entrance, still wearing that freaky smile of his. How had he beaten me here? I'd come straight from the stage and he'd still had to go around it, but he was here first? It didn't make sense, and I opened my mouth to say something when he produced the stack of bills from his pocket again, and I lost myself trying to calculate how much he held.

He tucked the bills back into his suit, but not before I'd gotten a good look. Shit, that was at least a couple of hundred dollars. I could get some damned good stuff for that and keep myself stocked up for a while. No more wondering if I could make enough to get my fix and keep myself fed.

I hurried down the long black hallway tucked neatly behind the stage. With its matching black paint, guests wouldn't see it unless they knew where to look. The first room was occupied, the door closed and locked, but the second was open a crack, the universal sign the room was available to whoever wanted to use it, however they wanted to use it. I hurried inside, gesturing Mr. Creepy-fucker-with-wads-of-cash in after me, and flipped the ratty cardboard sign on the door to display 'do not disturb' before slamming it with a rattle, twisting the copper lock into place. Maybe it was overkill to flip the sign, and lock the door—a combo usually reserved for orgies—but I wanted to ensure our privacy, and I didn't need some drunken John forcing the lock and stumbling in, wanting to join in the fun.

Something told me this guy wouldn't like that. I turned to face him and found him watching me. I was struck by how thin he was—his clothes tailored to fit his sinewy body didn't hang from him the way any normal garment would have. Tall too. I was above average height for a woman, but he was nearly a foot taller still, and I looked up into that ghastly smile of his, struggling to find one of my own. The thought of his money did it, and I managed a watery smile.

With a flourish of his hand and a small bob, he introduced himself.

"The name's Jack," he said in a surprisingly high-pitched sing-song voice. I caught the musical notes of an accent but couldn't place it. Not that I cared. His cash had been American, and that was good enough for me. He flashed his teeth at me expectantly. Shit, nearly all of his teeth were replaced by gold. I'd thought it was just a dozen or so before, but staring at them now, I couldn't see a single bit of enamel.

"Well, Jack, I just need a minute to freshen up. Why don't you make yourself comfortable?"

With a quick dip of his head, Jack crossed the room to sit on the chair by the vanity the girls used to freshen up before going on stage, one foot resting on the splintered old wood in a rude, entitled sort of way. His arm rested on his knee and he tilted his head as he watched me expectantly. Fuck that.

"A lady needs her privacy," I muttered, feeling annoyed, but Jack's smile only grew wider.

"Oh, but I like to watch, and I'll pay for your privacy."

Right, well, fuck him then. I moved to the rickety dresser in the corner and pulled out the key I kept tucked into the string of my bikini, unlocking the stiff top drawer and grabbing my stuff. I took it to the double bed in the center of the room, sitting on the edge of the dark brown quilted topper and set out my things on the night-stand.

I'd be damned if I was going to go to bed with a John sober. He watched me cook my drugs without comment, and I was grateful for that at least. The last thing I needed was some judgmental fuck giving me shit. With the blessed pinch of the needle, my uneasiness faded, and the tightness in my muscles loosened. I lay back onto the bed, letting the drugs soak into my system.

As if that was all the permission he needed, Jack removed his stiff purple jacket revealing a tailored white dress shirt and brown leather suspenders underneath. The shirt had flourishes of lace at the sleeve cuffs, previously hidden by his stiff suit. With more of his ghastly thin form revealed, Jack was truly terrifying—a stick man striding over to me with gold teeth flashing in the dim light—and the only reason I didn't cower in terror at his approach was the warm easy feeling of the drugs pumping through my veins.

A scarecrow, that's what he reminded me of, but one the farmer had neglected to stuff, full of sticks forming the basis of a man, but without any of the softness. With a firm grip like iron, he pulled me to the edge of the bed and unzipped his fly.

At least he was already hard, his cock just as stiff and devoid of life as the rest of him. It was like getting fucked by a skeleton, his body like a rigid pole, his grip rough. His head bobbed around as he fucked me without lube. I groaned at the rough friction, but quickly turned it to a cry of pleasure for his benefit. Thankfully, the act was over quickly, and in truth, Jack seemed to derive little pleasure from the encounter. He stared at me the whole time with his rheumy eyes dark and calculating, his grin much the same as it had been when he'd first approached me in the club, a grin that didn't falter, not even when he spilled inside of me. Fucker hadn't even worn a condom. The joke was on him—I had an itch in my pussy, and I hoped he caught it.

Jack returned to the vanity, carefully doing up his pants and resecuring his brown suspenders. While he busied himself, I prepared a pick me up. I deserved it after that weird shit. The whole while I cooked up the drugs, Jack watched me from his perch at the vanity, his horrid grin growing impossibly wider when I pricked my vein a second time. He almost seemed to be expecting something. He pointed to the nightstand, and I turned to see a pile of cash neatly piled on top of the peeling wood paint. When had he put that there? No matter. I counted it greedily. It was more than my quick calculation—at least four hundred dollars in crisp five dollar bills. Four. Hundred. Fucking. Dollars. Yes, I could get the really premium shit with this.

The money had been well worth a few moments of discomfort, and I smiled happily at the odd bird-man still watching me from the corner. "You know, Jack, at first I thought maybe you wanted to hurt me or something, but you're all right," I said, holding the bills up to him in tribute, the drugs leaving me looser with my tongue than I might otherwise have been. I eyed the locked door warily, hoping I hadn't put any ideas in his head, but Jack only chuckled, a strange sound that came from deep down in his throat.

"I wouldn't hurt a fly, my dear," he cooed.

I laughed nervously, watching him carefully. There had been another flash of gold from where he was sitting, but this time, the gold was in his hand.

What the fuck was that? It was so bright I could see it clearly from across the room. Whatever it was, Jack passed it from finger to finger over his knuckles so skillfully that I couldn't make it out. The dim lights glinted tantalizingly across its surface. "What's that?" I asked, struggling to follow the strangely fascinating object.

Jack stood up and held up a gold coin between thumb and forefinger. "Your tip, of course," he said. The coin shone like a beacon in the darkness, drawing me in effortlessly and immediately capturing my interest.

"It's mine?" It was so beautiful. I'd never seen anything like it. Normally, I would want to hock it in case it was valuable, but this time, I wanted to keep it for myself.

"Why, yes," hissed Jack, holding it out to me. Before he could change his mind, I scrambled off the bed and over to him, fumbling it from his outstretched hand and nearly dropping it in my eagerness.

I brought it back over to the bed and held it under the light so I could take a better look. It appeared to be some kind of an old coin. Warm in my hands, the metal was thicker than any coin I'd seen, and a cross was carved into it. A number of small, jagged lines formed the cross, making me think a knife wielded by a cruel hand had been taken to the soft metal many times. For what reason, I didn't know, and while I was curious, the question didn't stick in my mind, sliding across it as though coated in slippery oil. There one moment, and gone the next.

There were other symbols pressed into the coin as well—symbols I could almost make out. My eyes strained with the effort of tracking the patterns. I could follow the curve of a shape but would quickly lose it. Frustrated, I turned the coin over and over in my hands, holding it further under the light, desperate to see when a strange truth came to me.

It was the drugs, I reasoned. They'd worn off. I couldn't see the symbols because the drugs had worn off. They'd been helping my mind to focus at first, and now I couldn't see because I was sober. Fuck. Fucking Tom must've given me a weak batch. I needed them—needed to see. To make the symbols clearer like they'd been at the start. The need to see was an itch under my skin, and I had to scratch it. I prepped another needle with shaking hands. I needed to see. A circle? A star? A star within a circle? No, it was a square. Was that a letter or an eye? Where did that line go? I'd had it a moment ago. There. No, that wasn't it. Not a line at all, but a star. A star? No, the letter E.

My eyes briefly left the coin, and I barely felt the pinch of the needle as it dug into my vein. The pain didn't matter. Nothing mattered, not the way my limbs began to get heavy and numb, or the way my breathing was becoming more difficult. I just had to hold on. Almost there now. So close. I could almost see the patterns, and I knew somehow that when I did, I would know the secrets of the universe. The coin was everything—it was my whole world. I could almost make it out. With shaking hands, I prepared another needle.

Jack

I watched as the stripper turned the coin over and over under the lamplight, desperately trying to understand the thing she held in her hands. She would, and soon enough. I spoke to her, though she was past hearing me. It was always good to keep the niceties intact. What were we without our social graces?

"He, of course, is another story. I would never hurt you, my dear, but you see, I have the tiger by the tail with that one, and he needs to eat. So long as I keep the devil fed, he keeps old Jack in tip-top shape. Otherwise, it's the end for me, and we can't have *that* happening. The world needs old Jack, you see, and Jack needs the world."

I chuckled to myself, smiling with every one of my gold teeth—the naturals having been unaffected by the devil's magic and having long since rotted out—as she went to prepare more of the poison she was so eagerly shooting into her veins.

"Ah, an overdose!" I exclaimed to no one in particular. "How typical, how *boring*. I miss the good ole days before guns when he would make them set up a noose and hang themselves, choking to death with their eyes never leaving his pretty little coin. One time he even had a fellow call in his mother to be sacrificed in his stead! Killed her with a stapler, he did. What a slow way to go that was, and she begged him the whole time. The sacrifice didn't work, of course, and the fellow—what was his name? Ah, hell, I was never one for names. He did himself in the jugular with a ballpoint pen. The devil claimed two souls that night. Those were the days. He was always so much more inventive back then."

Cheryl

Desperate, I stared at the coin, begging it to tell me its secrets, to end my suffering. Just. A. Little. More. I was so close. I prepared another needle, hating the extra moment it took to do so with my shaking hands. Every moment of not knowing was agony, the itch beneath my skin now a searing pain.

The moment the drugs hit my veins, my breathing turned ragged and the patterns became clearer. There, there, another clue! The line I was following stayed in focus, and I craned my head this way and that, trying to find the right angle. No, not a line. Never a line. It was a curve. The curve of a horn—a horn? Yes, a horn. Then, with almost no effort at all, it came into focus like a lens snapping into place. I could see it, I could see at last. I could see... No. Oh no. Dear God, I could see... *him.*

Jack

I waited an extra moment after the girl had died before going to retrieve the coin from her outstretched hand. We were nothing without our manners after all, and I wouldn't want to interrupt such an intimate moment. A look of horror was etched on the face of the dead girl, her eyes stared unseeing at the ceiling while her mouth hung open, and saliva spilled from her slackened jaw. "Now you see him, don't you? Was he everything you expected him to be?" I grinned at the stripper's horror-stricken face.

The coin was hot to the touch, and I passed it over my knuckles a few times to cool it before slipping it into my pocket and doing up the custom zipper. Warmth seeped through the thick wool of my jacket from the coin regardless, and I chuckled to myself at the heat of it. The meal must've been better than expected, the girl's soul more blackened than I had first supposed.

"Yes, her soul was rather dark, wasn't it? But not quite dark enough. No, not quite dark enough." I gave my pocket a fond pat but yelped when the coin turned scorching hot and seared my hand. "Don't be salty now, you've had your fill. It's your turn to give Jack what he needs, or you won't get another." The coin cooled beneath my touch, and I felt energy pour from it to infuse my limbs with life once more. He kept a steady stream of it pumping through my veins and keeping me alive, but I'd begun to need these jolts of energy as well. I guess that was what happened when you were three hundred something years old. What the real number was, I didn't know or care. No need to keep track so long as I had my coin.

"There's a good boy. Now you have a little rest while Jack has his fun." I grinned to myself, knowing it was the stuff of nightmares. There was an Irish pub down the street I'd scoped out before coming to the strip club tonight, one with jaunty music and some fine-looking top shelf amber bottles set up neatly behind the bar. The place reminded me of the days of my youth, and I was eager to become one of its patrons, to lose myself in the drink now that my work was done.

They'd find the stripper soon—another whore dead of an overdose at the sleaziest club on the east side of town. Certainly nothing worth looking into. I left the door ajar, pulled down my hat with a courteous nod at the rotting corpse, and left the club like the whisper of a shadow.

On my way down the street, I passed a pumpkin smashed on the dingy sidewalk and thrown on its side—the once pristinely carved triangle eyes and nose caved in and giving the impression of a deformed figure. A chill went up my spine at the way my namesake had been treated, but after all it was Devil's Night, and the kids did have their fun. I laughed at the idea of this old pumpkin rotting and full of maggots in a week's time while I remained my sprightly young self for all eternity. Namesake, indeed. With a violent kick, I caved in the rest of its face, leaving a gaping hole in the middle—best to leave the maggots a larger door of entry. With a deep-throated chuckle, I headed down the street to find the pub.

Kimberly Shaw

I could never stand a drunk. Mama had always told me alcohol was a tool of the devil, and I reminded myself of her words as I headed down the plush red runner toward the stumbling man's door. Of course, things were different these days. A guest wearing a business suit with his head down walked past, and I paused to move around the variety of spray bottles in my cleaning cart as though I were look-ing for something, but the moment the edge of his shining shoes disappeared around the corner, I dropped the ruse and waddled over to the drunk's door, favoring my good leg. Here I'd been, minding my own business, just getting done with room 2C when he'd come stumbling out of the elevator, muttering about his coin and slurring his words. What a disgusting excuse for a man.

It would have been easy to dismiss him as just another despicable guest at this dingy hotel, but there then he'd taken something shiny out of his pocket and started talking to it like it was an old friend, passing it across his knuckles too quickly for me to see, but the way he'd talked to it, and the way it shined... well, something like that was bound to be worth something.

Everyone knew little knickknacks went missing all the time at hotels—it was just a fact of life. Small things got lost. Especially when you went flashing them around to the cleaning staff. I grinned to myself, pulling up to his room and parking my cart. I'd watched him tuck it into a zippered pocket in his jacket while he fumbled with the keycard at his door, but even the most sturdy of material could get a hole in it. I carried a pair of tiny scissors around just in case such an 'accident' needed to occur.

It'd been about fifteen minutes since I watched him tuck his shiny something or other into a zippered pocket and fumble with his room key at the door. Drunk as he'd been, sleep must have claimed him by now. Must have. The image of the object glinting in the low light called to me. I just had to get my hands on it. What could it be— shining like a diamond even in the dingy yellow glow of the few timid wall sconces? It must be something worthwhile, something precious.

My lips were dry, and I licked at them to soften the skin before taking out my skeleton key and reaching for the knob. I had to have it. If he was awake, or if he woke up, I was still a maid, and he had forgotten to hang the "do not disturb" sign on the door. I could just say I'd thought no one was in the room, never mind that I was always supposed to knock before entering, never mind that I'd watched him stumble his way into the room and knew for certain he was there.

My hand raised automatically to knock as I always did, but I caught myself, chuckling quietly and dropping it to my side. If whatever the man held was valuable, I could quit this shitty job and focus my energies on getting Ms. Harris to sign over her will. I'd been working for her for over a month now, and she was just starting to trust me. Soon, I'd start calling her Momma, just like the others, and she'd come around. It wouldn't be long until I could mix a few extra pills into her sweet tea and finish with her—just another old lady dying of natural causes. I'd cry to my supervisor and collect my inheritance once it was released to me.

Then, I could quit that fucking awful agency—*Oh, sorry, the grief, it's too much*—and skip town, join up with a different one, and start in on another old biddy.

The door unlocked with a soft click, but when I went to pull it open, the damned thing caught on a latch. He'd thought to latch it in the state he was in? Surprising. He must be a cautious sort. No problem. I'd done this before and knew my way around the extra security. I kept a screwdriver in my apron in case such an opportunity as this presented itself.

Opening the door as far as it would go to expose the latch, I hooked it twice through the chain and snaked the screwdriver around to pop it off. The door swung open on silent hinges—yes, so easy— and there the occupant lay, naked as a jaybird and stretched out across the bed with his ass hanging out, one leg hanging off the bed. His whole body was wrinkled up like an old prune left out in the sun to dry a bit too long. Weird, he hadn't looked that old in the face. He must've had work done. Extensive work. I wrinkled my nose with distaste. A drunk and a vain one at that. Terrible.

His clothes were thrown on the floor beside the bed, and I winced thinking about my old knees. As a woman of a certain age with a bit of extra fluff on her bones, squatting down was oftentimes a noisy endeavor. There was no help for it, and I held my breath as I squatted down. But my bum knees went down easy with almost no sound at all. Certainly not enough to wake the man on the bed, lulled to sleep as he was by the alcohol heavy in his belly. Carefully, I began to search his plum-colored jacket for where I'd seen him stash the coin. The zipper was as seamless as the hinges had been, opening smoothly beneath my skilled fingers with hardly a sound.

Reaching in, I felt inside the pocket for the coin. It was deeper than I expected, nearly consuming my hand before I felt something oddly warm meet my fingers. Pulling it free, I quickly tucked it into the front pocket of my apron and rose just as silently as I'd gone down, backing out of the room and watching the sleeping figure until I could close the door behind me. What luck, it closed just as quietly as it had opened. These doors were finicky at best and almost always made an annoying little creak just as they finished the swing, but not this one, not this time. I smiled at my good luck as the door clicked shut behind me.

Safe in the hallway, I started humming an old half-remembered nursery rhyme cheerfully, heading back to my cleaning cart and pushing it down the hall. It was break time by my watch, or it would've been if I'd been wearing one, and I couldn't wait to take a look at my prize. I took my cart down the ancient elevator all the way to the basement break room where the cleaning staff and maintenance workers came together to smoke a bit of pot, parking it outside the door. With the daytime shift barely started, I was sure to find it empty. Giddy, I turned the cheap brass knob and found the small room as empty as I'd expected, the cracked leather chairs with their sinking seats vacant, and the small coffee table devoid of flower and papers for rolling. The scent of pot still hung in the air, and office supplies lined the wall behind a tall couch. Cheap fuckers couldn't even give us a room to ourselves.

Muttering to myself about the management, I closed the door behind me and perched on the edge of a squashy chair. I was far too nervous to relax, and I fumbled the thick gold slab of a coin out of my apron pocket to hold it in trembling fingers.

I frowned down at the thing. It was beautiful, with strange symbols etched into the metal, but I couldn't make them out. The light in here was such shit. With a huff, I moved seats to position myself next to one of the two floor lights, but I still couldn't quite see.

It was almost as if the symbols shifted and changed. Every time I almost focused on a piece of it, the whole image would become something entirely different. What was going on? I needed to see it. The obsession to know what it meant, what the symbols were, overwhelmed my senses until it was all I could think about. I didn't care what kind of money the coin might fetch anymore, the secret was right there. I held the world in my hands, if only I could see.

I flipped the coin over and over in my jittery hands, holding it so close to the light that my fingers burned. The pain of my blistering flesh was nothing next to the coin. Was that a circle? A letter? A number? The blood pounded in my ears, louder and louder. The blood. Of course, my blood. I understood then, and the feeling of rightness washed over me.

Blood. Yes. That was the answer. The coin needed my blood. I just had to give it my blood, and it would show me its secrets... no— not it, *he*. He would show me his secrets. My gaze shifted at last, away from the coin and over to the office supplies on the shelf where my eyes fell on a large pair of rusty blue-handled scissors.

Becky Slater

No, no, no. This couldn't be happening. I stared down at Kimberly's twisted face with fear tight in my chest at her horrific end. I looked around me for the third time to find her assailant, but I'd already searched the room, and there wasn't one. Her face, her arms, her torso, every inch of exposed skin was sliced with cruel slashes, some so deep I could see glimpses of white bone. Her dark brown skin was stained crimson, and the dripping pair of blue-handled scissors in her hand told the story. Her face was the worst of it, one cheek sliced clean through so I could see her discolored tongue through the slash, and globs of yellow fat oozing out of the gash. An ear lay on the floor. *Her* ear.

Dear God in heaven. A delicate hoop earring encrusted with rhinestones still hung from the lobe. The only way I knew for sure who the woman was was by the blood spattered name tag still attached to her blood-drenched uniform.

To think, she'd gotten dressed for work today, neatened up her hair, put on her fancy earrings, and then done this to herself. Shivering, I wrapped my arms around my body in a steadying hug I was sorely in need of. Tears slipped down my cheeks.

I should tell someone. Her family needed to know what had happened to her. She must have been so sad to do this to herself, and I searched around her for a note. All I found was an odd little coin in her blistered hand. Had she burned herself as well? Poor, sweet Kimberly. The coin was some kind of thick gold, and I paused to stare at it. It looked expensive.

She didn't need it anymore. Lord bless her, she was in a different place now, free from pain, but me? Penelope needed her surgery to remove the poisonous tumor that was slowly killing her, and I would do anything to get the money to save my only child.

Including stealing from a dead woman? I looked again at the horrified expression on Kimberly's dead face, her mouth hanging open, eyes-filled with fear. With a nod to myself, I stepped forward and gently slid her eyelids close with the pads of my thumbs, saying a prayer as I did.

"I'm sure you would have wanted to help. Thank you." I took the coin from her hand and tucked it solemnly in my pocket. Courage bolstered, and with the promise of finding something with the potential to save my daughter, I left to go report Kimberly's suicide.

Jack

The hangover I woke up to was terrible—one of the worst I'd had in my many years. I pulled my heavy body up to sit and peered around with blurry vision. Blurry vision? What madness was this? I looked down at my hands, but I could barely make them out, almost as if I had a cloud covering everything to the front and right side of me. Something was wrong.

With a curse, I tried to spring to my feet but didn't quite make it, falling in a heap on the floor when my brittle legs snapped from the weight on them. I shrieked in pain and surprise, looking at my twisted limbs with shock.

"No! Where are you, you devil! We had a deal!" Mad with rage, I crawled through the excruciating pain of my broken legs over to where I had grown too hot and dropped my clothes to the ground. I fumbled for the zippered pocket angrily, finding it by touch alone, ready to scold the devil and threaten him with a fresh cross on his prison, but when I got it open, I found no coin within.

I howled my outrage into the empty room.

"Thief! Thief! I've been robbed! My coin! Where is my coin?" But there was no answer. Whoever had taken it was long gone. The force of my shrieks caused my jaw to unhinge, the cartilage in my body breaking down as the decomposition from the last three centuries caught up with me all at once. I might have had a chance of retrieving it if I'd woken up soon after the thief had stolen the coin, but instead, I'd slept through the first signs of its absence, and now?

My bladder gave way, and a puddle of urine stung my nose. I twisted reflexively to move away from it, but something gave way in my back with a pop, and I lost the feeling in my legs.

That was it then, no chasing after the thief and forcing the devil to restore my former glory. He'd won. That dirty old devil had bested me in the end. I laughed, the sound coming out as a horrific gurgle around my unhinged jaw just before the force of it caused my chest to cave in. My body convulsed as it gave way, and I embraced the darkness, knowing the devil might have a new master, but that he would still be trapped. The sound of my own distorted laughter followed me all the way down to the depths of hell where no ruler had dared to touch the devil's empty throne. Ah, old Jack had designs on that vacant seat. Perhaps it was I who would have the last laugh after all.

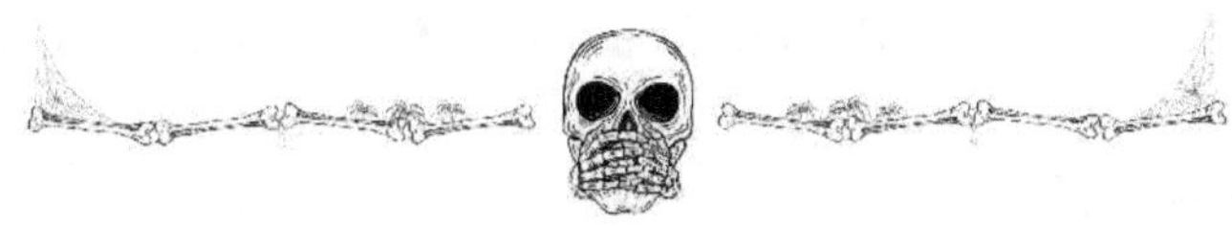

Becky Slater

The bus ride was bumpy, and I kept one hand in my pocket wrapped around the coin, the other gripping the crucifix I wore around my neck. It was such a strange little coin with a cross carved into it. Kimberly's blood had wiped clean off it without sticking. The thought made me clutch my cross all the tighter, the edges digging into my fingers painfully. We'd be there soon and then I could sell the coin and save Penelope. *Penelope.* It was her I was doing this for—I had to think of her with her soft red curls and trusting eyes. I'd told her Mommy would find a way to make her well again, and maybe Mommy had.

The pawn shop stood among a long line of small shops in the worst part of town. It boasted an old-style neon sign with the name "Pawnin 4 U" tastelessly lit up in highlighter yellow with a tenuous grasp on electricity, giving it the occasional flicker. It didn't look like the best place to be or the safest neighborhood, but it was the closest pawn shop I'd been able to find on my phone, and I wanted to just be done with this whole process, taking something from a dead woman and selling it was too much for me.

I got off at the next stop with a smile and a nod to the bus driver, not at all surprised when the man with deep acne scars covering his face and a permanent glower not only didn't acknowledge my farewell, but also nearly shut the door on me as I descended. How had I ever gotten mixed up in this? The hotel was sketchy, I'd known it when I'd taken the job, but it had been the only place hiring, and I'd been desperate enough to take it, as if the minimum wage I earned there would ever be enough to help save for Penelope's surgery. But after being laid off at the car plant, I'd needed to do something to make money, anything to tell myself I could keep us fed, housed, and somehow pay for the surgery. Every day that horrid thing was inside her was a day that she might not survive its removal.

A bell jingled somewhere overhead when I pushed open the cloudy glass door to the pawn shop. A heavy set man with beefy, hair-covered arms and a military haircut sized me up from behind a glass display case. He placed his meaty hands on the case in front of him and smiled over at me. It was the kind of sickening predatory smile that made me uneasy, made me want to find the nearest exit, and I would have, if not for Penelope.

"What have you got for me there, sweet thing?"

I glanced around nervously, considering going to find a different pawn shop, but doing so would take time, and Penelope was out of time. But it was more than that—I couldn't stomach the thought of taking the coin into my house, of holding it for a second longer. There was something wrong with it, something wicked, and I could feel it trying to grab a hold of me, trying and trying, the longer I had it in my possession. No. I needed this done today—now. My fingers tightened around the coin in my pocket.

With a confidence I didn't feel, I walked up to the display case where the man sat on a stool, his ample flesh spilling over the edges, unable to contain his girth, and slammed the coin down on the glass in front of him.

"This. It's gold, I-I think. I want to sell it."

"Hmm." The man picked up the coin and pulled over a lamp attached to the table, shining it across the surface. He started, humming deep in his throat appreciatively, and took out a magnifying glass. He looked at the coin under the light for a long few minutes, and I flexed my fingers, wiping the sweat off them and onto the coat I'd slipped on over my uniform. The glass case contained a number of oddities—ancient guns, a few sports cards, and, yes, some greening coins that looked old, very old. I thought of the shine on the coin I had brought—did that mean it wasn't as old and valuable as I'd supposed? A cold sweat gripped me while I waited for the pawn shop owner to decide.

At last, the man gave a low chuckle and turned from the coin to me. The strangeness of his chuckle surprised me, like he was sharing an inside joke with someone.

"What do you want for it, sweetheart?"

My mouth hung open. The way he was staring at me... I could name a number. Any number. He was dead serious. I thought back to the reports on Penelope and what she would need. The surgery, the radiation, the rehabilitation as she learned to use her legs again. "$125,000."

The man laughed, a laugh thick with mirth, his jowls and belly shaking so hard I thought the buttons on his white and red plaid shirt might burst and spill him out. "That much? Wow, you do need money, don't you, sweet thing?"

What did I even say to that? How should I answer? Was he actually considering it, or was he toying with me? How much could an old coin with a cross scratched into it be worth anyways? "Yes." *Oh, please.*

"Done. I have the cash in the back." My mouth hung open, and it remained open when he went into the back room and then when he returned with a crumpled brown bag packed nearly to the top with money.

"I... this..." Words failed me, as tears obscured my vision. "Oh, thank you, thank you." Then before he could say a word and change his mind, I rushed from his shop with the life-saving bundle clutched tight to my chest, sucking in the sweet air from outside as I tasted true relief for the first time in months. I'd done it. With this, I could save her. "Thank you, God, thank you."

The Pawn Shop Owner

I watched the young woman leave with a smile on my face. She thought I'd given her a good deal, but she hadn't known what she had. Money was nothing next to what sat atop my display case. The coin seethed with frustration, and I chuckled to myself, shifting on the stool to peer down at the devil trapped in the coin. It was the stuff of legends—the likes of which I'd never expected to see coming into my shop. I could see the devil within the metal, feel him reaching out to me, trying to ensnare me as he had so many others. I smirked.

"Was that one too good for you? Not a speck of darkness in her soul for you to latch onto was there? No, not like me. My soul's as black as they come, but you can't get to it, can you? No, you can't have me." I laughed again, holding my palms up to show the devil in the coin the pentagram scars I'd long ago etched into my hands. "No, you'll not have me, and how that must *grate* on you. What you will do is serve me, and serve me well. Do that, and I'll keep you plump and happy as you can be in your little prison." I could sense his dejection, and I wasn't at all surprised to find the coin cool to the touch when I reached for it.

"There's a good boy. You must be tired after exerting yourself. Don't worry, I'll get you something to eat soon enough. We've got to keep your strength up. I have much for you to do, and there's no shortage of twisted souls coming into my shop."

Just as I was musing to myself about what I would have the devil do for me first, the little bell on my door rang, and a tall wiry man in a cheap tracksuit with old oily stains standing out against the light grey stumbled through the door. His eyes were as wild as his bushy unkempt hair, and I grinned at him in way of greeting.

"Hi there, what can I help you with?" Quickly, I popped the coin into my display case—front and center.

"I'm here to-to sell this." The man held up a gold Rolex watch. He probably thought he'd cleaned it, but he was so strung out he hadn't noticed the drops of blood still clinging to the watch face.

Ah, he'd do nicely. Had to keep the devil fed, didn't I? Maybe the first thing I'd have him do was grant me anonymity. "Are you sure you wouldn't consider a trade, sir? Have a look in our display case and see if something catches your eye."

The man sputtered angrily, and his face turned red as he prepared to launch into a tirade, but he'd glanced into the display case when I'd mentioned it, and the words died on his lips. His face went slack, his eyes wide as he stared at the coin. "What's that?"

"It's just an old coin. An easy trade for that fine watch there. Would you like to have a better look in the private back room?"

"Yes, please, I'd like to see it." There was a note of desperation in his voice.

I waved the coin around, watching carefully as his unblinking eyes tracked its path. "Yes, I completely understand." I scooped up the coin and walked around the case to the wooden flip-up top piece to let him through. With a clap on the shoulder, I started to guide him toward the hallway leading to the storage room in the back. But then, I'd never seen the devil in action before, and I might as well make it a bit more interesting. "Don't go anywhere now." I held the coin up between my thumb and forefinger. His eyes were wide as saucers, his mouth parted in an 'o'—he wasn't going anywhere, the devil in the coin had him firmly in his grasp.

What to bring, what to bring. I scanned the display case and passed over an old revolver—too obvious. I snatched a thick gold chain, some marbles, a couple of calligraphy pens, and after a moment's hesitation, a rusty pair of pliers still covered in black gunk from when I'd used them to unplug the sink. I couldn't wait to see what he picked. This was going to be fun.

I returned to the man's side, cheerfully resting my arm across his shoulder as I steered him toward a more private space. He moved easily with a slight bit of pressure on his arm to guide him forward.

"By the way, I don't think I introduced myself." I smiled, but the man didn't care. He wasn't paying attention to a word I said. "The name's Jack."

About the Author

In addition to writing horror, and organizing anthologies as a co-founder of *The Sisterhood of the Black Pen*, Faye also writes dark and gritty fantasy with strong romantic subplots. Her readers can expect dark themes, high stakes, soulmates, and fierce heroines who struggle through their broken pasts to find connection and salvation. Faye's works regularly feature non-human characters with entirely human feelings and weaknesses, offering her readers a compelling mix of escapism and relatable characters.

Enjoy the 'what if?' nature of Jack? Check out Faye's dark and spicy Aladdin retelling, *Lamplight*, which asks the question, 'what would have happened to Aladdin if the genie had been evil?'

Follow Faye on tiktok (faye.knightly.writer) and instagram (@faye_knightly_writer) for updates on her January 2024 release of *When the Stars Whisper*, a lion king inspired dark fantasy that is best described as *Dune* meets *Game of Thrones*, with a bisexual female dom lead and lion shifters. Or check out her kinky werewolf write-and-release, *Breeders*, airing weekly on radish fiction.

Faye shares her writing space with a wildly supportive husband who regularly leaves her 'cofferings' (the last dredges of his coffee left out on the table for her to find), three tiny humans who provide just the right amount of distraction, and a former Egyptian street cat who warms her lap to the purrfect writing temperature.

DON'T LISTEN

KRYSTYNA LEE

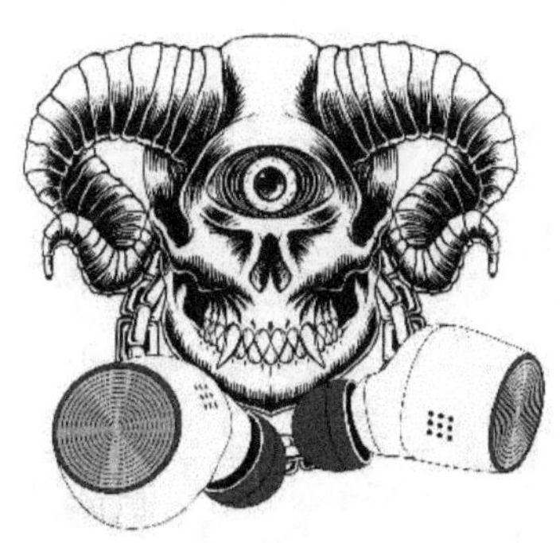

Ana

H ey, Ana," a voice called from behind. I took out my ear buds and began to turn around, the cool October breeze blowing my hair lightly across my face. Ben was running straight toward me, his blond hair flying wildly around as he jumped over cracks in the uneven sidewalk. He was a senior, like me, but just transferred to our school last month when his dad got a job here. I found him the first day of school looking bewildered in the hallways, trying to find his classes. We'd been hanging out ever since.

"Hey, Ben, what's up?" I said, putting my earbuds into their case.

Small beads of sweat were trickling down his forehead, as if he'd been running a few blocks to catch up to me. Taking deep breaths, he began to steady himself. "I wanted to ask if you were going to Michelle's tonight," he said, becoming restless. He began shifting his weight from one foot to the other in nervous anticipation.

I sighed, adjusting my backpack to my other shoulder. Every Halloween, Michelle, the mayor's daughter, held a giant, stupid party at her dad's mansion filled with alcohol and everyone praising her for being 'so cool.' The mansion was one of the oldest houses on Main Street, built around the 1800s or something. Everyone said it was haunted by the angry spirit of the first mayor of Saint Charles, who was murdered for money. Of course, that was just a legend, though. "I don't know. The party is always booze and hook ups... and at some point, Jason will pop out from somewhere screaming he's the 'ghost of mayors past' or some shit. It gets kinda repetitive year after year. I'm not friends with them anyway." I noticed Ben's face beginning to fall as I quickly continued. "Also, my parents are out of town, and they told me to stay in to watch the house for 'troublemakers.'" I rolled my eyes, thinking of my parents' version of troublemakers being kids with Silly String to spray all over the door. One wipe, and it was all gone.

Ben nodded and looked down at his still shuffling feet. His shoulders began to sag, and he looked defeated. He was taking this way harder than I thought. He threw his head back wildly with the most dramatic expression of anguish. "Oh, what to do! I was just looking forward to a fun Halloween party. And I'm new here, so I don't want to go alone... I could get lost... or worse, hazed! If only my dear friend Ana had gone with me to keep me safe." He spun on his feet, flailing his arms out to the side. Landing on his knees, he threw his head to the sky and, with his best Shakespearean impression, continued, "Oh, woe! What is poor Benjamin to do in these circumstances!"

I began laughing at the absurdity as I noticed an old lady across the street stop in her tracks to turn and look at the high school boy, appearing as if he was performing *Macbeth* in the middle of the sidewalk. She watched us disapprovingly before turning and stalking away. Still laughing, I reached over and pulled Ben's arms back to his side. "Fine, fine! I'll go! Just to protect the 'poor Benjamin' from harm," I said with my own attempt at a Shakespearean flair.

He stood up, beaming with excitement. "Perfect! I knew I could count on you! So, what should we go as? We could do a little... Bonnie and Clyde thing? Or—ooh! What about we dress as each other! Or..." He began rambling ideas so fast I could not keep up. After about a minute or two more of "ideas" being thrown out, I finally raised my voice to cut him off.

"Or! We could just go in normal clothes? That's an option."

He was looking at me in shock, then his entire body sank in disappointment. I began to ready myself for another soliloquy on the horrors and inhumanity of my request. "Come on, Ana! It's Halloween! You don't want to have fun? This is the one night a year where we aren't considered weirdos for dressing in crazy clothes!" he said, completely exasperated.

I shrugged and looked past him in the direction of Main Street. Even from two blocks away, I could still see the high roof of Michelle's house.

Ben sighed again. "Fine, you can wear normal clothes. But at least have some fun makeup," he pleaded, returning to his kneeling position, "or goofy hair? Something!"

I inwardly sighed as I gave him a curt nod. He brightened as he hopped up and started to run back the direction he came. He turned one final time to look at me, his face gleaming with excitement.

"See you tonight! Nine o'clock in front of the State Capital!" He kept running.

I continued to watch him until he turned the corner, past a blue Victorian house. Sighing again, I turned back around and re-opened my earbud case. Putting them in, I pressed play and resumed my walk home.

"Welcome to Lore Obscura! The show where we find the most obscure legends and folklore from across our country. Tonight, for our Halloween Special, I am taking you to the center of America. The Gateway to the West! We are going to Missouri. Specifically, Saint Charles, right across the river from Saint Louis!"

I paused for a minute. Really, Saint Charles? Were we even good enough to be on a podcast? What legends did we even have? The podcast was hosted by some kid at school, so maybe he was trying to make Saint Charles sound cooler than it actually was. Turning the volume up, I continued my walk, my Converse crunching over fallen leaves. Two kids, about seven years old, ran past me with their backpacks flying behind them, probably rushing home to prepare for a night of trick-or-treating.

"I am sure many of our listeners have not heard of this place, but Saint Charles is very important to Missouri history. The First State Capital was located there! And they make sure you never forget it!"

Snorting, I continued up the steps to my house. Unlike Main Street, my block was not littered with Victorian or Colonial mansions. Instead, there were a bunch of one story houses that all looked similar with the same boring beige paint job. The music began to deepen, becoming menacing as I reached the red wooden door to my house. Sliding my key into the lock, the music hit a deep, eerie note as the voice picked back up.

"But we aren't here to discuss their impressive history. We are here to look at their dark side! Saint Charles has a historic Main Street where the first State Capital building is still located. And that street has a pretty creepy legend associated with it. One of the scariest legends I have found to date!"

I paused while opening the door. What was this legend I'd never heard of? Why didn't I know anything about this stupid town I'd been stuck in my whole life? Entering the living room, I closed the door and sat down on the sofa to listen. The ceiling fan made a rhythmic clicking sound that was barely audible over the dark music.

"We found a short poem associated with this legend. Now, listeners, we have to tell you. Warnings were all over this poem saying to never read it out loud. Especially if you live in or near Saint Charles. Apparently, reading, hearing, or even thinking about the poem will bring 'it' to you. And no one knows what will happen past that. You just... disappear!"

Rolling my eyes, I stretched out on the sofa, readying to hear this "legend."

"But we here at Lore Obscura are not easily frightened. Not only will I read this poem out loud for everyone to hear, but I am doing it LIVE in Saint Charles! So, if anything spooookyyyy happens, you will be the first to know. Now, let's... begin!"

As I rolled onto my stomach, the sofa softly creaked beneath me.

"In all accounts and all its names,
Do not respond to it calling your name.
In the alleys of St. Charles, avoid saying a thing,
Or else it will follow, calling your name..."

A loud pop snapped me from the poem. I let out a scream as the room plunged into darkness. Light filtered in through the window blinds from the streetlamp, casting tall shadows across the ceiling. Standing up, I looked around the living room. The only sounds heard were my ragged breathing and the clicking of the fan. Looking at the ceiling fan, I saw that the light bulb directly above my head was blown out. Finally, after what felt like ages, the voice returned, causing me to jump.

"Whoa, guys, that's creepy, but not as creepy as what just hap—"

I ripped the earbuds out and threw them across the room, still shaking. I began listening to my surroundings. Click. Click. Click. I stayed there in the center of my darkened living room, steadying my breathing to the rhythm of the ceiling fan. After a few moments, I picked up my cell phone. 8:00. Shit! Shaking myself free of the spook, I ran into my room, flipping on every light along the way. Thankfully, the bulbs remained intact, and I quickly threw on clothes. I found some black tights and an oversized orange sweater dress to pull on over them. There, orange and black, that's Halloweenie enough. I looked in the mirror and sighed. My long, copper hair fell flat around my face. Looking at my makeup, I contemplated attempting some fun eyeliner, maybe batwings or spiderwebs, but remembering the time, I decided on the ole tried and true cat eyes liner. I tried to make something of a cute hairstyle, but in the end, I gave up and just pulled it all into a ponytail.

Exiting the house, I shivered as a cool breeze blew along my back. I considered running back inside to grab a jacket but checking the time on my phone, I noticed it was already 8:45. It would take me at least fifteen minutes to reach the Capital. Huffing, I began my walk toward Main Street. Kids in colorful costumes ran by giggling as their parents followed behind, laughing and talking amongst themselves. No one paid me any mind as I continued past them.

Reaching for my pocket, I remembered that this outfit didn't have any. Crossing my arms to help them remain warm, I trudged on. Really wish I remembered my earbuds. I thought I left them on the floor. Another strong breeze picked up, and I ran into an alleyway to avoid it.

"Ana," a voice called softly behind me, barely more than a whisper.

I paused, remembering the poem. *Do not respond to it calling your name.* Shaking the thoughts away and scoffing at myself, I kept going through the alleyway, walking out onto Main Street. About five more minutes to the Capital, I noticed Main Street was oddly empty for Halloween night. North Main Street was littered with bars and restaurants hosting Halloween parties and events, but I, however, was on the furthest end of South, where the only businesses were mom and pop antique stores and craft shops. Having their Halloween events earlier in the day, they were now all locked and dark.

Lampposts illuminated the brick-lined street as I carried on. The occasional breeze lifted strands of my hair that had managed to fall loose from my ponytail. I stepped in front of an alleyway when I saw something move out of the corner of my eye. I turned to look, but there was nothing. Just a dark, empty, narrow alleyway.

"Ana."

Fear shot up my spine as I froze, cold sweat beading on my face. Taking a shaky breath in, I took another step forward. I walked faster and faster, listening for another set of footsteps following behind, but all I heard was the voice becoming louder and more insistent.

"Ana! Ana... Ana!"

The voice continued as I picked up my pace. Panic began to take over. Finally, I broke into a sprint toward the Capital. Still no feet pursued me, but the voice remained.

"Ana!"

Screams from the voice echoed across the empty street as my foot twisted on an uneven brick. I tumbled hard to the ground, my knee striking the edge of an exposed brick. Hot pain raced through my body. Sucking breath in through my teeth, I looked down. My tights were ripped, blood dripping onto the bricks.

"Ana," a familiar voice said behind me.

Anger flashed through me when I recognized Ben's voice and realized what just happened. "Ben, I swear! If this was your idea of a Halloween prank, I will..." Spinning around, I found myself alone in the middle of the street. Everything was silent, even the breeze had paused. "Ben?" I called out shakily. "Hello?"

"Ana," the voice called again, quietly this time.

I whipped my head around just in time to see a shadow dart behind a building. I could feel the heat rising again. This was the stupidest prank someone could pull right now. Angrily, I stood up and limped into the alley toward the shadow, yelling at Ben the entire time. "Ben, this isn't funny! I actually got hurt! What is wrong with you?" I turned the corner, stopping dead in my tracks. The figure in front of me was not Ben. I wasn't sure I could even call it a human. It appeared to be made of a solid black material in the shape of a human. It towered over me, at least seven feet tall. I let out a small gasp, stepping back to the safety of the street. It seemed to be looking directly at me, but it had no eyes. No features. Just a blank, black face.

The figure took a step toward me, sounds of cracking bones filling the empty space between us. My blood turned to ice. I couldn't move. The thing... smiled. The smile grew and grew, splitting completely across the face. Shadows pulled away to reveal long, sharp, brilliantly white teeth. As it opened its mouth, I saw another set of teeth behind the first, just as sharp and deadly. Its body began to morph as it grew larger, more sounds of cracking and popping joints echoing around me. The arms melted into shadows, racing across the ground toward me. I wanted to run, to scream, but something was holding me silently in place as the shadowy tendrils wrapped around my ankles, making me feel like my feet had been plunged into ice water. Pain creeped up my legs as the thick threads of inky black followed behind it, slithering around my body until all I could feel was a deathly cold. The form continued morphing in front of my eyes. I heard the sound of flesh ripping as gigantic wings with glossy black feathers burst forth from its back. The wings extended to the sound of sickening pops as they wrapped around me. Something wet and cold oozed down my back where the wings touched me. The mouth with its two rows of teeth continued to elongate, becoming a demented snout. The smile was ever expanding, showing more and more never-ending teeth. Then, the forms shifted to show... eyes. Not just two, but eight red eyes, glaring at me, filled with hunger.

I realized that I'd been holding my breath throughout the transformation. Trying to suck in a large gulp of air, I panicked when something stopped me. I couldn't move, I couldn't breathe... My heart pounded wildly in my chest as my lungs burned, begging for oxygen. The creature glided closer to me, all eight eyes watching me gleefully. The mouth opened and blocked out my view of... everything.

Everything except the pitch black darkness inside the monster's mouth. My vision faded as I felt my heartbeat slow, the burning in my lungs overtaking my senses. I heard a deep voice rumble one final word, causing my skull to vibrate before darkness took over.

"Ana."

Ben

I looked at my watch for the hundredth time—9:20. Can't believe Ana would stand me up. I glanced around for one final try, still unable to see even the slight outline of her red hair or slim frame rounding a corner. Reluctantly, I began walking to Michelle's alone. Not only had I been stood up, but now I had to go into this stupid party as the 'new kid with no friends.' I ground my teeth as I walked the final block. Other teens from school were passing by, many in couples' costumes or group outfits. Some looked at me as I walked, their faces clearly questioning my presence, but one girl ran up to me.

"Hey! Ben, right?" she said. She was wearing a short frilly black skirt, a white flowy blouse with a very plunging neckline, and a red hat. I was guessing Little Red Riding Hood.

"Yeah, uh..." I trailed off, realizing I had no idea what her name was.

"Oh, Rachel! I sit behind you in Davis's math class," she said. "Aren't you friends with Ana?"

I nodded, feeling a small amount of heat rising to my cheeks as I remembered that I was alone at the biggest party of the year. Rachel seemed to notice my discomfort.

"Hey, don't feel bad. I used to be friends with Ana too. She does this kinda thing. Bailing on parties and such. How 'bout you join us? We are doing a 'fairytale' theme, and you could fit in perfectly!" she said brightly.

I remembered at that moment that I was dressed in my old Renaissance outfit that could be mistaken for "fairytale character." I looked past Rachel to her group of friends. One guy was wearing a werewolf mask with a shirt and jeans. A blonde girl standing next to him was wearing a short pink dress with a sparkly pink, squiggly... pig tail... attached to a belt. Another girl stood next to them, wearing what looked to just be a medieval-esque dress. Her long, black hair was intricately braided, like something out of *Lord of the Rings*. I looked back at Rachel. "Okay, sure," I nervously responded.

She gave me a small smile back. "Come on, I'll introduce you! Your costume goes so well with Natalie's outfit! If I didn't know any better, you two could have been wearing a couples' costume!" Rachel rushed me over and introduced me to the group. Werewolf Guy, I learn, was named Eddy.

"I like the outfit, dude! Looks way more interesting than this cheap mask. I can barely breathe in here!" Eddy said, beginning to take off the mask when the blonde girl, whose name was Elizabeth, slapped his hands away.

"Keep it on, Eddy! We have a chance to win the couples' costume," she said earnestly. Rachel laughed and pointed at the final girl, who I took to be Natalie. "Lizzie, you have some competition now with Ben and Natalie wearing those outfits!"

Natalie turned a slight shade of pink and looked down at her feet. "I used to work at the Ren Faire," she mumbled.

My ears perked up hearing this. "Hey, I did too! Back in Seattle! That's where this is from. It was actually my work outfit," I said excitedly.

Natalie looked up in surprise. A bright smile quickly took over her face.

Rachel looked back and forth between us and then laughed again. "Oh, this is great! I'm a matchmaker, I'm calling it," she said while bouncing on the balls of her feet.

I felt myself blush and noticed Natalie looking back down. Eddy laughed.

"Come on, guys. Michelle isn't gonna wait for us!" We all filed into the house. Music was loudly playing, the walls vibrating to the beat of rapid dance music. People were packed into a giant living room, holding cups and bottles. The room was filled with the smell of various cheap alcohol. High ceilings towered above us with intricate crown moldings of flowers and filigree. Hanging in the center was a giant chandelier with hundreds of crystals dangling from the bottom in an almost waterfall pattern, causing rainbow lights to be reflected everywhere. Staring at the light reflections, I felt an almost magical trance wash over me.

"The chandelier is supposedly from the 1700s and came with the original owner all the way from France," a smooth voice said.

I turned to see a tall girl with strawberry blonde hair and intense green eyes looking directly at me. She was wearing a figure hugging black velvet gown that fell all the way to the floor. She smiled and handed me a red plastic cup.

"You must be Ben. I haven't had a chance to meet you yet. I'm Michelle," she said with a welcoming smile that oozed the kind of warmth you would expect to see on a politician's face. All smiles and bored eyes. She really was the mayor's daughter.

I took the cup and tried the smallest of sips. A cool liquid went down, burning my throat in the process. I began coughing, and Michelle laughed.

"Not big on vodka, I see," she continued giggling as I sucked in air. Before she could continue talking, the music cut out. Michelle spun around in surprise and raised her voice above the crowd. "What do you think you're doing?" she yelled.

A guy wearing a red and green striped shirt with black pants hopped up on top of the coffee table. Michelle scoffed, heading toward him. "Everyone, everyone! Listen! Something happened!" he shouted.

Others began sighing. "Get off the table, Jason, you're drunk!"

"No, no, this is serious! Not a prank! The police just said someone is missing!"

The room fell into an uncomfortable silence. We all began looking at each other, questioning whether to believe the ravings of a drunk Jason. Could it be Ana? I looked toward Rachel, but she seemed just as confused.

With the room silent, Jason continued. "You know Todd? The geeky junior who runs that podcast practically no one listens to? What's it called, Lore... something... Well, his parents just reported him missing!"

Some people rolled their eyes. Michelle was now standing below Jason, next to the table. Her shoulders were so tense with rage that I could see their muscular outlines from across the room. "That's not funny, Jason. Now get off the table before my dad kills me," she snapped while reaching for him.

Jason side stepped her. "I'm not joking, it's on the news! See for yourselves! His parents said he was recording a live Halloween episode and then disappeared mid-recording! Apparently, someone else who was listening to it is now also reported missing!"

Rachel seemed to have enough of Jason's games. She stood up on her tiptoes as if to help boost her voice across the room. "Well, if he disappeared while recording, then we should be able to hear it if you play the episode," she shouted. Others nodded, talking amongst themselves.

Michelle, thoroughly aggravated, stepped up on the table beside Jason. "If I play the stupid episode through the speakers, can we get back to the party?" she asked, exasperated.

Jason nodded and hopped off the table. Michelle sighed and pulled out her phone. Walking to the speaker, she began searching for the episode. Quickly, a new voice filled the room.

"*Welcome to Lore Obscura! The show where we find the most obscure legends...*"

We all found places to sit to listen to the episode. Michelle remained near the speaker, glaring at Jason. The room was quiet as we all listened, eager to hear how Todd disappeared. A shiver began at the base of my spine—an uneasiness that I couldn't seem to shake. I tried to ignore it and focus on what Todd was saying.

"*I am doing it LIVE in Saint Charles itself! So, if anything spoooookyyyy happens, you will be the first to know. Now, let's... begin!*

In all accounts and all its names,

Do not respond to it calling your name.

In the alleys of St. Charles, avoid saying a thing,

Or else it will follow, calling your name..."

We all scream as a light bulb popped, and we were thrown into darkness...

About the Author

Krystyna Lee, going by the pseudonym Kalee, is an Art Historian who con-
ducts research and hosts a dark history podcast called Macabre Matters.
Her podcast can be found on Spotify, Apple Podcasts, and Google Podcasts.

TRISTAN AND SABINE

MICHAL LEIGH

Reverend Sabine Baring-Gould

Years ago in college, I read about Reverend Sabine Baring-Gould, the man most famous for writing the well-known hymn, "Onward Christian Soldiers." In addition to being a hymnodist, he was a celebrated historian and prolific writer of original fiction and collected folk lore. He was rumored to give lectures at Cambridge with a pet bat on his person, and also to be the inspiration of the professor in George Bernard Shaw's Pygmalion. My character, Sabine Hastings, while inspired by Baring-Gould, is entirely a fabrication. The real Sabine Baring-Gould wrote a book entitled The Book of Were-wolves, which is now in the common domain and can be read in its entirety online or in various printings. Within The Book of Were-wolves there is no indication that Sabine Baring-Gould ever believed in werewolf lore, and to the contrary, he gives many rational explanations as to how people in certain cultures may have come to believe in them, or where the tales may have originated. I have left the events of my story open to interpretation. Is evil a choice, an inherent attribute, or merely a function of one's environment? Is there a monstrous werewolf in this story, or are we all monsters given the right impetus? Within the pages of this homage to the classic horror of Poe, Lovecraft, Stoker, and Baring-Gould. It is up for you to decide.

Tristan

Y ou've forgotten the lights again."

"Hmm?" I sigh. I must have actually dozed off without realizing it. I wish to God he hadn't woken me. There are precious few nights I fall asleep restfully. And I know damn well I left them all lit.

"You've left the lamp lit and several candles too. I'm afraid that if every innkeeper on the continent charges us for refilling the lamps every night, it will eat up any savings of sharing a room. We may have to cut our travels short and return to Cambridge with barely a pamphlet's worth of research."

"Oh, sorry, Professor. I assumed you would be along shortly, so I left it as a courtesy."

"I've explained to you before that if you retire early, as you make a habit of doing, that I don't need you to leave the lamps and candles alight. I don't have a complicated routine of an evening, Tristan." He splashes some water from the basin on his face and dries it. "And I should think that the innkeeper would likewise prefer that their establishment to not be burnt to a crisp on my account."

"Of course. Terribly sorry." I make an effort to channel my genuine shame into the appearance of repentance, wracking my brain for how I can contrive to keep the lights on again tomorrow without arousing suspicion.

"I'm well aware of my privilege in being able to afford to travel abroad for my research, but I am not so rich as to not notice the extra charges laid on us for the extra candles and oil."

"Of course." I'm running out of ideas, and I know that the professor is right. It's exceedingly wasteful of me to light the lamps while it's still daylight and to leave them lit while no one truly needs them. "It was terribly forgetful of me. I will try to remember to extinguish them tomorrow."

"You can blow them out now. I'm done washing up."

I blow out the lamp on the table and all but one of the three candles around the room that are burning low as he climbs into the bed across the room. I glance over my shoulder to make sure Sabine isn't looking before I hold my wrist over the flame—just long enough to remind me of the light and make me feel as though a part of it is still with me through the night. It hurts, but I won't be able to sleep anyway. Because God knows I'm a liar. And I know what liars deserve.

Sabine

"Not the box," Tristan whispers. Box? I don't have the foggiest idea what he's going on about, but he's had a funny look to him since we lost sight of the village. He just looked a bit white at first, which I attributed to the cold and damp. But then he just stopped walking and stood perfectly still like a man whose soul had left his body until he whispered those words. He doubles over, breathing so hard that it must surely make him dizzy, but he pants for air as a man who is drowning.

"Slow down, man. You're all right. You're all right." I uselessly reassure him until the spell passes. "Are you sure that you're well now?" My voice feels flat in the stillness of the marsh air around us. The innkeeper told us this morning that no one but the Widow

Ciobanu lives in "the Waste," the name by which the locals call this boggy stretch of earth, nor do they have any business here. The innkeeper assured us that she was very knowledgeable on the folklore surrounding werewolves, the subject of my newest collection. Perhaps it is only the knowledge that there is not another soul for miles around us, but I had not accounted for how lonely it would feel here. The atmosphere feels like it's never been disturbed in the history of man, and it seems to take no notice of us even now.

"I shall be," Tristan replies, yet his eyes say otherwise. He's young and strong, but he doesn't look well at all. Perhaps some rowdiness from the inn's common room kept him awake, but this is something more. His jaw and neck muscles are tense, and his skin has a clammy pallor that cannot entirely be accounted for by the ever present fog. Perhaps it is fear of losing our way.

I am not prone to the shivers myself, for I bear my faith as an inviolable shield, if not against physical harm, then against anything that might affect my eternal soul. Though, I am wary that we shouldn't stray off the path through the Waste. It's only just made visible by the many years it's been traversed by the members of a single family. The dense fog hangs about us like a white curtain, rendering any objects or persons completely obscured as if they were behind a wall of plaster. I wouldn't like to think of how long a man might wander in the fog if he were to stray but a little.

"I can still see your unease. Is it the fog that troubles you?" I ask.

The path we walk is an unpleasant, almost marshy thing. Grasses grow to either side of it only just visible through the opaque gloom. The ground squelches with our every step. It soaks through my boots and wool stockings, though the rest of me is scarcely drier. The mud and the mist give the impression that they are one and the same—still, stagnant, and unwholesome. A miasma of decaying things hangs about the place.

"No, sir. Well, yes, in a way."

"Do not fear. We shall stick to the path and trust in God to guide us safely. And to guide me in the use of my revolver if necessary. I'm a terrible shot." I would not be eager to use lethal force on a fellow man, of course, particularly not for the mere loss of goods when the man at the receiving end could lose his eternal soul with his last act being one of a sinful nature. But I hope that the appearance of a gun might be enough to deter a highwayman, and it seemed prudent when venturing into old and wild places, such as this, that I should have some means of protection against wild beasts.

"It is not fear, exactly. I have a particular discomfort of not being able to see. So, yes, the fog discomfits me, but it is of little consequence. The innkeeper informed me that the Waste where the Widow Ciobanu resides is more often shrouded in fog than it is not. It cannot be helped." His jaw is set and his eyes downcast. I haven't seen him look so scared, so small, since the first day I saw him at the university.

I had just entered the library for some research on comparative tellings of various bits of Eastern European folklore for my thesis. A boy sat alone at a study table, reading. He was small and thin, verging on frail, but his eyes sparkled with joy. He read as a man who had entered the gates of heaven. He soaked up the delights of the words on the page before him as though they filled a great need. The world around him had ceased to exist entirely. I watched him for a time, wondering what text could enrapture a young man so completely.

"Might I ask what you are reading?" I asked.

At first, the boy did not react to my approach. He was still adrift in a sea of words.

"Excuse me."

He continued reading.

I tried louder. "Excuse me."

He jumped as though he had been caught at something rather shameful and quickly closed his book, sliding it beneath the larger tome chained to the desk.

"*Oh, goodness. You gave me quite a start, Professor... I'm sorry, I don't believe we've been introduced.*"

"*Hastings. Forgive me for startling you. I noticed that you seem to be enjoying your book a great deal. Might I ask what you are reading?*"

"*Oh, yes. Of course.*" The boy proceeded to show me the impressive looking tome that he had placed on the much smaller book he had been reading.

"*Ah, yes. Summa Theologica, the great work of Thomas Aquinas. What is your favorite part?*"

"*Um, yes, well, the theological premise on the whole, I should think.*"

I had to bite my tongue not to laugh out loud and scare the little rabbit away or I would have never found anything out about him. "*Ah, yes. The theological bits are rather the whole point. Though, to be honest, I find them as dry as tombs.*" I couldn't help but smile at the boy who was clearly hiding an earnest love for something with an equally earnest ignorance of theology. "*But what is this bit sticking out from beneath?*" I simply had to know at this point, even if I had to wrest it away from him.

"*It,*" the boy's lip trembled, "*it's nothing.*"

"*Come now.*" I smiled in what I hoped was a disarming and not at all accusing way. It must have worked too, as he handed me the book. It was barely more than a pamphlet really, with a cover of thick paper rather than bound leather. He cringed as I observed it, as though he were expecting a whipping. It was a collection of children's stories, translated from German. I couldn't contain my laughter. "*Is this what you were reading?*"

His face glowed with shame. "*I don't expect that—*"

"*Young man,*" I interjected, "*there is no shame in taking joy in children's stories. I collect them myself. Children often don't realize how complex and wonderful they are. In fact, I need an assistant to accompany me on an upcoming sabbatical to conduct some research. I would be honored to have such an enthusiastic reader of children's tales to assist me in my own studies of folklore, especially if you have any skill as a translator. What is your name?*"

"*Tristan, sir. But aren't you terribly upset with me for my duplicity?*"

"*Nonsense. I couldn't have a better assistant than one who genuinely loves stories as much as I. What sort of research are you doing here?*"

"*I'm afraid, I—well, none, sir.*"

"*Reading solely for pleasure then?*"

"*Yes... No... Well, not solely. You see, some of the men in the commons were discussing a lady of their acquaintance who was much changed in appearance of late. Merriweather Fortescue likened her to a 'cinder maid,' and they all laughed when I asked why. Apparently, it is a childhood tale.*" *He lowered his eyes to the ancient oak desk again.*

"*One with which you were not familiar, I take it. And you are taking steps to remedy this?*"

"*Yes, sir.*"

"*There are many reasons why a scholar might reference records of folklore and fairytales. I myself make a study of recording them. But I see no reason why a man should try to hide it. The Cinder Maid is a common enough tale, but there are as many variations on it as there are civilizations in the world. Perhaps you know it by another name.*"

"*No.*" *There was a finality in his voice. Not like someone putting their foot down, but like someone who had only just accepted a deep loss and had been asked to exhume it. He did not speak again for several moments. I didn't pressure him. He looked as though he might begin to sob, but he merely sat in silence until he was able to say with all appearances of decorum, "My nurse was... unkind."*

Tristan

We reach the home of Widow Ciobanu after midday, though it's hard to be certain with the sun hiding behind the Godforsaken fog. I know I shouldn't think such things. I must render every thought captive unto Christ, but I struggle to see Him in this place. The thought makes me shudder.

The widow does not speak a word of English, having spent all her life in this hovel on the marsh. While the professor employed me as his assistant partly because he loved how I saw folklore with such novelty, in reality, I mostly work as his translator in his travels. The professor has spent most of his studies in Latin rather than modern languages, as my tutor had seen fit to teach me in my youth.

My parents spent much time abroad and left me in the care of my nurse, Katie. I was too sickly a child to attend boarding school with other boys my age, so a tutor was arranged for me when I turned ten, and my parents decided I needed a more learned instructor than Katie. The reason for my sickliness became apparent when my new tutor, Mr. Henshaw, decided as a part of my education to develop my physical abilities as well as my mental faculties. We took a walk on a warm day, and he thought it a prime opportunity for a swimming lesson. I shall never forget the look of horror on his face when I removed my shirt. My chest and back were a mass of bruises, young and red, old and yellowish green, deep violet in the intermediate stage. I knew no different. My tutor saw to it that my nurse was dismissed that very day. He was a kind man and a skilled educator, but much damage had already been done to body, mind, and soul.

Hardly a day passes which does not reveal an undiscovered crack that woman left behind in my shattered self. I'm ashamed of my spell in the marsh today. In the past, I've only known myself to have my episodes in the most utter darkness, but apparently, I can lose myself in fog as well. I hardly know what the professor said to me while I was awash in my own brokenness. On a few such occasions, I have gone so far as to...

But that is in the past. I must try to do better.

I start as a figure appears in the mist not five feet in front of me. It can only be the Widow Ciobanu, for the innkeeper explained that her family has been the only people to live in the Waste and that no man who values his horse would dare to take it here. She apparently heard our approach and awaited our arrival.

I introduce myself and the professor and explain his aspiration to complete an exhaustive treatise on the folklore surrounding werewolves, indicating that the innkeeper in town had recommended her in particular as something of an expert on the topic. She smiles with teeth broken and worn and bids us welcome into her home.

The hovel of weathered boards, thatch, and mud is scarcely drier than the waste beyond its walls. But there is a fire. The woman's bed lies in one corner, and a table sits before the hearth. It's stained a dark and hideous shade of red that would be shocking had I not, in recent weeks, become inured to the ubiquity of the beetroot in nearly all of the regional dishes. It isn't a vegetable I particularly enjoy. I take the seat I'm offered as graciously as I'm able, even though the table looks like it belongs in a slaughterhouse, and I produce my writing implements from my coat pocket while translating the professor's gratitude at our hostess's kindness. The stickiness of the beet juice combined with the smell of decay wafting from the marsh leads my mind toward the disturbing images I so often struggle to keep at bay. Things I probably deserve. Things Katie deserves too, for her duplicity and sinfulness is at least as great as my own.

"Madam," the professor begins, "I would be so pleased if you would tell us what you know of werewolves."

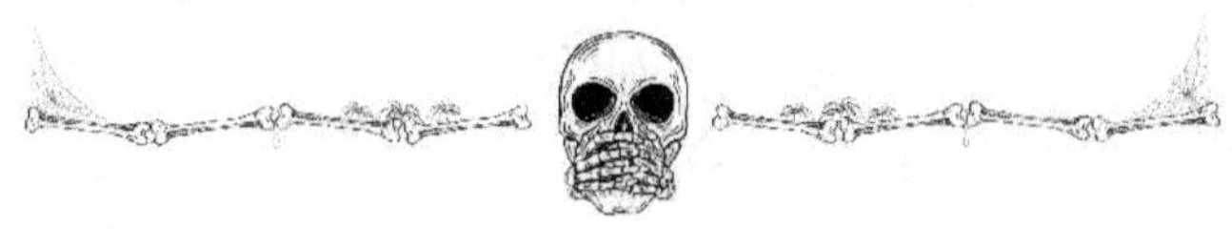

Sabine

"The vârcolac is of the devil," the woman begins.

Though Tristan translates our words, the woman's demeanor and her tone speak for themselves, yet I cannot put my finger on what emotion she portrays. Fear? Anger? Sadness? Those would make sense, but they don't match what my senses are telling me. Her eyes shine brightly with a strange passion. Though I can't make heads or tails of it, her expression seems more akin to eagerness, but eager for what, I can only guess.

"The vârcolac can be immense in stature, neither man nor beast, but a nightmare from hell. They can appear as a natural wolf. They can even appear as a man, with all of his weakness and frailty. Monsters, all. Hosts of Satan. They consume flesh and soul alike. The moment a vârcolac bites, the soul is damaged by a festering evil that will consume every ounce, every drop of goodness, and replace it with a raging famine until you become like them. One with darkness. If bitten, the pope himself would slake his thirst with the blood of those he loved best."

She tells tales of men, women, and children who were turned or slain. Tells how those slain by the vârcolac are buried in the area, or more often, the few remaining pieces of them. The stories are incredibly detailed. A young girl long ago whose mother told her not to play too long out of doors, recognized only by the smear of entrails found on her very recognizable red cape. A son, in more recent times, who came home with strange bite marks. His family was found the next day, torn limb from limb and hearts pulled from their chests.

"Where did you learn these tales, madam?" I ask. "Were they passed down from your mother?"

"My mother? No. These were my friends and neighbors," she says with a bizarre smile. "I saw with my own eyes when my husband was taken. Oh, how he screamed!"

Something in my stomach turns completely at this revelation. I would think this must be in jest. But in such a jest, I can find no humor. How can she say such awful things, and with that strange grin upon her face, all the while talking about the dismemberment of dear friends? This woman is clearly demented. A sad fate for a woman living on her own, but not one I feel equipped with the proper knowledge to address. It's surely my duty to immediately alert the folk of the village that this woman is not in her right mind. Though it pains me to think it, I can only imagine that she will be confined.

I give my excuses and stand to take my leave, bidding young Tristan with my eyes to do the same.

"Darkness will overtake you," Tristan translates for me in a weak whisper, though the widow is looking at him as if this is a message meant for his ears alone. He freezes to the spot. The walk from the village was not a short one, and Widow Ciobanu's tales were long, but something in her strange smile tells me that she is not speaking of nightfall.

"She's right. The night will come upon us on our return to the village. We have stayed too long." His eyes widen as it sinks in that we must complete our return journey in the dark.

"Tristan, this woman is obviously deranged." I would not normally say such things in her presence, but for now, I am grateful that she does not speak English any more than I speak Romanian. "I feel that we ought to take our leave. Immediately. Perhaps we can alert someone in the village to her condition so they may see that she is cared for in her declining mental state."

Ciobanu speaks again. And again, she looks directly at Tristan. "The night will be eternally black," he translates. His pulse is thrumming so violently I can see it in his neck. "She has offered to let us sleep here tonight and return in the morning light. Please, Professor, I do not think I can bear a night so black as this one where not even the stars shine."

"Do you really want to stay here?"

"No. But I cannot abide such darkness. I cannot. I *cannot*." His voice breaks with panic. "Please, Professor."

I relent despite my misgivings and nod before addressing the widow. "Thank you for your gracious offer of accommodation. We will gratefully accept."

The widow opens a rough-hewn antique chest, worn smooth in places by generations of use, and makes ready some old blankets on the floor for us. She does not offer us any supper, which would not go amiss after our long walk this morning, but I don't protest. Perhaps she does not possess any food to offer. I wouldn't wish to shame her for her lack, especially given her apparently delicate mental state. The fire burns low, and Tristan keeps glancing at it nervously.

Thus far on our tour, Tristan has always asked to retire early. I have always found him abed with a lamp or candle still aflame, which I would extinguish before retiring. But he is so wide-eyed tonight that I doubt sleep will find him.

"I won't leave your side." I sit beside him on our makeshift pallet. He glances up from his ruminations. The darkness outside the dimly lit room weighs upon him as though it's a solid expanse of iron threatening to crush him. Only a few sticks of thatch and some glowing peat embers hold it back.

"Yes, all will be well in the morning. Perhaps the sun will burn away the fog at last." He looks as though he cannot remember the sun and scarcely believes in mornings at all.

I take his hand in mine as I would a child's. "Did you know that Mrs. Hastings makes the very best strawberry scones?" I ask him, reaching for the sunniest topic my mind can call forth. "Of course, you haven't met my dear wife. On the morrow, we shall cut short our travels and make our way to my home, where you shall stay with us for no less than a fortnight. And I shall ask Mrs. Hastings to supply you with as many strawberry scones as you can eat, my lad." This thought seems to penetrate his fear, and he even ventures a weak smile, which warms my heart. If anyone could make someone smile in this place, it would be her. "Come, let's go to sleep so that we can leave this place as soon as day breaks." Tristan nods and lays down. I do likewise.

"Surely, I could not put you and your wife to such trouble, Professor." Something tugs heavily at my heartstrings. The same tug I experienced when I saw him devouring fairytales in the library. The same tug I felt as I heard him explain why he'd been reading them so studiously. I wanted to help him. I wanted to protect him from harm. As I do now.

"Nonsense. We have traveled together for over a month. We are friends, you and I. And you must call me Sabine." I pat him on the back like I imagine someday doing to my own son. "Good night, Tristan."

I lay quietly for a moment before hearing, "Professor?"

"Sabine," I remind him.

"Sabine," he amends. "Would you... Forgive me. It is of no consequence."

I take his hand and see something deep within him wound tight to its breaking point begin to loosen. "I won't let go."

Though I do not know when I fall asleep, I dream of unholy altars to an unholy god, of blood and teeth and snarls. Of bones snapping and flesh tearing. I open my eyes with a start, relieved that it has all been a nightmare. But then... I hear something that isn't a dream. Something animalistic. Something wet. And the pace of my heart tells me that I am very much awake. From the light of the embers of the peat brick that Tristan added to the fire, I can just make out the figure of the Widow Ciobanu wrestling with something in her pallet. I fear that an animal has breached the hut while we were asleep and attacked her. I sit up finding my hand still entwined with Tristan's. He rouses while I reach for the pistol in my coat pocket, but I freeze as the widow turns toward me, dropping the lifeless body of some unknown creature. The body is too far mangled, and the room too dark, to make out whether it is man or beast.

My thundering heart stops cold for several beats. She grins broadly, and rivulets of blood trail down her chin, oozing thick and black in the dim light. She begins speaking, and Tristan's eyes widen, but he does not repeat what he hears for me.

"Run, Tristan!" I take my coat in one hand and his hand in the other, and we don't linger long enough to gather any of our other belongings. We tear out of the door, barefooted and panting with fear. The fog has not thinned, but rather, in the absence of the sun, has become a featureless, solid thing of pure black. Tristan's hand lays limply in mine, though I clasp his tightly, dragging him as quickly as I can run. I am not a runner though. My lungs burn. The ground fights my every step as the cold, black mud pulls at my bare feet, squelching between my toes. I pour every ounce of effort into making my feet move faster. Faster. I must go faster.

Do I hear another set of splashes? My jaw clenches. I cannot pause to find out.

Tristan's hand wrenches out of mine as I stumble on an unseen object. The impact jars my toes as I fly long enough to wonder if the impact will hurt. The mud absorbs much of the shock that my face and hands would have received otherwise as I roll and tumble through the muck. My stubbed toes start to throb before I can get up, and my foot aches, but it could be worse. I gingerly put weight on it and wince.

I cannot see Tristan. I cannot see my own hands. The world has closed in, and I am alone in it.

"Tristan!" I call at a stage whisper. He cannot be far, and I don't want to draw the attention of that woman... if she is indeed human at all.

Tristan

My head hurts, and my ears are ringing.

"Please, Katie, I won't say anything to anyone about your visitors."

"My what, you insolent little thing?" Katie asks quietly. "I haven't the faintest idea to what you are referring." Her tone shifts slightly, not louder, but more dangerous. "But you are right that you shan't be talking to anyone at all for some time, Master Tristan. Who would believe a lying little rat like you anyway? You know that lying is a grievous sin, don't you, Master Tristan?"

"Yes, but I—"

"Then, you know that liars ought to be punished for their sins lest they burn in the eternal pit, don't you?" She sneers primly, as though she would like nothing better than to observe my eternal torment.

"Oh, please, Katie! I didn't mean to lie, I only–"

"And you won't make any noises, either. What should befall your eternal soul if I accidentally dropped rat poison in your tea before you should repent? And don't forget who watches you in your sleep, young master, lest you smother yourself in your soft, warm pillows at night."

I feel my breath catching, but I mustn't cry.

"Box," she says softly. *The word is a sentence.*

"Please, Katie, anything but the—" *My vision goes blank, and my legs buckle beneath me from the force of her slap. She shoves me into the empty trunk before I can recover. The narrowing band of light is the only thing I can see as she lowers the lid and locks it. The band of light disappears next. Presumably she puts a quilt or something over it to cover the gaps and muffle any noise I might make.*

I cannot straighten my legs or move my arms. The blackness surrounding me is absolute. The closeness of the walls around me squeezes the very air from my lungs. I'm going to die in this box. But that's probably a better fate than to disobey Katie. I mustn't cry, yet I can't help but cry. I mustn't be heard crying, so I open my mouth wide to gather the air my wracking sobs require in perfect silence. I'm going to die in this box.

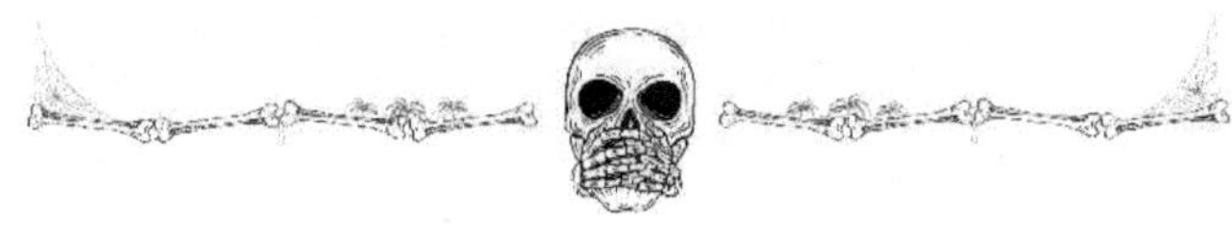

Sabine

I have no idea whether I am facing the way I was running or the way I have just come. "Tristan! Tristan!"

I stop to listen and hear nothing but my heart pounding in my chest. Then… snarling, tearing, wet sounds. Bones breaking. But no screams. It sounds as though a wolf were tearing into a fresh carcass.

Tristan

I mustn't cry.

I mustn't cry.

I'm going to die in this box.

Sabine

I pull my revolver from my coat and aim it blindly into the dark. A whine, a splash, and silence.

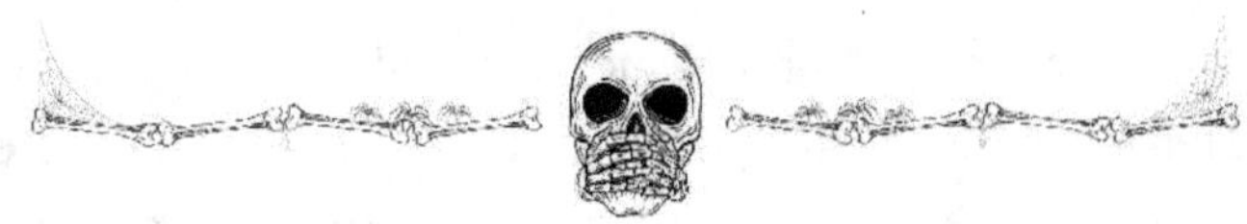

Tristan

It hurts so much. I mustn't cry.

I am going to die in this box.

I know what I deserve. Things Katie warned me of. The hounds of hell, the blood running from my veins into the cold earth, crows claiming my eyes, my flesh rotting away. I've seen it so many times in my mind's eye. Blackness. Darkness. Blood. So much blood.

But If I am going to hell anyway, maybe I can take her with me. Two can die in my box. I can see her. I can hear her. I can almost taste her blood.

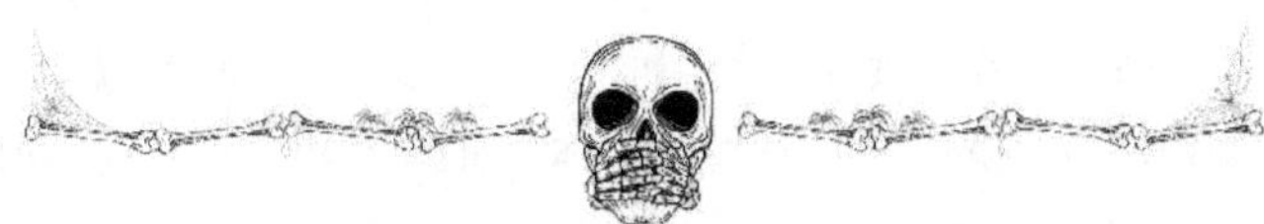

Sabine

"Katie."

I hobble toward the whispered name, and the fog clears just enough that I can make out a dim shape of my friend and a great wolf lying beside him. Tristan is mangled, but somehow, he sits up. The look in his eyes is wild, made all the worse by an unearthly smile. It is not the smile of a friend, but the smile of a predator, or perhaps of an eldritch thing that ought not to exist.

"The whole world is a box," he says with a dangerous glee. "Welcome to hell." He grabs at my arm and begins to claw at me and fight me with a demonic strength despite limbs that are bent in places God did not intend. He rolls on top of me and pins me to the ground. Blood from his wounded face and pours onto mine. I feel his hot breath closing in on my neck. His teeth just make contact as the revolver goes off, leaving my ears ringing as Tristan goes limp.

Oh God. Have I killed him? "Tristan? Please, God. Tristan!" I cry in the darkness until my eyes feel like the driest part of the whole gruesome, invisible tableau.

As day begins to break, I can see that my foot is likely broken. Fear alone granted me insensitivity to it. I cannot... I cannot carry him. Nor can I leave him just yet. I sit in silence, listening to the rhythm of my heart in my swollen foot and the absence of his in his chest. As my grief gradually gives way to other sensations—pain, hunger, sleeplessness—I realize it's time to move on and hope against hope that I am hobbling in the direction of the village.

In an hour or so, I come across a path which I can only hope to be the right one. I choose a direction based entirely upon chance and, in a few more hours, find myself stumbling out of the waste, out of the fog, and into the village.

I wake several hours later, not knowing what has transpired. Using mostly gestures and some poor sketches, the innkeeper and his wife inquire about Tristan. Tears well up in my eyes, and they look at each other knowingly.

A villager is produced who can speak some words of what one might call English. He tells me that three men have left to search for Tristan. They do not find any sign of him or of any wolf, nor of Widow Ciobanu, though they do report that many bones and unidentifiable bodies were found strewn about her home. They search again the next day, but do not return. No further search parties venture out.

I cannot convince myself one way or another whether Tristan was afflicted by a true evil or if I was. Perhaps I am a little mad. Perhaps I imagined it all. If he were indeed a werewolf, such a thing of evil ought to not be permitted to exist. But perhaps I killed my best friend in his utmost time of need. Or perhaps I did not kill him after all. Not really.

With my foot now on the mend, I'm heading home tomorrow. A translator was sent for, and statements were taken. I have not yet written to Tristan's family. I don't know what I would begin to say. That I killed their son? The room feels too small. Not a room... a box. I pull the covers up, knowing full well that sleep will not find me. Not real sleep. Not rest. I turn my back to the lit lantern on the table and face the three candles flickering on the dresser, then close my eyes.

About the Author

Michal Leigh occasionally leaks stories from her brain. This is probably a good thing, as it might explode otherwise, which would be a real chore to clean up. Aside from writing for kids and adults, Michal enjoys hiking, creating stuff, imagining naps, and ignoring housework. Twitter @Michal_Leigh and Insta @michal_leigh_writes

LEGACY

KRISTIN CRAGG

he Brown Family Legacy

In 1892, the Brown family was plagued by tuberculosis. hree members had died, and a fourth had been infected. With little understanding of medicine, the small Rhode Island town of Exter looked to unusual methods to save George Brown's only son. After exhuming George's wife and one of his daughters, they examined the body of his other recently-deceased daughter, Mercy, who was found to have color in her cheeks and blood in her veins. Ignoring the doctor's explanation of what happens to a body in a northern winter, the townspeople attempted to create a cure by burning Mercy's heart and feeding the ashes to George's son, who died shortly thereafter. Mercy was buried and eventually became known as America's last vampire. But what if that wasn't the end of the story?

From the Diary of Dr. Matthew Johnson
January 8, 1892

The townspeople have gone mad. A wave of consumption has washed through Exhall, and they've decided the culprit is a vampire. No one here is willing to look at the science and logic of the thing. Despite my best efforts, they're determined to lean on superstitious nonsense. The focus of their investigation is Temperance Shaw. The poor woman is already dead—I examined her myself. I'm not sure what else can be done. Perhaps, I will just sit back and let this insanity pass. There's no reasoning with a mob.

Present Day
Los Angeles

Luke's phone buzzed in his pocket as he unlocked the door to his dorm room. He was grateful to be out of the gloom and into the bright artificial light. The weather had been weird lately—unseasonably cool and cloudy for October in SoCal. His brown eyes sparkled as he thought of the message waiting for him. His physique spoke of his dedication to the gym, as did his loose athletic clothes.

After setting his bag down, he fell into his chair and pulled out his phone. *Vanessa.* He smiled involuntarily and scanned her newest message:

Still on for tonight? I thought we could catch the new Shriek movie.

Luke's fingers flew across the keypad.

Sounds good. What are they at, like 8?

Probably. I don't care though. I love me some horror.

I know. Class okay?

Same as usual. Dinner?

Absolutely.

Dining hall or splurge?

How about the Greasy Spoon?

Ooh, you know the way to a girl's heart.

He sent a smiling emoji.

Movie is at 8. Dinner at 6:30?

Sounds good. See you then, Ness.

Looking forward to it.

Luke smiled and tossed his phone on the couch gently, then headed to the kitchen to grab a drink.

January 15, 1892

Just as I thought the vampire fervor was dying down, they've come up with a new idea: exhumation and examination of Temperance Shaw's body. I thought suspicion and wild accusations were enough, but they are determined to take action. They believe that her coffin will be empty. It won't be.

Leaning back in his chair, Luke sighed contentedly. There was nothing like a good burger and fries, especially on a day like today. Fall in LA was usually pretty temperate, but it had been more overcast than usual. He had even considered grabbing a hoodie but decided against it. There was a chance of rain next week, but he doubted that would happen.

He glanced around the restaurant, if you could call it that. It was more a hole-in-the-wall—a tiny place where students congregated. He ran his fingers over the surface of the table, sticky from grease and oft-spilled condiments. The once-red booths were cracked and faded, and the smell of fried food seemed to permeate every inch of the place. There was a pathetic attempt to decorate for Halloween—faded decorations likely bought at a dollar store many years past—but that merely added to the ambiance, although no one would ever use that word to describe this place. No one had any idea how they managed to stay afloat in L.A. with the cheap prices they charged, but they did make up for the quality through the quantity.

Luke realized he'd been lost in his thoughts and looked up to see what Vanessa was doing while he had spaced out. He glanced across the table to find her absent-mindedly stirring the remnants of her milkshake, frowning into the silver cup. Her black hair spilled over her shoulders onto the table in soft waves.

"Penny for your thoughts?"

Her head jerked up, and she smiled, but her emerald eyes were filled with panic. She looked as if she had been caught doing something wrong.

Luke's eyes narrowed for a split second. She had been doing more of that lately. It was weird. They seemed to be growing closer, but at the same time, the closer they got, the further she seemed to pull away.

Vanessa half coughed, half laughed. "Sorry, was just thinking."

"What about?"

She let out a shallow breath as she looked toward the ceiling. She was thinking about something, but he couldn't quite get a read on her expression.

"My dad's in town." Her voice was flat with no hint of excitement. Almost as if she were commenting on the color of the napkins.

"Hey, that's exciting!" Luke paused. "I mean, is it? I don't really know much about him. Actually, I don't know anything, come to think of it."

Vanessa sucked on her bottom lip. "He's, um, how do I put it?" Her eyes searched the space between them, as if she was scanning a dictionary. "Intense." She began to drum her fingers on the table.

Luke reached out and took her hand, calming her nervous energy. "So are you, Ness."

She laughed, and Luke felt the tension dissipate.

"Good, then you won't mind coming to lunch with us this weekend?"

"Like, this weekend, this weekend?"

"Yeah. He really wants to meet you."

Luke smiled. "Should I be worried?"

She hesitated for a second, then laughed again. "No, of course not." Her smile remained for a second, then dropped. She picked the smile back up so quickly Luke wasn't quite sure he saw it missing at all. "So, we better get to the movie if we want good seats!"

He stood, walked around the table, and helped her slide out of the booth. There was an uneasiness between them, but it was probably just his anxiety. That, or the weight of the greasy food.

January 20, 1892

As expected, Temperance Shaw's body was exactly where her family had left it: in a wooden coffin housed in a crypt in the White Church cemetery. When we opened the top of the coffin, she looked exactly the same as when we buried her a month ago. Upon examination, we found that there was still blood in her body and her face was flush as if she were still alive. Neither of these facts should be a surprise: there has been snow on the ground for weeks, making it impossible to dig up the ground to bury the coffin. Of course the body looks well preserved: the snow is preserving it! But that's not enough to satisfy these lunatics. Based on some folklore they gathered from Lord-knows-where, they plan to burn the body and feed the heart to Temperance's brother, Christopher, who has regrettably been stricken by consumption like the rest of his family. Christopher is just on the cusp of adulthood. Too young yet to have a family, but old enough to know that he would make a good man. He is determined, dependable, and kind, yet these qualities already seem to be slipping away. It's a shame that he will not be with us long enough to become someone worth knowing. Consumption is a terrible disease with which to be stricken.

Saturday came quicker than Luke would have liked, and the California sun was back to its usual shine. After taking care to shower and shave, he searched through his closet and found the one pair of tan slacks he owned, figuring the black might've been too formal. Or something. He threw on a polo shirt, said goodbye to his new roommate, and headed to town to meet Vanessa and her father.

She'd chosen a popular chain restaurant, serving a little bit of everything, but nothing spectacular. It was a step up from the places they usually frequented but wasn't fancy or intimidating. Hopefully just right for a parental meeting.

As Luke turned the corner to the restaurant, he felt a buzz in his pocket.

Hey, table was ready, so
we're already sitting down.
We're opposite the window
in the back.

So much for making a good first impression. Despite having arrived ten minutes early, Vanessa and her father had beat him there.

Luke entered the restaurant, nerves on edge. It was as if his whole body was buzzing. He wished there was some way to skip the interview and just get to the part where Ness's dad started to like him. Parents always liked Luke. He was a likeable guy.

He barely glanced at the black spooky decor draped over the entryway. Wound tighter than a spring, he wove his way through the tables, chairs, servers, and handful of children waving their arms wildly into the aisles. The bright light of the window spilled into the room, illuminating nearly every table except a few tucked against the far wall. They were so masked in shadow, it took a minute to find his girlfriend despite knowing exactly where she'd be.

Once he found her, he felt his steps falter. She hadn't been kidding. The man next to her was intense.

He was tall, rigid, with angular everything—jaw, ears, shoulders. It was almost as if he had been drawn with a ruler by some art student experimenting with different styles. The light pouring in from the nearby window hit in such a way that the angles were accentuated, and his face was partially covered in shadow. His hair was powder gray, held firmly in place with just a bit too much gel. But it was his eyes that worried Luke. They were cold, icy blue, seeming to pierce straight into his soul. Luke felt a shiver pass through his body, but he shook it off, smiling as he approached.

"Hello, Mr. Johnson. I'm Luke. It's nice to meet you."

Vanessa's father stood. He was tall. Very tall. Despite standing just over six feet, Luke felt small next to him. The older man did have a few inches on him, but it was more the condescension, as if her father was looking down on a disobedient child.

Luke felt his smile falter but held out his hand. Vanessa's father stared derisively at it until Luke retracted his hand, brushing the sweat against the side of his pants. So much for calling her father by his first name.

The two men stood, sizing each other up. It had become a battle of wills, both waiting for the other to sit.

Vanessa stood, touching her father gently on his arm. "Daddy, this is Luke. My boyfriend."

Her father grimaced. This was not going well.

"Luke, this is my father, Marcus." Her father bristled, but it didn't seem to bother her. "Why don't we all take a seat?" She smiled encouragingly at Luke. She must've been modeled after her mother in both appearance and personality—it was clear she inherited very little from her father. There was a softness in her voice and posture that melted Luke. He slid into his seat as Marcus uncomfortably folded himself into his.

"Tell me about your family," Marcus said. It wasn't a question.

Luke shifted uncomfortably. *Down to business, I guess.* "Well, my family is from Rhode Island. Been there for a long time, actually. My great-whatever grandfather settled there after the Civil War."

Marcus cocked his head to the side. "Rhode Island, huh? Tell me about the people in your family."

Vanessa giggled nervously. "We're from Rhode Island too. I think Daddy just wants to know if we share any ancestors."

Marcus leaned in. "Do you have any Christophers in your family?"

Luke shrugged. "Maybe a long time ago. None living, that I know of."

"What about—"

Once again, Vanessa laid her hand on her father's. "Maybe we should order first, Daddy?"

Marcus glared at no one in particular, then dove into the menu as if it were an ancient text, pouring over each menu item carefully. Luke, having been to this restaurant several times, already knew what he wanted.

The server approached and took their orders. Luke finished up the group, ordering lemon garlic chicken.

As soon as the server left, Marcus leaned in, eyeing Luke. "So, you like garlic. Interesting."

Luke had noticed that everything was a statement with this man. Never a question. As they waited, the silence grew unbearable.

Luke broke the tension. "So, Ness, I haven't really talked to you about my new roommate."

Marcus's eyes narrowed. "Ness?"

Time to backtrack. "I meant Vanessa." He glanced at his girlfriend, then over to her father, then back to her. "Anyway, the guy is really cool. He was just transferred in. He said he was majoring in history."

Marcus took a deep breath in through his nose. "What happened to your prior roommate?"

Vanessa grimaced but didn't interrupt.

Suddenly, Luke's mouth felt very dry. "I don't like to talk about it." Marcus's eyes seemed to bore into him, and Luke continued as if he couldn't help himself. "He was found on campus. They said he was murdered."

"Interesting." Marcus stroked his chin. "How did he die?"

Luke swallowed hard. "The blood was drained from his body."

"How do you know that?" Marcus narrowed his eyes.

"News reports." Luke hazarded a glance as Vanessa, who was watching the verbal tennis match carefully. Her knuckles were turning white as she wrapped her hands around her cup.

"And they didn't find the murderer?"

"No."

Marcus arched his eyebrow. Unblinking, he leaned toward Luke.

The sense of being interrogated was too overwhelming. Words fell out of Luke's mouth uncontrollably. "I... they questioned me." It was getting hot. Luke tugged at his collar. "It was lucky I had an alibi. It seemed like the description of the eyewitness pointed to me."

Marcus opened his mouth to respond, but was interrupted by the waitress who had arrived with their meals.

Luke breathed a sigh of relief. He was about to dig in when he heard Marcus clearing his throat. He looked up to see Marcus with his hands folded. He set his fork carefully on the edge of his plate and lowered his head. After a brief prayer, both Vanessa and Luke began to eat. The food on Marcus's plate sat untouched.

"Vanessa, your mother wanted me to give this to you. You must've left it at home last time you visited." Marcus held up a glittering silver cross necklace.

Luke glanced over at his girlfriend. She looked as if she'd just taken a bite of something bitter. Maybe she'd left the necklace behind on purpose.

"Here, Luke, you should look at the detail. It's exquisite." Marcus offered the pendant to Luke for inspection.

Luke hesitated. This was an odd shift. It was almost as if Marcus was being nice. Suspicious, but unwilling to tempt fate, Luke took the necklace in hand, held it to his eyes and counted to five, hoping that was long enough to appease Marcus. "It's lovely," he said, handing it back.

Marcus passed the necklace to Vanessa without looking at her.

"See, Daddy, I told you he was fine."

That was an odd statement. Vanessa didn't seem religious before. Maybe it was important to her family.

Marcus cleared his throat. "I've told you time and again, Vanessa, don't take off that cross. It's important."

Luke watched the interaction feeling as if he was missing a critical detail that no one was planning on sharing with him.

"I don't need to do everything the same way as you, Daddy." Vanessa glared at her father.

"You do if it keeps you safe," Marcus shot back.

"I'm perfectly safe with Luke."

Marcus's nostrils flared. "Perhaps. For now."

Despite his discomfort, Luke spoke up. "Mr. Johnson, I would never do anything to hurt your daughter. She's too important to me."

Marcus ignored Luke and looked over at Vanessa. "You know as well as I that a relationship between the two of you cannot happen. It's entirely inappropriate given his background."

Luke wracked his brain trying to figure out what Vanessa might've told her father that would make him think such a thing. Given the importance of the cross, maybe his objections had to do with his atheist parents.

"He is more than his family, Daddy. Things have changed."

"Nothing has changed. You need to keep your distance. It's critical to remain impartial."

Luke shifted in his seat. Despite the fact that the conversation centered around him, neither Vanessa nor her father acknowledged his presence. He might as well have skipped lunch and let them argue without him.

"That's no longer a possibility. Luke and I are together, and there's nothing you can do about it."

Marcus stood, slamming his hands on the table. "Just watch me." He stormed out of the restaurant, leaving his still-untouched food on the table.

January 23, 1892

Christopher held on longer than I expected. Once they fed him the blackened mix of Temperance's charred heart and lungs, he quickly took a turn for the worst. I'd like to say that his death was painless, but in truth, it was agonizingly slow. He seemed to be in excruciating pain most of the time, delirious as well, passing in and out of consciousness. It was likely a great relief to no longer struggle with his breath nor cough up blood. May God rest his soul.

You did good, babe.

Luke stared at the message on his phone. He took another sip of the beer he'd snuck into his dorm room.

You weren't kidding about your dad being intense.
That was the most uncomfortable meal I've ever had.

I'm sorry about that.
I thought my dad could keep it together
for one meal, but I guess that was too much to ask.

What is his problem with me anyway?

Don't worry about it.

Kinda hard not to.

Can't you let it go? For now at least?

He hesitated, then typed:

Yes, but only because you're the one asking.

I guess I'm lucky you love me.

You have no idea.

"What up, roomie?" Kit plopped down in the chair next to Luke. He ran his fingers through his soft brown hair. His chestnut eyes twinkled as he gently punched Luke in the shoulder. "Vanessa again?"

Luke smiled. "Wouldn't you like to know." Kit was easy to talk to. Warm. Like a soft blanket wrapped around you during a thunderstorm. He seemed to put everyone at ease.

Kit laughed. A gentle chuckle this time, not like the roaring fire of true amusement. "I do know, Luke. You make this face." Kit fluttered his eyes and made kissing sounds.

"Aw, shut up, Kit."

"Come on, Luke, it's sweet. I'm glad you're happy."

Luke shook his head, frowning. "I'd be a whole lot happier if I didn't have to deal with her father."

"That bad, huh?"

"You have no idea. He spent the whole meal looking like he wanted to leap across the table and stab me with his butter knife."

Kit relaxed into his chair. "Hey, speaking of stabbing, did you hear there was another body found? This one was down in the Village."

"I didn't know you knew about the first one."

Kit shrugged. "I checked up on this place before I moved in."

"How did this person die?"

"Well, just like the other, they say she was drained of blood. Rumor has it that there were puncture wounds on her neck. Some say it's the work of a vampire."

It was Luke's turn to laugh. "A vampire? Really? Come on, I know it's October, but that's ridiculous."

"There are more things in heaven and earth, Luke, than are dreamt of in your philosophy."

Luke raised his eyebrows. "You're quoting *Hamlet* to me?"

"Yup."

"In reference to vampires existing?"

Kit shrugged again. "I'm just saying, it doesn't seem that far-fetched. There are all sorts of things out there that can't be explained."

"Yeah, but again, vampires?"

Kit leaned in. "Don't you think it might be nice, living forever?"

"Not if I need to kill people to do so."

"Eh, I don't think it'd be so bad. After all, you wouldn't need to kill good people. You could stick with killing people who deserve it."

Luke turned around and stared hard at his roommate. Kit's exterior was languid, as if any stressor could roll right off him. But there was something serious lurking behind his eyes. Like he was waiting for Luke's response. As if that response was very important.

Luke cleared his throat. "Look, I need to do some reading for class." He turned back to his desk and slid his headphones on as he tried to stop thinking about vampires, murders, and most of all, Vanessa's dad.

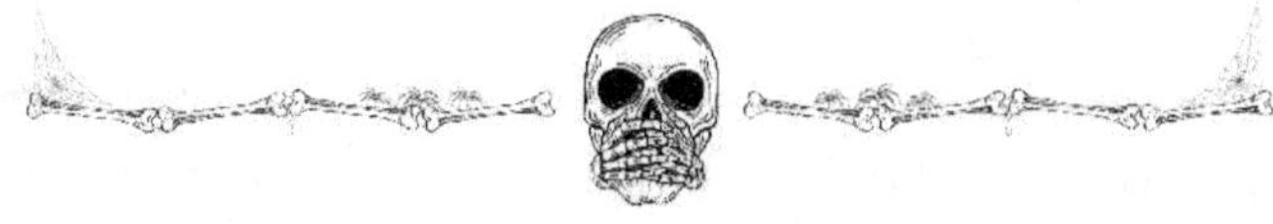

February 10, 1892

With all the fear of the supernatural, we seemed to have forgotten that normal humans are capable of great evil. The oldest Shaw son, Ezekiel, was murdered last night. Worse still, the murderer drained the body of blood and left two puncture wounds on the neck. It seems someone has not just a murderous streak, but a flair for the dramatic. Why else would someone stage a vampiric killing? Such a shame about Ezekiel. He was a good man, and he leaves behind a wife and two children. He will be missed.

Luke woke up to the sound of thunder. The sky was dark, much like his mood. The lunch with Vanessa's father still weighed heavily on him, despite several days having passed. He tried to shrug off the melancholy, but it was tough with the weather the way it was, not to mention the day ahead of him. Thursday was his busy day. He had an early morning class as well as one mid-day and one in the early evening, so he usually packed his things up for the day and ate lunch on campus. The rest of his time between classes was spent in the library. Especially on a day like today, when it was pouring rain, it seemed prudent to do as little walking as possible.

After his first class ended, Luke braved the rain and made his way to his favorite desk in the library. He pulled out his books, setting them carefully on the table and was about to put on his headphones when he heard a whisper from across the table.

"Hey, Luke. Fancy meeting you here."

Luke looked up to find Kit with his lopsided grin. He reminded Luke of a lost puppy. "Hey, Kit," he whispered back. "Doing some studying?"

"Nothing for class. More for fun." He tapped the book in front of him. "Reading up on vampires. Our conversation the other night made me curious."

"Ah, huh," Luke said dismissively. He didn't have time for such nonsense. He had an exam tomorrow. He opened up his book, hoping to clue Kit into the fact that he wanted to get some studying done.

"Look, I know you're busy, but I thought you might want to look at this." Kit slid a book across the table to Luke and pointed at a picture.

"Doesn't she look like Vanessa?"

Luke started. The girl did look like Vanessa. Strikingly so. If not for the poor quality of the photo and the fashion of the clothing, it might've been taken yesterday. Not-Vanessa was seated between what Luke assumed were her two parents, who were flanked by two younger boys. Not-Vanessa was in sharp focus in the black and white photo, though the rest of the family was a bit blurred. The caption on the photo read: "Virginia Johnson, alleged victim of the Rhode Island Vampire, posed post-mortem with her family. 1892."

Luke shivered and shoved the book back at Kit. "What is this?"

"The diary of some old doctor. Pretty cool, huh?"

"No, it's not cool. It's morbid."

Kit laughed. "Come on, the only certainties in life are death and taxes, right? Might as well laugh at them since they can't be avoided." He laughed again. The librarian walked toward them, her heels clicking on the wooden floors.

"You better go, Kit. Ms. Mackenzie looks like she's ready to chew you out."

Kit stood, tucking the book under his arm. "See ya later, roomie."

February 19, 1892

My heart has been broken into a million pieces. My precious daughter, Virginia, has been murdered. She is the latest victim in a string of unsolved murders. Like the others, she was drained of blood. I'm starting to think there might be something to this vampire hysteria. Mind, I don't believe in vampires, but I do believe there might be a disturbed individual who does.

The sun was just setting as Luke finished his final class of the day, though you wouldn't have noticed with the dark clouds looming overhead. The rain had briefly let up, which was a blessing. He hated walking back to his dorm in the rain. The campus had poor drainage, and his shoes took forever to dry out. In fact, they were still damp from his morning walk onto campus.

Luke headed toward his dorm, distracted with thoughts of wet shoes and exams. He took the elevator up to the second floor. As he turned the corner near his room, his phone buzzed in his pocket. He pulled it out, but before he could check the message, he heard someone clearing his throat.

Luke looked up to find a police officer waiting at the door. His stomach flipped, and he tasted bile in his mouth. It was Lt. Quinn, the same man who had taken him in for questioning when his last roommate had died.

"If this is about the body you found in the Village, I had nothing to do with it, I swear." Luke tried to push past the officer into his room, but Lt. Quinn shifted into his path. He was broad shouldered, with every muscle tensed, including the ones on his face. He seemed to be frowning, clenching his jaw, and grimacing all at the same time.

"Hey, I'm not here to arrest you," he said grimly. "We already know you didn't do anything. First thing we did was check in with your professors. You're in the clear. I'm here to warn you. This is the third murder—"

Luke interrupted. "Third?"

"Another body was found near the Santa Monica Pier. Same M.O." Lt. Quinn lowered his voice. "But that's not why I'm here. I'm here as a favor. All the victims seem to have some connection to you—your roommate, one of your TAs, and now your lab partner. I'd be extra careful, Mr. Shaw. Maybe consider walking with campus security until we find the culprit. Don't go anywhere alone."

Luke opened his mouth to speak, but his throat was parched. He smacked his lips, trying to conjure up some saliva to moisten his dry tongue.

"Oh," Lt. Quinn added, "the identity of the most recent victim hasn't been released yet, so don't say anything. I shouldn't have said anything to begin with, but I'd feel awful if something were to happen to you. You might be at the center of this mess, but it's not your fault."

March 3, 1892

Something unbelievable has happened. I scarce know how to put it into words. Ezekiel has been spotted wandering outside town. I would not believe it had I not seen it with my own eyes. After a late-night visit to Ms. Morris, I was on my way home when I found Ezekiel shadowing Isaac Greene. When I called out to Isaac, Ezekiel turned to look at me, then fled. There have been rumors of sightings of Christopher as well, but I have yet to see him. I cannot imagine how Ezekiel is once again walking this earth, but it cannot be for good. I suspect that the rash of murders might be connected to the Shaw brothers. I plan to conduct an investigation of my own.

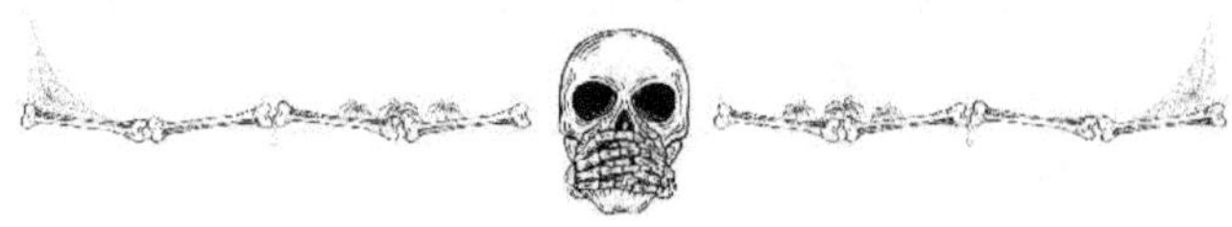

Luke woke up shivering. He'd never felt so cold in his life. And thirsty. And there was a hunger—a gnawing hunger. Worse than any he'd ever experienced. His throat was parched. He felt like a dried-up riverbed, anxious for each and every drop of water. He sat up, trying to remember why he had fallen asleep on the floor, especially with the fluorescent light glaring down at him. Seated, his head began to swim. His eyes blurred, and he couldn't feel his fingers or toes. His senses were all out of whack. As if someone had put them in a blender, mixed them up, and redistributed them. He yawned, battling exhaustion, then tried to stand. His legs refused to obey, shaking as if he'd just finished running a marathon.

"Woah, Luke, take it easy." A hand reached out to steady him. *Kit.* Where did he come from?

"Kit, I think I need to go to the doctor."

"No, you just need a bit of time to adjust. Just breathe."

Luke tried to focus on the air moving in and out of his lungs, but his body kept swaying. Kit placed one protective hand over Luke's chest and the other over his spine. The grounding helped Luke focus. He stared down at his chest, focusing on breathing. He tried to take a deep breath in, but his chest didn't move. He tried exhaling, but that didn't work either.

"Kit, I-I can't breathe!"

"Looks like you're doing just fine to me."

"You told me to breathe, but my chest isn't moving! How am I breathing if my chest isn't moving?"

Kit shook his head. "Nothing to worry about. You're breathing, and that's all that matters."

"Yeah, but *my chest isn't moving!*"

Kit patted him on the shoulder gently. "You're just in shock. I meant, you need to calm down. Panicking isn't going to help anything."

"Why would I be panicking?"

No answer.

"Kit, why would I be panicking?"

"No reason."

That wasn't convincing.

"Kit, what aren't you telling me?"

"Nothing, Luke." He paused. "How are you feeling?"

The room started coming into focus. "Better. I think. Hungry."

Kit laughed. "Yeah, that's pretty normal."

"What do you mean?"

"Well, you nearly worked yourself to death. I came in and found you on the floor. You must've fallen asleep studying."

Luke glanced over at his desk, where the pages of an open book fluttered with the movement of the fan.

"It might be best if you just went to bed, Luke. You need to get some rest."

"But I'm so hungry," Luke said, smacking his lips.

"You need sleep more than you need food right now, trust me," Kit replied.

Luke looked out the window. The sun was just starting to rise. "I need to get up. I have class at eight."

"I don't think you're going to want to head out right now. Maybe later. Trust me, you need some sleep."

Luke blinked absently as Kit helped him into his bed. The hunger gnawed at his insides, but the exhaustion overpowered him, and he soon succumbed to sleep.

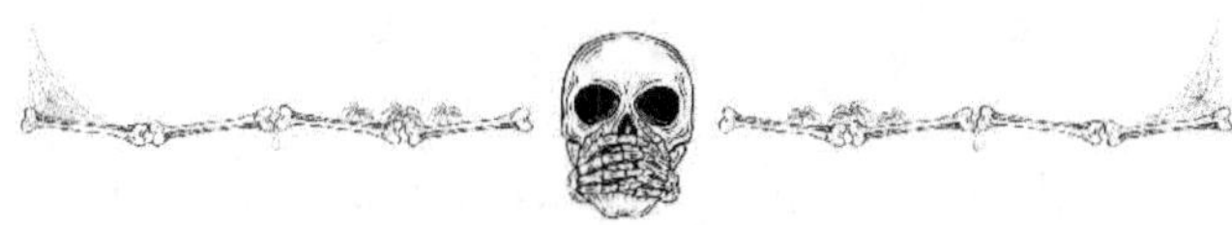

March 15, 1892

I cannot believe I am writing this, but I have confirmed the existence of what I suspect to be vampires. Last night, I was lurking in the shadows, waiting for Ezekiel, or possibly Christopher, to make a move. Down a dark alley, a woman of questionable moralities wandered, looking for customers. A dark figure followed her, and I heard her cry out. I rushed to her aid and uncovered my lantern, which revealed Ezekiel crouched over the body of the woman. His mouth was pressed to her neck, and at the sound of my footsteps, or perhaps the light of my lantern, he looked at me. Blood dripped down his chin. It was, without a doubt, Ezekiel Shaw, or someone identical to him. He rushed off, melting into the darkness. I attempted to provide aid to the unfortunate victim, but she was too far gone. Tomorrow, I plan to meet with the men of the village in the hopes of forming a party to flush the creatures out and destroy them.

The sun sneaked through the blinds when Luke awoke. He stumbled out of bed, the hunger still present. He made his way to the window, sneaking his fingers between the slats to peek through the blinds. Almost immediately, he yanked his hands back. His fingers felt like they were on fire. Luke retreated back into the shadow of his room. The light from the sun was blinding—uncomfortably so. It had to be midday. Luke had an exam to get to, but it now felt unimportant, as if there were bigger things happening, although he didn't know what.

He opened his mini-fridge and pulled out a snack pack of cheese and meats. He ripped it open and took a bite, then spit it out. Disgusting. He unlocked his phone to see if he'd missed anything while asleep. A conversation with Vanessa popped up.

How are you doing? Ready
for your test?

       Yeah, I think so.

Hey, have you seen
your roommate?

       No, why?

I was hoping we could
get some alone
time. ;-)

       Sounds good to me!

You're sure he's gone?

       Yup.

Where is he?

> *He said something about*
> *going down to Third Street.*
> *He's been down in Santa*
> *Monica for a few days now.*

I guess he doesn't worry about class
attendance then?

> *Guess not.*

Luke frowned. He didn't remember sending any of those messages. And hadn't he just seen Kit this morning? He shook his head, trying to clear the cobwebs, but everything still felt fuzzy. He decided to lay back down.

March 24, 1892

I do not think my heart can take any more pain. My eldest son, Jacob, has been claimed by the demon. I was away from home with a search party when my son was taken from me. A few other men were patrolling with me, and we had cornered Ezekiel. It seems ludicrous, but we had come as prepared as we could, having only the stories of vampires in our children's fairytales for reference. Issac pressed forward first, brandishing a cross. Ezekiel drew back with a hiss, but Issac pursued, pressing the cross into his arm, scorching the flesh. Ezekiel screamed in pain, and I made my move, driving a stake into his heart, turning Ezekiel to ash. I returned home, victorious, only to find Jacob, my son, lying at our front door completely drained of blood. Why didn't I think of protecting my home and my son with garlic? Thankfully, my wife and other son stayed indoors. All vampire lore says that they must be invited in, and thankfully, my wife knew enough to refuse Christopher entrance. It is Christopher Shaw, as I suspected. Constance, of course, is completely distraught. I cannot imagine what it was like to see that monster murder our child. My greatest regret is allowing the hysteria of the town to culminate in feeding Christopher the heart of his sister. I fear that, in trying to prevent a thing, we in fact caused that thing to come into being. Mark these words: I will not rest until Christopher, and any others he may turn, are eliminated.

Darkness had fallen by the time Luke woke up again. Kit was nowhere to be found. Luke's head was pounding, and it felt like his stomach was trying to claw its way out of his torso. The hunger was unbearable. He glanced at the clock: 8pm. The dining hall was still open, but not for much longer. He glanced out the window to check the weather. Still raining. He picked up his umbrella, and his phone buzzed with a text from Vanessa.

Hey, you okay?

Yeah, just hungry.

*I might be coming down
with something*

Been worried about you.

*I'm fine. Going to head
to the dining hall to
grab some food.*

*Wish I could be with you tonight,
but I gotta help my dad.*

What are you doing?

Some work thing.

This late?

Yeah, he works the graveyard shift.

But he needs your help?

A long pause.

Yeah.

What does he do?

Another long pause.

Hard to explain. Hey, Kit still gone?

Yup.

Let me know if he turns up.

Why?

I can explain later.

*You're being awfully eva-
sive, Ness.*

*Sorry, I can explain it all tomorrow.
Breakfast?*

Let's make it dinner.

It's a date. Love you!

Love you too.

Luke pocketed the phone without responding. He grabbed his umbrella and took the elevator down to the ground floor. It was a short walk to the dining hall, but it was more lonely than usual, probably due to the rain. He walked slowly, his body shaking with hunger and pent-up energy. Distracted by the gnawing of his stomach and the sound of the rain splattering against the pavement, he slammed into someone.

Luke looked up to see an ashen face. A toothy smile sneered at him, fangs laying uncomfortably against the man's lower lip. "Watch where you're walking. I could use a bite to eat," he snapped at Luke. A black cape fluttered around the dark figure.

Luke froze. It couldn't be. Vampires weren't real, no matter what Kit had said. He stared at the teeth, glimmering in the moonlight. Teeth that could pierce skin. That could drain a body of blood. He shivered, trying to will the frightening thoughts away. He tried to respond, but his mouth felt dry, and his tongue felt like sandpaper. A cute blonde poked her head around the terrifying man standing in front of him. Wearing red leather pants and a sleek black shirt, she held up a wooden stake. Laughing, she said, "Hey, want me to stake him for you?"

The vampire laughed in response and pulled the girl closer. He looked at Luke. "You're lucky Buffy is here to protect you."

Luke didn't answer.

"Hey, ease up, man, it's Halloween."

"Yeah, where's your costume?" the girl added.

"I, uh..." Luke was at a loss for words.

"I guess you've been pre-partying, huh?"

Luke nodded blankly, searching for an escape. How was it Halloween already? Had he been sick for that long? He tried to form a response, but his brain felt like mush. Laughing, the couple left Luke in the dark as they headed back to the dorms.

On edge, Luke resumed his walk toward the dining hall. The wind shifted, and his nose caught a whiff of something more appetizing than pizza and hamburgers. Luke couldn't pinpoint the scent, but it was intoxicating. Almost unconsciously, he pivoted towards the smell, following his nose into the darkness of the trees behind the dorms. A path led down to the village below—a poorly-lit shortcut women rarely took for fear of what might happen there.

From the shadows behind the trees, Kit emerged.

"Hey, roomie. Hungry?"

Luke heard his stomach growl. "Famished."

"I know the perfect place to catch a bite. Follow me."

Luke followed Kit into the darkness, where he crouched behind a tree. Hunkered down next to him, Luke asked, "What are we doing?"

"Patience."

"What does that mean?"

Kit held up a finger and pointed. Two scantily-clad co-eds were climbing up the stairs. Both were dressed as cats with pointed ears and furry tails swinging from their too-short skirts.

"Purrfect," Kit purred. He jumped out from behind the tree and, seconds later, had one of the girls trapped with her arms pinned behind her back. The girl screamed. Kit opened his mouth, and his canines grew into two long fangs, which he sunk into the helpless girl's neck. The other girl slammed her purse into Kit, trying to get him to let her friend go. Kit's eyes smiled at Luke as he sucked the life out of his victim. The second girl froze as her friend turned white and went limp in Kit's arms. Screaming, the survivor took off running at full speed.

"What the fuck are you doing?" Luke yelled in horror.

Kit pulled his mouth away. Blood trickled down his chin. "Just getting a bite to eat. Want something?"

Luke was frozen to the spot. Before he could process what was happening, Kit had run after the second girl. He caught up to her quickly and dragged her kicking and screaming back to Luke. Again, Kit pinned the girl's arms behind her back. He pushed her toward Luke. "Take a deep breath. Doesn't she smell delicious?"

Against his will, Luke found himself tasting the air. It was the same scent that had drawn him away from the dining room. He felt a sharp pang in his mouth as his fangs grew for the first time. He lost control of his body, the intoxicating smell of blood drowning out all other sensations. He opened his mouth wide and bit down on the shrieking girl. Her cries were soon silenced, and Luke finally felt satiated.

"Well done, Luke," Kit said. "Well done."

December 13, 1934

This will be the last entry in my diary. I fear I don't have much time left. I have spent the last forty-odd years searching for Christopher, but to no avail. I've come close several times, but the monster always manages to elude my grasp. I have managed to dispatch several of his vampire children. He seems to enjoy turning his brother's descendants; probably out of some twisted desire to create a family legacy. As for me, I leave behind a legacy of vampire hunters. I know that my family will continue the work I have begun, working tirelessly to hunt down any undead member of the Shaw family. I must trust my family to do what I have not be able to: kill Christopher.

Luke awoke to the sound of pounding on his door. He sat upright, trying to locate himself. What a weird night. He'd had the strangest dream about him and Kit... but he couldn't finish the thought. It was too gruesome. Besides, there was his health to worry about. Against all reason, he felt fantastic. Everything still felt off-kilter, as if reality had recently shifted. Everything, all of his senses, were in extra-sharp focus. He could smell and see things he had never dreamed of before. Even now, his tongue tasted metal, and his nose picked up the scent of copper in the air.

He swung his legs off the bed as the pounding intensified.

"Just a minute," he called. His voice was gravelly, somehow deeper. Much closer to a baritone than his usual tenor. He glanced down at his clothes, trying to decide if he was presentable.

His once-white shirt was sprayed with red splatter. Gingerly, he brought the shirt up to his nose. Blood. That's where the smell was coming from. He felt a pain in his teeth—a pain that was somehow familiar, terrifying, and thrilling all at once.

Luke quickly examined himself, starting with his mouth. His canines felt strange, longer, more violent. The taste of blood lingered on his tongue, but there were no injuries that he could find. And if the blood wasn't his, then... His blood ran cold. It couldn't be.

"Luke, it's me, Vanessa!" came the voice from the other side of the door. "Are you okay?'

"Sorry, Ness," he called back. She was so demanding. He needed to think. "Just woke up. Give me a minute."

Luke rushed over to the mirror, but there was an empty spot where it used to be. He frowned. More pounding at the door. "Just changing!" he yelled back. He tore off the bloodied shirt and replaced it with a fresh one, then wiped his face, neck, and arms down with wet wipes. There was a lot of blood. It was everywhere. Luke felt his stomach churning, sick at the thought of death, and sicker at the hunger that accompanied that thought.

"Luke, I need you to open the door now." Vanessa's voice was higher-pitched than usual, panicked.

Luke rolled his head, trying to calm down. He needed time to think. Think about the blood and the hunger and what he'd done last night—no, he hadn't done anything. He couldn't have. It was a dream. Just a dream. He must've had a nosebleed or something. Yes, that was probably it.

He steadied his breathing as the pounding continued at the door. He strolled over and opened it as casually as he could. Instantly, he recoiled. The smell of garlic was overpowering. He gagged.

Vanessa stepped into the room, smelling like a mixture of lavender and garlic. Her hair was piled messily on top of her head, exposing her long, thin neck. Luke licked his lips subconsciously. Before she could say anything, her father pushed her to the side.

"Where is he?" Marcus demanded.

Luke narrowed his eyes. "Where's who?" There was an edge to his own voice he hadn't heard before.

"Christopher!" Marcus shouted back. "I know you know where he is."

"Daddy..." Vanessa began.

Her father held up a hand, cutting her off. Marcus's eyes settled on Kit's desk. He rushed over and picked up the book. "Where did you get this?"

Despite being confused, he was grateful for the change in focus. "It's not mine. It's my roommate's. Some diary he found."

"Christopher," Marcus growled. "Where is he?"

Luke's nostrils flared. "I don't know any Christopher."

"Don't be daft. Your great, great, great uncle."

"Now who's being daft?" Luke laughed. It sounded cruel. Luke was startled by his own voice, but even still, he was filled with a sense of power. Vanessa drew back, clearly confused. Luke rolled his eyes. "Anyone that old would need to be—"

"Dead?"

Their heads swiveled to find Kit leaning against the doorframe casually.

In one swift motion, he rushed behind Vanessa, pinning her arms to her back with one hand. "Now don't do anything stupid," he said, looking at Marcus. "You too, Luke," Kit added as an afterthought.

For a brief moment, all four stood assessing the situation.

Kit spoke first. "Johnson, I presume?" The question was directed at Marcus, who glared in response. "No need to answer. It was a rhetorical question. Your daughter here looks just like her great, great, great aunt."

Marcus opened his mouth to speak, but Luke cut him off before he had the chance. "Kit, I don't know what's going on, but you gotta let her go," he said with a growl in his voice.

Kit laughed cheerfully. "What's going on? Have you forgotten already? Vampires are real, Luke. You had quite an experience with one last night." He winked, still holding tight to Vanessa.

It was like a veil had been ripped from Luke's eyes as everything seemed to click into place, like the world had suddenly shifted from black and white to color. The dream had been real. He felt sick to his stomach. He had murdered an innocent girl. But a contrary feeling quickly arose from his gut—satisfaction. Hunger. Enjoyment. Yes, he had killed the girl, but she had been delicious. With his stomach nearly growling in excitement, Luke cracked his neck side to side, reveling in the relaxing crunch of his vertebrae. A movement from beside Kit drew his attention. Vanessa. Luke blinked, trying to regain control of the monster buried inside himself, trying to claw its way to the surface.

"This is the monster behind the recent string of murders," Marcus explained, glaring at Kit.

Luke looked at his roommate, curious rather than upset. "You? But those were my friends..." He was trying very hard to focus, but the sounds of both Vanessa's and Marcus's heartbeats were calling out to him. Luke hung on to the question, his inner monster battling what was left of his humanity. "Why would you kill them?" he added, putting his energy into the mystery rather than his gnawing hunger.

"He was trying to frame you," Vanessa answered.

"No," Marcus countered, "he was taunting us."

Kit smiled with an affectionate grin. "You know me so well, Johnson. Tell me, what is my next move?"

"It doesn't matter. I have you now." Marcus edged toward him.

Kit held up a finger and wagged it in front of him. "Uh, uh, uh. I still have your sweet, innocent daughter trapped in my evil clutches." His voice dripped with mockery. "What will you do to get her back, Johnson?"

"Nothing. She will become another casualty in the war against you and your kind. She will make the sacrifice if it stops you."

Luke stepped forward, but Kit didn't notice him. Luke could hear Vanessa's heartbeat pounding like a siren's song. He had no affection for Marcus, but he'd be damned if Kit was going to kill Vanessa.

"Yes," Kit continued, still using Vanessa as a shield, "but can *you* make the sacrifice? Like I said, she is the spitting image of her great aunt. She was *delicious*. I wonder if Vanessa here will taste as sweet." Without breaking eye contact, Kit ran a finger down Vanessa's neck, from earlobe to clavicle. Luke saw her shiver and felt a wave of jealousy course through his stomach. Relishing in her fear, Kit turned and licked her bare neck, giving Marcus just enough time to make his move.

He reached into his left pocket and retracted a large silver cross, which he held up toward Kit. In his right hand, Marcus clutched a wooden stake. He leaped toward Kit, who pushed Vanessa out of his way into Luke.

She fell into Luke, her arms circling his neck. She was warm. He felt the pulse of her blood through her wrist resting on his neck. He inhaled deeply, wanting to consume her, but the smell of garlic in her blood was overpowering. He dropped her onto the carpet and tried to take a step back, but the room was cramped enough to only grant him a few inches of space.

In the meantime, Marcus had pushed the cross into Kit's face. There was a hiss, and the smell of scorched flesh as the metal made contact with his skin. Kit shrieked and brought a hand to his cheek as he used the other to push Marcus away with a shove to the chest. It looked like a small motion, but Marcus flew into the chair behind him, knocking it over and collapsing on the ground. Vanessa rushed over to help her father.

Kit laughed. "Aw, poor Daddy got knocked down, huh?" He dropped his hand, revealing a cross-shaped burn. Luke watched in fascination as the blood began to congeal. Marcus struggled to get to his feet. He glanced at Vanessa as he tried to catch his breath. "I'll take care of the demon. You take care of this."

"Daddy, I can't."

"You can. This is the reason you were sent here—to keep an eye on the Shaw descendant."

"But I love him," she whispered.

"*It.*" Marcus's gaze softened. "You may love it, but it can't love you back. You know what you need to do."

"Aw, so touching," Kit mocked.

Marcus turned toward the vampire, brandishing another stake. His strength now gathered, he leaped at Kit.

"Sorry, kid, you're on your own," Kit called to Luke, dodging the attack. "If you make it out of this, meet me in New Orleans. Good luck." With a cocky smile, Kit tipped his imaginary hat and took off running down the hall.

Without another word, Marcus rushed out, close on Kit's heels.

Slowly, Vanessa rose from the ground. There were tears in her eyes.

"Don't cry, Ness." Luke pushed through the pain of the smell and opened his arms wide, ready to wrap her in a hug. His mouth began to open involuntarily as he bared his teeth.

She took a step closer to him, a cross in her left hand, just like her father. She handed it to Luke.

Unconsciously, he reached out, taking the cross in his hand. Immediately, a wave of pain rushed over him, and he dropped the cross, shrieking. It had seared his flesh, leaving a cross-shaped imprint on his palm. Purely on instinct, he reached for Vanessa, unsure of what he was going to do.

She took a step back, tears streaming down her cheeks.

Luke felt torn. The last remaining bit of his heart seemed to be breaking, but the thumping of *her* heart—the pounding of the blood in her veins—drowned out all reason. His mouth widened, and his canines began to grow into fangs. With a smile, he lunged at his girlfriend, who threw her left hand up in defense.

Pressing his chest against her hand, he tilted his head, searching for the right angle to sink his teeth into her neck. He was all monster now. No love, no sympathy. Just hunger. Pure, violent hunger with a helpless victim in his grasp. She wasn't his girlfriend. There was nothing between them anymore. There never had been. She was a stranger. A delicious, mouthwatering blood source. His teeth found their mark, and he bit down gently on the soft flesh, savoring the initial puncture of the skin.

He took a deep drink, but a sharp pain forced him to retract his fangs. Staggering, he looked down to see a stake embedded between his ribs. His vision began to blur.

"I'm so sorry, Luke," she whispered. "I'll always love you."

Her image faded away, like dust in the wind. Then, there was only darkness.

Kristin Cragg began telling stories as soon as she could talk and set about writing them down as soon as she learned to spell—and she hasn't stopped since (well, except for those pesky few years of depression, but who's counting?). She is currently writing and submitting new stories, editing her novels, and doing other author-y things. Kristin writes short stories in a variety of genres, though her novels in progress are all satire. Her first short story can be found in Twisted Tales of Holiday Horror, *published by the Sisterhood of the Black Pen, while other stories have found homes in diverse publications.*

Kristin has been a voracious reader since the age of seven when her teacher read Charlie and the Chocolate Factory *far too slowly, and she finished it on her own. She delights in grammar (for some odd reason) and is obsessed with collecting antique books. She is happily married with three kids, two cats, a tortoise, and books in every room of the house. If you enjoy classic literature, microfiction, crocheting, cats, irregular blog posts, Jesus, stuff about epilepsy, and oddly specific lists, you can find her at kristincragg.com or catch up with her on Facebook, Instagram, Twitter, and Tik-Tok, all under the username KristinCragg.*

OUIJA BOARD

KARI ROBINS

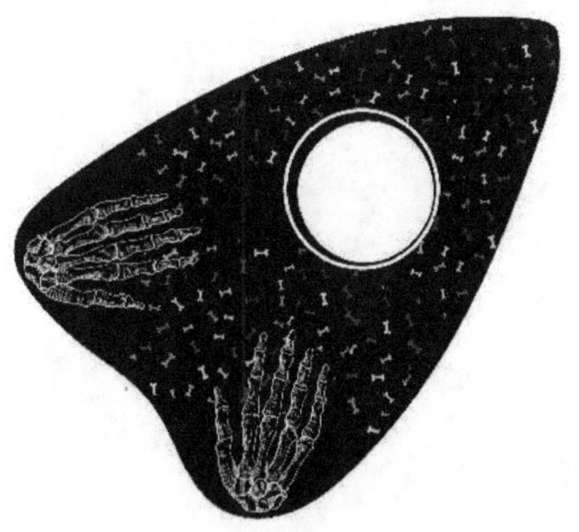

The Ouija Board

The Ouija board is one of the oldest board games. To many, it's just a silly game pre-teen girls play to scare each other. But what if it wasn't? To many, this piece of cardboard is a path to darkness.
Legends of witches have existed since the dawn of time, and many believe that the Ouija board is a tool of witchcraft.

If you belonged to a group of friends that believed in witchcraft, the last thing you'd want to do is keep a secret from them. Right? Even one involving murder and a coverup? And definitely don't sit down on All Hallows Eve to try an Ouija board with them. You never know what door to the Underworld you'll open... or who might waltz back into your life.

My heart thrummed in my chest as my hands moved across the board.
A secret so deep that even I believed my own lie bubbled to the surface.
'Katie' the board said.
His name flashed before me, and the lie came unwound.
I was caught, the board knew the truth and would see that I'd pay for my crime.

They were all crazy. We could have been out at a party in slutty costumes, but instead, we were sitting at the coffee table in my apartment living room. The darkened room was lit with candles surrounding us in a circle. A Ouija board sat in the middle of the table. They all stared at it like it was going to move on its own. I stood several feet away from them, refusing to sit.

"This is crazy! It's just a stupid kids' game." We were juniors in college now, not teenage girls playing at witchcraft anymore. "I thought we'd given this nonsense up?" I asked them.

"No!" they all shouted at once.

"I know we haven't done this since our last All Hallows Eve in high school, but we've been doing it since we were fifteen years old. We've been so distant since graduation, and we need this," Sara said, her face held in stone with the seriousness of a heart attack.

I threw up my hands in defeat. "Fine," I grumbled, as I sat with them.

"What should we ask?" Jess started.

"How about we talk to Brittany Murphy," Alice suggested. We'd never been really close until we became roommates freshman year, and I couldn't imagine my life without her. Most days, she would be in tights, a hoodie, and a messy bun, but other days, she could be a runway model with her hair and makeup done to perfection and her thousand dollar dresses. But she'd always just be Ali to me.

"Girl, you've been obsessed with her since you were eight years old. Time to let that one go," Sara said, and Ali's face dropped.

"How about we try and contact the lady from across the hall?" Amanda asked. "You know, the one whose husband murdered her and her lover before killing himself?"

"Hell no," Alice and I both said together. That apartment creeped me out more than any horror flick ever could.

"I've got one," Jess said, placing two fingers on the planchette and eyeing us. I rolled my eyes but joined in with the rest, placing my own fingers on the small plastic triangle.

Jess closed her eyes and tilted her head to the ceiling.

"Oh, goddess of the multiverse. We come to you on this All Hallow's Eve for your guidance. Be with us on our journey and lead us to the answers we seek." She rolled her neck around before dropping her chin to her chest. "Is someone here hiding any deep secrets from the rest of us?" she asked and immediately the pointer moved to the 'yes' and stopped. "Who?"

It moved again.

K

A

T

I

E

All eyes shot to me.

"I—it's just a game," I stuttered out.

"What is her secret?" Ali half-whispered.

My heart stopped as the pointer slowly moved.

D

Y

L

A

I yanked my hands away and bolted to my feet. "It's just a stupid game. Who was pushing it?" A crash of thunder made me jump out of my skin.

Sara stood slowly to her feet and took a step back. "D—Dylan? Do you know what happened to Dylan?"

Dylan had been her high school sweetheart until he disappeared on prom night. No one knew what really happened that night. No one but me. Or so I thought. One of my friends must have found out what happened to him, and they were messing with me now.

"You know I don't know what happened any more than you do. We all were interrogated by the police. He was your boyfriend. Wasn't he supposed to be with you?" I asked Sara, trying to divert her line of questioning.

Tears formed in her eyes as she shook her head. "He told me he got a text from his little sister. She was drunk. But the cops said that she never sent him one."

Ali, Jess, and Amanda were standing now, wrapping Sara in a hug. She never got over his loss. It'd been three years, and she still hoped he'd come home. But I knew he never would.

"I'm sorry, Katie. I didn't mean to accuse you of anything. I know you don't know what happened. It's just been so exhausting not knowing," she said.

"I can't begin to imagine what you've gone through, Sara. I'm sorry."

She nodded. "I think we should call it a night."

"Yeah, maybe," I agreed. I peered down at the board, and a shiver crept down my back. It's not real. The voice in my head didn't sound convinced as I tried to reassure myself.

Jess led Sara to the door, whispering their goodbyes before heading out into the hall. The moment the door clicked shut, Ali turned on me, all trace of sweetness gone.

"What the hell was that?"

"What do you mean?" I asked.

"What do you know? You can't lie to me." Her small frame stood toe to toe with me as she crossed the room.

"I—I don't know anything," I lied.

"You're hiding something, and I'm going to find out what." She turned and stormed off to her bedroom, slamming the door behind her.

I shook off the chill and trudged to my own room.

The guilt welled in my gut when I shut my eyes and his face haunted me. His angular jaw and perfect smile used to make my stomach flutter. The soft curls of his blond hair against my skin as I dug my fingers into his scalp would always get me, but the way his big hands gripped my ass as I rode him... that was what every girl dreamed of. He was my best friend's boyfriend, and I was just his fuck buddy.

Until prom night.

The high buzzed through me like an electric wave, pushing me ever closer to him. Dylan's sunkissed hands yanked up my dress, ripping the tiny thread of underwear from my hips. His lips found my neck, nibbling on the skin below my ear. I dug my nails into his shaggy blond hair.

"Bend over," he whispered.

I turned around, pulling the dress up over my ass, pushing into the crotch of his tux. His fingers gripped my hips, pulling me into him harder.

"Fuck me, Dylan," I begged.

He pulled me off him enough to undo his pants and slid them down to his knees. I gripped the metal beams of the bleachers and rubbed my ass against his cock.

Between the booze and the pills, my head was spinning, but when he pressed the tip of his cock to my entrance, fireworks exploded in my core. He slammed into me as I braced against the beam.

The scream that tore from my lips could have woken the dead. Thankfully, the DJ's music would drown it out. He pulled out and pushed back in until we were both breathless. He didn't slow his pace until he was on the edge.

"Fuck, Kat, I'm close. You ready?" he asked.

"Um-hum," I gasped.

"Ugh." He pulled out, and I dropped to my knees, taking his cum in my mouth, sucking it all down as my fingers rubbed at my own clit until I was coming along with him.

I woke in a cold sweat, remembering that night. My panties were a little more than wet. Dylan could make just about any girl drop her panties. Too bad he was gone.

Shaking off the feeling, I crept back to the living room. The Ouija board still sat on the table. Out of sheer stupidity, I knelt, placing my fingers on the pointer.

"Dylan?" I whispered. It shouldn't have worked with just me, but it moved.

Yes.

A cold shiver ran down my spine, sending every tiny hair on end and goosebumps across my arms.

"I miss you."

Me too.

"I'm sorry." A tear dripped down my cheek.

The pointer moved again.

Goodbye.

My blood ran cold. I stood, picking up the board and running to the kitchen, stuffing it in the trash can and closing the cabinet door. I stared at the cabinet door for a long moment before opening it up and pulling the bag from the can—headed to the dumpster.

The hairs on the back of my neck stood on end the moment I stepped out into the parking lot. A shiver ran down my back as I walked to the dumpster. I shoved the bag in and waited a moment before turning around again. The lot was lit up with street lamps, so I scanned the area for any signs of someone watching me, but I was the only idiot awake at this time of the morning.

Rolling my eyes at my own imagination, I walked back into the apartment building. Just as I got to my door, the adjacent door opened and out stepped tall, dark, and handsome. Ali and I had been in this building for almost two years, and we still didn't know the guy's name, but we enjoyed watching his ass as he'd walk away. His deep umber skin and bald head reminded me of my favorite TV portrayal of an FBI crime fighting superhero, and I'd daydreamed of him calling me 'baby girl' in bed.

His eyes met mine, and he grinned. "Morning, Katie," he said. "Nice pj's."

I looked down, slightly mortified. My cheer shorts were riding up my crotch so hard you could see everything, and the plain white tee I was wearing did nothing to hide my cold nipples.

"Oh my god." I quickly covered my chest and pulled the shorts out of my ass.

He stepped closer and whispered into my ear, "I've been watching you watching me. Name's Derek if you want to moan it next time you play with that sweet pussy of yours." He straightened, grinned at my dumbfounded face, and walked away.

I gaped at him as he walked out the front door and off into the night. When my senses cleared and my pussy unclenched, I stepped back into my apartment and sank down on the couch. He knew my name. And what's worse... Could he hear me getting myself off at night? Sitting up, I rubbed my eyes, trying to clear the thoughts from my mind. When I opened them again, a blurry image on the table turned my stomach. I blinked quickly as my eyes focused.

The Ouija board.

"What the hell?" I jumped to my feet.

"What's wrong with you?" Ali's voice called out from behind me.

"The—the board. I threw it away..." I pointed to where it still sat.

"Where's the fucking coffee? Clearly, we both need it. Why the hell are you awake already?"

"I—nightmare." I walked back over to her. "But the board. I took it out to the dumpster, and it's still here."

"Are you sure you didn't dream it?"

"No, I ran into the neighbor on my way back."

"Which neighbor?" She asked like she hadn't been secretly stalking him too. "God, never mind. Go back to bed. I gotta go to work." She ignored me and walked into the kitchen and started the coffee.

Maybe she was right, and it was all in my head and I just needed sleep. I trudged back to my room and crawled under the covers.

A knock at my door woke me hours later. The sun peeked out from behind my dark curtains. The pounding grew louder, pulling me out of my bed and toward the front door.

"I'm coming. I'm coming." With a click, I unlocked the door, opening it a crack.

"You better not be coming without me." Derek's dark form loomed in the doorway, filling it. "I can't get that image of your perky tits and tight pussy out of my mind." He pushed the door open and stepped inside, shutting and locking it behind him. "I can't concentrate until I've tasted all of you."

He reached out, grabbing my wrist, pulling me into his strong arms before I could protest. I'd been watching this man for months and fantasizing about him when I was alone in my room, but I'd only just met him.

"What are you doing?" I finally asked, pushing against his chest to no avail.

"My plan was to do *you*." He pressed his lips to mine, sending heat to my core. Against my better judgment, my mouth moved with his, and I parted my lips, breathing him in. His tongue darted inside, licking the roof of my mouth. His fingers snaked up my shorts, gripping my bare ass as he lifted me off my feet and carried me to the couch.

"Derek," I breathed out. "I don't... We shouldn't..." But my pussy protested. It'd been nearly a year since anyone but B.O.B.—my battery operated boyfriend—had gotten me off, and she was weeping for this stranger now.

"I can smell your desire." He pulled my shorts down before setting me on the back of the couch and kneeling before me. His hands gripped my thighs, parting them before burrowing his face in my core. A moan escaped me as his tongue traced up my slit. "And you taste as delicious as you smell." He plunged back in with two fingers, rubbing at my insides while his mouth sucked on my clit.

"Derek," I moaned.

"That's it, good girl. Moan for me."

I wrapped my legs around his head and brought my hand to my nipple, pinching it hard.

"God, I want you to come on my face," he breathed on my stomach, as he pumped faster.

"Won't have to wait long," I gasped, as he lapped at my wetness. "Fuck, I'm coming," I screamed. My pussy clenched around his fingers as the wave flooded me. When I relaxed, he pulled out and stood, pulling me off the couch.

"Bend over," he whispered into my ear.

I did as commanded and bent over the couch. The sound of his belt sliding out of the belt loops had my thighs quaking. I jerked slightly at the light smack on my ass that followed.

He growled, and I stiffened. He hit me harder this time, but I didn't flinch.

"Baby girl." He rubbed at the tender spot. "What do you want?"

"I—I want your cock."

"Can you handle it?"

"Yes," I said, a little too smugly.

"Yes, what?"

I'd had guys like him, and despite what the 'Karens' of the world thought, it was a major turn on for me. "Yes, sir," I purred.

His hand moved to my core, twirling around in my slickness. "You're so wet for me."

"Please," I begged.

He moved the tip of his cock to my center, sliding it up and down before thrusting inside, stretching me.

"Derek," I groaned at his girth.

"Are you going to take it like a good girl?"

All I could do was nod as he slammed in and out of me. He pounded my pussy until tears streamed down my face, but I wasn't about to break.

"Fuck, I'm so fucking close," he finally said. "You going to swallow my cum like a good girl?"

"Yes, sir," I managed to say.

"Get on your knees," he barked, as he pulled out.

I knelt in front of him, seeing the size of his dick for the first time. It was nearly as thick as my wrist and a good ten inches long. I gulped before opening my mouth for him. He guided his cock inside, fucking my face, making me gag as he slammed into me.

"Fuck!" He moaned as hot cum shot down the back of my throat.

He pulled out of my mouth slowly, leaving me to lick every last drop of cum off his shaft. When he finally pulled away, he yanked up his pants and buttoned them before helping me to my feet.

"That's my good girl, Kat. You did so good. I'll come back for you tonight." He kissed my neck before walking out the door.

After pulling my own shorts back on, I slumped onto the couch, wondering what in the hell just happened. I hadn't cum so hard in a long time, and I'd hardly known the man, but I also couldn't wait for round two.

I must have zoned out, though, because the next thing I knew, Ali was shaking my shoulder.

"Katie!"

When my eyes focused on hers, they were wide.

"What?" I asked.

"I've been calling your name for ten minutes. What the hell happened to you?"

"What do you mean?"

"There's blood all over the back of the couch and your lap."

I looked down to see a few spots of red on my shorts and shrugged. "Oh, that was Derek. We got a little rough," I said, not bothered by the blood.

"That's a bit more blood than just rough sex, Katie. Who the hell is Derek?"

"You're exaggerating. It's not that bad, Ali. And Derek is our neighbor, 3B. I ran into him this morning in my pj's, and I guess it really turned him on." I leaned against the armrest.

"Derek? 3B?" Ali sat on the edge of the couch, placing a hand on my knee. "Honey, no one's been in 3B since we moved in."

I laughed. "Of course there has been. Who have we been gawking at?"

"Katie, I'm gay, remember? I don't gawk at guys."

"You are?" I paused, chewing on my lower lip. "I mean, I know you are, but we've been watching him. Haven't we?" I sat up.

"We're the only ones on this floor. No one wants 3B no matter how cheap it is."

"They don't? Why?"

"Katie, are you sure you're feeling okay? How can you not remember what happened there? The murder? That's why our rent is so cheap."

"Murder? No one said anything about murder." I stood, thinking she knew the truth.

"The triple homicide across the hall? You know the one we were just talking about last night? That murder?"

I dropped onto the couch. "Oh, that murder."

"What murder were you thinking about?"

"Nothing. I guess I'm really out of it."

"I'd say. You lost a lot of blood. You really should go to the hospital."

Glancing back down at the dots of blood on my shorts, I frowned. Slowly, I knelt on the couch and peered over the back to where a bloody kitchen knife lay. I clamped my hand over my mouth and ran to the bathroom. I sat on the edge of the tub and ripped off my shorts. My stomach churned as I gaped at the long cuts along my inner thighs.

"What the fuck?" Bile crept up my throat, and I spewed it into the sink. The bleeding had stopped, but three gashes spread over my legs right up to my core. I sat there frozen in place for a long moment. How had I allowed a stranger to cut me while screwing my brains out?

The images of Derek between my thighs finally spurred me to action. I wanted to wash away everything that had happened. My hands shook as I turned the tub faucet on, waiting for the water to warm up.

"Katie! What's going on? Why's there a knife? Are you sure you're okay?" The handle jiggled but didn't budge.

"I'm okay! I-I promise. Just going to take a bath." I plugged the tub and let it fill before sliding in. The water stung the cuts, bringing up fresh tears.

"Katie, I'm worried about you," Ali called again.

"I'm fine, really!"

After a long pause, she said, "Okay, but I'll be here when you get out."

The water boiled all my fears to the surface. They knew what really happened prom night and were somehow messing with me. But it wasn't my fault. He could have said no. He took the damn pills. I just...

Dipping my head under the surface of the water, I imagined what it would feel like to be Dylan. Somewhere in the Colorado River, a black Honda Civic lay with the decomposing body of my best friend's boyfriend, and only I knew. Or so I thought.

Did Ali see? Or had Sara followed him? "Oh, sweet little Kit Kat." Derek's voice pulled me out of the water. He sat on the edge of the toilet with his legs spread wide, leaning his elbows on his knees, staring at me.

"What the hell?" I jumped back, trying to cover myself. "How'd you get in here?"

"Haven't you figured it out yet, pet?"

"Figured out what?"

"Who I really am?" He grinned.

"Ali said no one's in 3B, so how'd you get in there?"

"Walls mean nothing to me, Kit Kat." He stood over the tub, taking me all in before walking right through the door.

I jumped to my feet, yanking the towel from the rack, wrapping it around me before cracking and peering out the hallway.

When he was nowhere in sight, I breathed a sigh of relief and crept from room to room searching for him, but nothing.

Ali stood abruptly at the table when I snuck into the kitchen.

"Where'd he go?" I whispered.

"What? Who?" she asked.

I shook my head. "Is anyone else here? I-I thought I heard someone?"

"No, just me. You're dripping water everywhere. What's going on?"

"N-nothing." I turned to leave. I must've imagined it...

"It's not nothing. You've been really freaked out since last night. Do you know what happened to Dylan?"

"I—it wasn't my fault. I don't know where he is." It wasn't entirely a lie. I was so high that night that I really don't remember where

I sunk his car. I only remember walking back to the gym barefoot because my heels were killing me. I had rejoined my date, explaining my absence with a sour stomach, and he drove me home.

My parents woke me the next morning saying that something happened to Dylan. The whole town was in chaos. The cops had search parties stretching out from the high school to the river. Apparently, it had rained after I'd gotten home and washed away any trace that I'd been at the river.

Dylan's home life wasn't that great, so in the end, the cops said he had run away and that he'd eventually resurface. He was eighteen, so they said that if he ran away, they couldn't force him to come home anyway.

Everyone eventually stopped looking for him. Everyone but Sara.

"Katie?" Ali waved her hand in front of my face. "Hey, Katie, you zoned out there for a minute."

"Sorry, it's just... remembering that day we all searched for him. I can't imagine that one of us would mess with that stupid board to bring this all up again. Poor Sara."

"I don't think anyone pushed it. Everyone was pretty freaked out."

"So, you really think it was Dylan's ghost?" I scoffed. We'd been pretending like we could talk to the dead and cast spells since we were twelve, but I never really believed it. "I bet it was Jess. She was the one to ask the question, and she's always been jealous of me."

"What would she gain by accusing you of keeping secrets?"

"I don't know. Maybe she doesn't want Sara hanging out with me anymore."

"That seems pretty petty. Even for her."

"Maybe, but do you really think it was Dylan?"

She didn't say anything, but I saw the truth in her eyes. She really believed it was him.

"Whatever. I'm going back to bed." It was only noon, but I was exhausted, and I didn't have any classes today. After applying a few bandages to my legs, I crawled back into bed.

My sleep was plagued by images of Dylan. The way his eyes rolled into the back of his head. His weight as I dragged him to his car. Everything came flooding back in my dreams.

Then, Derek showed up. Derek was a regular in my dreams but he was typically half-naked. This time, his arms wrapped around me so tight I could hardly breathe.

"I know, Kit Kat. I know what happened," he breathed in my ear.

"H-how?"

"Kit Kat, I thought you were smarter than this." He smiled and spun me around in his arms. "I remember that night under the bleachers as clearly as you do."

My heart froze. I tried to pull out of his grasp, but his arms tightened around me, squeezing me like a vise.

"Dylan didn't OD." He leaned down, kissing my neck. "He drowned."

My throat burned from screaming when I bolted out of bed. My door slammed open, and Ali came running in.

"What the hell?" she asked.

"S-sorry... nightmare." I leaned back against the wall, my whole body shaking. "It's fine. Go back to what you were doing."

"You sure?"

"Yeah, it was just a dream," I lied, but she left, closing the door behind her. It was just a dream. I repeated this mantra in my head trying to convince myself. Derek was my adult African-American neighbor, and Dylan was my Caucasian high school crush. But Dylan was dead. *Wasn't he?*

I hugged my knees to my chest and let the tears fall.

He was dead.

I *killed* Dylan.

It was my fault.

Everything fled from me, ripping my soul from my body. I sat there and cried silently for what felt like hours.

A soft knock on my door finally stifled my tears.

"Yes?" I called.

"Can you come out here, Katie? We need to talk to you," Ali said.

We? Who the hell was out there? I threw the covers off me and crawled out of bed. When I stepped into the living room, my four childhood friends all stood there waiting for me. "What is this?" I asked.

"Please, sit. We need to talk," Ali said before she sat at the coffee table. The rest followed, and I only now saw the Ouija board sitting on the table.

"About what?" I made no move to join them. My heart beat so loud in my ears I feared they'd hear it.

"Will you just come over here, please?"

Reluctantly, I moved to join them but sat on the edge of the couch instead of on the floor.

"What is going on?" Ali asked.

"I've told you. Nothing." I crossed my arms.

"Then, what's with the nightmares, and the phantom guy, and the blood?" Ali asked.

Neither Jess, Amanda, nor Sara's expressions changed at her words.

I stood. "You told them?"

"I had to! You're scaring me." Ali looked at me with wide eyes.

"I can't believe this shit! What the hell are you saying?" I bit the inside of my cheek so hard I tasted blood.

"You're hiding something." Anger replaced fear in Ali's face.

"What are you accusing me of?" Tears burned my eyes.

"You know what happened to Dylan!" Sara shouted.

"I... I... what?"

"You know, don't you?" She stood, glaring at me.

My heart jumped to my throat. "You're all fucking crazy!"

"Then, tell us what's going on."

"I don't have to explain anything to you!" I stomped off to my room, throwing on sweats and shoes before heading back to the living room.

"Don't you dare walk away from us. You need to tell us!" Jess said.

"I don't know what you're talking about, and I'm not about to stand here and get yelled at in my own home!" I pushed past them and out the door.

The cool evening air sent a chill down my spine, but I kept walking. I needed to put some distance between us. My feet found the walking trail before my brain registered where I was going.

"I can't believe they all came at me like that. I mean, they're right, but still..." I paced on the path. "How do they know?"

"I might have an answer for that." Derek's dark form strode up next to me.

"No, you can't be here. You're not real," I choked on my words.

"I'm as real as you are."

"No!" I ran. My heart pounded in my throat.

He didn't need to run to keep pace with me. He was just there.

"Go away!" I covered my ears, trying to block his voice out.

"Hear me out."

I stopped running to catch my breath. "What?" I gasped.

"Tell them the truth, and I'll go away," he said.

"What? You want me to admit to pushing Dylan's car in the river with him in it?" I laughed out loud.

"Haven't you figured out who I am yet?"

I stared at him.

"I *am* Dylan." His dark skin melted into a muddy beige and his eyes flashed a bright blue before liquidating, leaving hollow husks in their wake.

I ran faster than I ever had. He couldn't be Dylan. Derek was a solid person. *Wasn't he?* I had touched him. His lips had been on mine. The orgasm he'd given me was real. *Derek's real.* I repeated that over and over in my head as I ran, trying to convince myself.

My feet didn't stop until the path ended.

The rushing water froze my veins. A tall concrete wall ended just feet above ground level holding the river at bay.

My heart stopped beating, watching the river flow before me. The car hadn't sunk right away like in the movies, and I stood there, watching, unaware of what was happening inside it. Until now.

Images of what really happened that night hit me hard, bringing me to my knees. A drugged out Dylan waking up when the water hit his skin flashed before me. The panic in his eyes turned my stomach.

He struggled to get the seatbelt off, but it wouldn't budge. His hands fumbled around the car, looking for something sharp to cut it, but he came up empty. The water rushed in, pressing against his chest. The car shifted and jolted forward, plunging the car into the water that started filling the cabin. Panic constricted his breathing, leaving him gasping for air.

Pulling and yanking on the belt only tightened its hold on him. Water reached his neck. He stretched and lifted his head, sucking in the last of the oxygen on the roof of the car as the water overtook him, covering his body. His eyes went wide as he held his breath, praying for someone to rescue him.

But there was no escape. I knew he would die there, and I now knew it was my fault.

He clawed at his throat, desperate for the air he would never reach. When he couldn't hold on any longer, he gasped in the water. The more he struggled, the more water poured into his lungs.

He breathed in the river until he breathed no more.

I stared at his lifeless body for a long time before the images vanished and I was left standing beside the very river where Dylan had drowned.

"I... I'm sorry, Dylan," I whispered.

"I've waited three long years to hear you say that." Derek... No, Dylan said just before he grabbed me by the hips and pulled me back to him. "God, Kit Kat, how I have missed you." His perfect lips nuzzled into my neck, and I let myself pretend for just a moment he was really here but didn't dare turn around to confirm that.

"I missed you too," I said.

"But now we can be together forever."

A chill ran down my spine just moments before his strong hands shoved me hard. I lost my balance and stumbled forward, tumbling head over heels into the river. My arms flailed around, trying to keep afloat as the waves pounded against me. The concrete wall stood between me and safety, and I knew there'd be no way I could climb it.

"Help!" I screamed, but no one would hear me over the sounds of the rushing water.

My eyes scanned the area, praying for something to hold on to or some way to reach the shore. No debris floated by, and only the smooth concrete walls surrounded the shore.

A shadowy figure emerged just above the wall.

"Help!" I yelled.

Through the haze of the water splashing around me, the figure simply stood there, watching me.

"Help me!" I called out to them again, but the person remained silent.

Why weren't they moving? Why were they just standing there?

"Please!" I kicked and waved my arms, struggling to stay afloat.

The shadow knelt, and Derek's brown face came into focus. My heart jumped to my throat as I pushed away.

"No," I cried.

"There is no one to hear your cries just as there was no one to hear mine."

My stomach sank as something brushed my ankle and latched on, yanking me down. I gulped in a breath just before I slid under water.

He appeared beside me in the water. "Oh, Kit Kat. I would have made this easier if you had just confessed." His dark bald head changed to that of Dylan's tanned blond head as he pulled me closer, gripping on tight. "Just breathe it in. It will hurt less."

I shook my head and tried to kick out of his hold. My lungs screamed for air, but I couldn't break free.

Please, I begged the universe, wishing for anyone to save me. *I thought you OD'd, Dylan, really I did. Please don't let me die!*

But no one would save me, just as no one had saved him.

I closed my eyes and breathed. Gulping in a lungful of water soothed the ache in my chest. I breathed in more until the pain stopped.

About the Author

Kari Robins has always preferred the written word to the spoken word. She has been writing flash fiction since she was in middle school when she would write stories instead of taking notes in class. A high school teacher encouraged her to become a writer but feared her grammar wasn't good enough. But now she pays an editor for that! She graduated from college in 2019 to become a teacher for Technology and Engineering, but the COVID-19 pandemic changed her plans, and she started writing again.

She released her first paranormal fantasy romance, The Rise of the Vördur, in 2021. Its duet book, The Battle for Yggdrasil, was released in 2023 as well as her first dark fantasy romance, Scarlet. The next two books are set to release in early 2024. The Twisted Tales of Halloween Horror is her first venture into the horror and short story genre. She is also working on a fantasy series where each book follows a different character, but they are all fighting the same enemy. She is really excited about this new series and hopes to have the first one out sometime in the summer of 2024.

If you enjoyed this story follow her on TikTok @kari.robins.writes or check out her website (KariRobins.com) and newsletters for special offers.

NEVER RUN OUT OF CANDY

SARA CLEMENTINA

Samhain

Samhain is an ancient Celtic festival marking the beginning of winter. The boundary between worlds thinned, and the Aos Si, or spirits or fairies, can enter through the sidhe, or fairy mounds. In order to not offend the Aos Si, people left out food and drink. Soul cakes were initially used to appease the spirits. Later, mumming or souling was common during the festival as people dressed in costume and went door to door singing songs or reciting verse. Soul cakes were given as payment for the entertainment and thought to be the origin of modern trick-or-treating.

Fiona," John calls over the racket, trying to get my attention from the other side of the porch. Between the heat, the birds, and my deep desire to shoo John and the kids out of the house, it's hard to focus. The rosé is already chilling in the fridge, and all I have to do is hand out a little candy. I might finally be able to read a chapter in my book.

"Are you sure you don't want to come with us?" he asks, raising his voice above the din of crows. Sitting in rows along the power lines, they fidget and shift, trying to keep their balance in between urgent and perfectly timed screams. They've been here all day. "It isn't the end of the world if we don't hand out candy."

"I don't know, it might be. The Jacobsons got egged last year when they went to Cabo," I reply. I'm not really worried about that, but Mommy needs a little alone time. The idea of tromping around the neighborhood in this stifling heat, the streets filled with candy-crazed kids, is not appealing. Plus, I already stocked up at Costco.

"Do you think you have enough candy?" he asks, helping Sophie put on her fairy wings for the third time. She wriggles out of them again and kicks off her shoes. John sighs.

"I have three big bags, but please make sure you leave your phone on, just in case," I say a little too loudly. I look up at the menacing chorus. I've seen crows around the neighborhood, but never like this, never this insistent. The rhythmic caws are rough and abrasive, as though their vocal chords are made of sandpaper. They twist and turn in the wind, ruffling their ink black feathers, but never fly away. In fact, I think their numbers are growing. Maybe it's the strange weather we've been having. They're probably hot as balls like the rest of us and can't stop complaining.

Xander is already in the front yard wielding his cutlass, whacking at the bushes while trying to keep the hook from falling off his other hand.

"Not the roses, please," I call out. His velcro sneakers and the ragged bottoms of his pirate pantaloons are already covered in mud. It rained for a week straight and finally stopped today in time for trick-or-treating. But instead of a crisp and clear fall day in Los Angeles, we were treated to a muggy, once-in-a-century heat wave. Oppressive leaden skies, triple digit temps, and enough humidity to make a Florida summer seem dry. The brutal heat pushes its way into the house, pressing up against the air-conditioning in a war for real estate that the heat will win if I keep the door open much longer.

"Okay, call me if you want to switch places. You have to go. Maybe she can be a fairy that doesn't fly," I say, herding them off the porch. I hope he doesn't call. I need a break.

I shut the door against the oven-hot air and retreat into the coolness of the kitchen. Maybe I'll have a little bit of time to myself before the trick-or-treaters arrive. John left early, with daylight left to spare, hoping to get Sophie back for an early bedtime. She's a nightmare without a good night's sleep and only a bad dream when she gets her full eleven hours. The terrible threes, I laugh to myself.

I pour the rosé and have downed half the glass when the doorbell rings. A few tiny voices call out.

"Trick or treat!"

Fudgeballs. Even in my mind, I'm trying to practice not swearing. I need to leave my F-filled youth behind and grow up. I'm a gosh-darned mother of two, living in the suburbs and driving a white minivan for balls' sake. The rest of the wine will have to wait.

There's a steady stream of fairies, princesses, and superheroes. The sun sets and makes no contribution to cooling off the sticky air. It's so thick I think you might be able to swim through it. Every time I open the door, there is a blast of muggy swamp accompanied by the constant screeching from above. Why are their eyes so beady, and why are they always looking at me?

I consider putting out the candy bowl so I can hide in the house, read my book, and drink my wine. John and the kids should be back soon. Despite my earlier desperation to get them out of the house, I'm already missing them. Xander's ongoing soliloquies about dinosaurs, Sophie's still-pudgy baby body snuggling up against me, and the way John makes me laugh.

Maybe I should join them for the last half hour. It isn't that big a deal if I miss handing out a few more chocolate minis, right? My pits are sweaty, and I'm a little light headed. Too much wine and not enough water. Despite the humidity, the heat is sucking out not only all my water, but the marrow from my bones. I need to hydrate. I head to the kitchen to get some ice water, but the doorbell rings again before I can make it.

"Trick or treat," a deep gruff male voice calls.

I open the door and suck in a little gasp. A mountain of meat and muscle dressed in some sort of viking costume stands on my porch. There is an inordinate amount of aged leather and antique brass studs. He wears a terrifying mask that completely obscures his face. It's black and red with deep polished obsidian eyeballs that, despite a lack of iris or white, seems to stare at me, hungry. A huge stylized hook nose arches over an open-mouth grin filled with tiny pointed teeth. They are polished with some shiny material that makes them appear wet, like real drool is covering them.

He takes a step closer and is now standing right on my doormat. Doesn't he know the etiquette? And where is his kid? We get the occasional adult trick-or-treater who puts out their own bag along with their children and more than a few teenagers. But a grown man in a grotesque mask? We stare at one another, neither able to end this tête-à-tête. He leans in a little closer, an almost imperceptible movement, and holds out a dirty pillowcase.

My heart pounds, and my stomach clenches. My eyes dart to the street, seeing who else is around, but it's maddeningly empty. The only sounds are the loud buzz from the street light, which blinks overhead, the yellow light hazy in the still thick, wet air, and the incessant cawing of those darned crows. Why are they still cawing? It's already dark. I don't know anything about birds, but don't they shut the farts up after dark? Bright blue electricity crackles along the power lines, but the crows don't seem to care. They stay stubbornly fixed to the buzzing wires, staring at me with tar black eyes, eerily similar to the beast's mask.

The man looms above me, standing way too close. I instinctively take a step back. He thrusts his pillow case out farther, clutching it with dirty nails, sharpened to points. He waits expectantly, the grimy gray fabric of the sack inches from my body. It is limp, and holds no candy. Maybe I'm his first stop? I frantically scan the street again. Who will hear me if I scream? Finally, I grab a handful of candy and stuff it into his case.

My heart pumps too much blood through my veins while I wait to see what he is going to do. *Take your candy and go, dude!* Thankfully, he nods and turns to leave. I let out a breath and hurry to close the door. Once there is solid wood between me and him, I look through the peephole and watch him walk down the mud stained path. Too many kids have been cutting across the lawn. The whole city is a muddy swamp after so much rain.

My heart still races. I hit the *John Mobile* icon on my phone and try to breathe along with the rings. Five deep breaths before it goes to voicemail.

"It's John, leave a message."

Fudge on a biscuit. I let out a little shriek of frustration. He always does this. Why have a phone if you never freaking answer it? I need to calm down, I need to get that water, and maybe just a little more wine. I take three steps towards the kitchen before the doorbell rings again. *Carbonated crap in a can.*

"Trick or treat!"

Another deep voice. Do I open the door? I'm probably overreacting. People have all kinds of reasons they trick-or-treat. I shouldn't be so judgy... or terrified. He didn't do anything. He took his candy and got the duck off my porch. But is it the same person back again, only a few minutes later? Maybe he's back to rape and pillage now that he knows I'm home alone. I peer through the peep-hole.

Another mask, equally horrible. This one is smoky gray with rolls of fat and huge polished round cheeks. The mouth is full of rotting jagged teeth, a mix of yellow and brown set into putrid black gums. The beady bloodshot eyes move back and forth. How is it doing that? Is it motorized? Or is it not a mask, but some elaborate special effects makeup? Or could it not be make-up or a mask at all? Maybe there really are monsters or demons, and I've been lucky enough to never see one. At least, not until now.

"Trick or treat," he demands.

I'm being ridiculous. A judgy, uncompassionate, snobby, nervous mother truckin' Nellie. Sure, those masks are really gross, and they seem inappropriate to be wearing with so many children around, but I should be more understanding. I remind myself I can't control people, only my reaction. Committed to a more generous heart, I slowly open the door. I smile awkwardly and hand him a few pieces of candy. Like the other man, he nods and turns to go.

Relieved, I run to the kitchen to finally get my ice water before that duckin' doorbell rings again. I'm worried I might faint. Who knew tending to the trick-or-treaters would be so taxing? Granted, I might have aged myself a few extra years by freaking out about those weirdos. Sorry, unusual gentlemen. I should try and be my best self. It's what every mother should do, right?

There is a faint whiff of rotting food in the kitchen, but I don't have time to investigate. The garbage probably needs to go out. I fill a glass with ice and water from the fridge dispenser and suck it down in one long gulp. It tastes like a moldy cooler or like freezer-burned vegetables. Maybe something is wrong with the ice maker. I add it to the mental list of things to investigate later. The doorbell rings again.

The river of children and their families continues. I can't stop thinking about those masks. I decide they have to be masks, any other alternative doesn't mesh with the reality I am determined to stay grounded within. Maybe they were teenage boys playing a prank? I don't really get it, but maybe it's for TikTok or YouTube or whatever the cool kids are doing these days. I shrug off my earlier fear as heatstroke and vow to stay more hydrated.

I'm running low on candy. I try John again. No answer. He does this all the time. It annoys me all the time. Why can't he pick up the ever lovin' phone? Why aren't they back? Has something happened? I hear a siren in the distance, barely audible over the constant chorus of caws. Should I be worried? I send a curt text. A few more children arrive, and I hand out the last of the candy.

Before I have a chance to close the door and turn off the porch light, a trio emerges out of the darkness. The crows let out one last shriek and, in unison, close their clapping beaks. Finally, I think, but my relief is short lived.

I ignore the smaller figures as my eyes dart to the towering man, the red mask with the sharp teeth and hooked nose. The glassy black eyes peer down at me. I force myself not to say *You again*, but that's all that races through my mind.

"Sorry, we-we've just ran out," I stutter, staring up at the mask.

"You ran out of candy?" a bright and sweet voice with a thick Irish accent asks.

The man recedes in my vision as a golden spotlight appears over the speaker. I know it's only my porch light, but she's illuminated with an otherworldly glow. Her glossy red lips press together into a forced smile. Her porcelain skin is flawless, the color a uniform alabaster except for a smudge of smoky lavender around her eyes. Her eyes—I can't look away. They draw me in, making me forget the heat, and the candy, and the enormous masked man looming above us. Her eyes are a piercing green, the color too vivid, like wild clover or fresh cut grass in the sunshine. She has thick copper hair pulled up into an elaborate hairdo woven with burgundy flowers, twigs, and tiny delicate vines that trail down her back and frame her face.

She wears an emerald green velvet fitted corset bustier with intricate botanical embroidery. Her skirt is short and flared, made of some light and gauzy material. Forest green leather braces lace up her calves and forearms. It looks like a costume from a movie set.

"That's quite a costume," I say, not sure why she isn't leaving. There's no sugar left to be had from this house. *Time to move along, lady, and take that mound of flesh with you, please.*

She smiles. Her teeth are tiny and shaved into points. They are arctic white, almost translucent, set against diseased gums mottled a grotesque yellow and black. It has to be some type of special effects make-up, but it doesn't look like a prosthetic. It looks real.

I turn away from the teeth, and the little girl catches my attention. She mirrors her mother's hideous grin. Thankfully, her tiny pointed teeth are set into healthy pink gums. She shares her mother's otherworldly beauty, the large wide-set eyes, the flawless china doll skin, and rosy red lips, although hers aren't painted that color. The child is familiar somehow, and I look again at the mother who still stands there staring, waiting. She looks oddly familiar too.

"Do I know you?" I say stupidly. Somehow, despite being an O'Brian neé MacDougal, I have never met an actual Irish person.

"Do ya?" she says and lets out a tinkling laugh. "Beautiful family you've got there, love. Are they all out trick-or-treatin'?" She nods over my shoulder to the family portrait that hangs over the entry way table. I breathe a sigh of relief that the layout of our house doesn't let someone at the front door see the rest of the way in. I don't know why, but I don't want this woman knowing what the inside of my house looks like.

"Yup," I say, instinctively turning to look at the portrait. We're all dressed up in our fanciest clothes. Xander is four, and Sophie is only five months old. We're sitting on top of a grassy knoll in a nearby park. Xander calls it the fairy hill because of the time we found a mushroom ring around the top. The sun is shining through the trees, casting dappled light behind us. I love that portrait. By some magic of the universe, we were all smiling and looking at the camera, even the baby.

"Are ye Irish as well, love, or is tha' just yer husband's family? The O'Brians, right?"

How does she know? But then I remember the gaudy mailbox John insisted on, with its ridiculous four leaf clovers and a rainbow, and *The O'Brians* in big green cursive blazoned on the side.

"Yes, I was born a MacDougal actually, but it's been a long time since any MacDougal, or O'Brian for that matter, has lived in Ireland."

"Aye, but ye should know yer roots, love. Know the stories from the ol' country. Even if ye don't live there anymore. Like tonight, yer should know of Samhain, and the mummers begging fer cakes of the soul. Too many people lose the old ways. It's amazin' what can be lost in a generation, never mind ten or fifty. It's a real shame," she sighs wistfully, as her clover eyes stare into my own. "A real shame."

What on God's green earth is this woman talking about? Why won't she leave?

"Yeah, well, like I said, I'm so sorry, but we just ran out of candy. John is on his way home, though, and he's bringing more," I lie and start closing the door, hoping she gets the hint this time.

She cocks her head to the side and frowns. I remember now who she reminds me of. It's Alison from the preschool co-op. But Alison isn't Irish, and she isn't as beautiful, and she doesn't have those clover eyes. Plus she has a son, not a daughter. I look down at the girl again.

Alison's child is not as achingly beautiful, and he's a boy. But I suppose this child could be a boy. Dressed like a tiny woodland sprite with long luxurious curls, I had assumed. But these days, maybe I shouldn't. All this kid has done is stand there and blink her big green eyes. She is very unlike the boy whose name I can't remember, who runs around like a banshee and bites people sometimes. I feel bad, but Alison has asked for a play date a few times.

I've always found a way to say no. You can't mess around with biters, raising a toddler has enough challenges.

"Okay, maybe we'll swing by later," the woman says, startling me out of my thoughts. What an odd thing to say. Why would she care? Why would she come back? There are a million other houses giving out mountains of sugar. Why does she need my candy?

"Okay, he should be back real soon," I say dumbly, closing the door a little more.

"Oh by the way, love, I think some kids have gotten into some mischief with yer mailbox," she says and turns to go. They seem to float down the path while the huge man lumbers after them. The crows begin their cacophony with renewed vigor. They caw and caw, and the electricity buzzes in the humid air.

I wait a few more beats to make sure they are well and truly gone before walking down the path to see the mailbox. The post is askew, the door hangs open, barely attached by one remaining hinge. The top is smashed in. What appear to be claw marks are scraped into the wood where our name used to be. *The O'Brians* have been obliterated, only a mess of green flecks and deep gouges remain. The crows let out a wet, gurgling cry, followed by a long drawn out caw of a different and more desperate pitch. *What the fudge is Samhain?*

I shut off all the lights except the one reading lamp in the back sunroom. I curl up on the couch and start to Google. The words accumulate in my brain as I open tab after tab. I burrow deep into this rabbit hole.

Samhain, the fae, malevolent beings, supernatural powers, grudge holders, shapeshifters, mummers, soul cakes, Celtic pagan rituals, faerie mounds in which you should never trespass. The more I read, the more a hot fiery itch creeps up my neck. My skin is wet with perspiration, my underarms, hot and clammy with a sour sweat made from fear, not exertion.

Could that woman be a faerie? Did we inadvertently trespass on her mound? Maybe Xander was right, and our photo shoot desecrated her holy place. I picked the spot, and I think I might have changed Sophie's diaper up there. Is it possible that Alison from preschool is a grudge-holding faerie queen who's mad because I snubbed her offers for a playdate? Then, she gave me a chance to make it up to her on Samhain, but I ran out of sweets. What is going to happen if she comes back and I still don't have any candy?

I frantically look up a recipe for soul cakes. Maybe I can whip something up to appease her before she comes back. Who am I kidding? How can I measure anything in grams? I don't regularly stock sultanas. My pulse spikes until I read a little further. They're just raisins. I need to calm the fudge down. I'm overreacting.

I check my phone—no word from John. I take a deep breath and try to convince myself I'm letting the internet get the best of my common sense. This is twenty-first century Los Angeles, not ye ol' timey times of yore in ye ol' Ireland. She's just some weird lady who really likes Halloween. As for Alison from preschool, maybe I should give her a chance. But is it fair to Sophie to subject her to a biter? I'll have to circle back to that one.

The lamp flickers and buzzes. It's a miracle there hasn't already been a power outage. Why is it so darn hot in here? I'm burning up. I've been so worried about the evil faerie queen, I forgot all about how strange it is that John won't answer the phone. Sophie is late for bedtime. I try him again. Voicemail. *Duck, duck, duck!*

This heat is making me crazy. I need more water, even if it tastes like balls, and maybe something to eat too. I can't seem to shake this dizziness, the feeling like I might faint at any moment. I head to the kitchen. The smell is stronger now, and it's definitely coming from the fridge.

I open the door and hot putrid air hits me in the face. All the food is rotted beyond anything that could have happened in the last few hours. The strawberries are covered in thick gray fuzz. The eggs have exploded in their fancy clear case, a putrid yellow slime drips from the container. The milk carton has been ripped open and clotted clumps of rotting cheese spill out over the edge. The ground turkey I bought yesterday is slimy and an iridescent green, like the inside of an abalone shell. When a fat wax-white pus filled maggot crawls out of the meat. I gag and slam the door closed. *WTF*. She must be really mad about me running out of soul cakes.

There is no way. Even if the fridge lost power this morning, the food would not have gone bad that fast. In desperation I send more texts to John.

CALL ME
CALL ME
CALL ME
CALL ME

The phone stays ominously silent. No frickin' answer. I shriek in frustration. I go back to the sunroom to turn out the light. I'm taking matters into my own hands. I'll walk around the neighborhood until I can find John myself. Is it too soon to call the police?

Before I reach the lamp, it flickers again, emits a few blue sparks, and goes out. It takes my eyes a moment to adjust. I can see outside the panoramic windows now. The neighbors still have power. Between the light pollution in LA and the full moon, the backyard is lit in a gloomy dim light. A shadowy figure moves towards the window, its gray face, or rather its mask, familiar.

All the things happen in my body all at once. My heart rate triples, my stomach twists into a tangle of knots, I choke back the contents threatening to erupt from my mouth, and I clench my bowels, trying to prevent myself from having an accident right there on the den floor.

I go to call 911, but the screen is dark. I frantically press the power button, but nothing happens. The battery is dead. I press it again. Nothing. I curse John and myself for not keeping the landline.

Before I have a chance to turn and run for the neighbors', the mask appears in the window. The gray one with the rotted teeth and the bulbous cheeks. I swear the lips stretch into a grin as he lifts a finger and taps gently on the glass.

"Trick or treat—"

I scream and turn to run for the front door. Another masked figure appears in the next window, and the next, and the next. Green, yellow, purple—a rainbow of horror fills every window. The faerie queen's entourage.

I scream all the way to my front door and skid to a halt. Through a blur of tears, I force myself to peer through the peephole to make sure the coast is clear. The biggest and meatiest of them all, the red and black mask with hooked nose and sharp teeth is peering back.

"Trick or treat," he growls.

I run to the bathroom and slam the door, shoving my finger into the button to lock it. The window in here is small and frosted, but I can see movement outside, the shadow of a mask scratching against the glass.

I bury my face in my hands and scream again, hoping my neighbors will hear me. How can they not notice my house being surrounded by crazy people in scary masks? Where the hell is John?

I collapse on the floor and let the tears flow. Eventually, my screams ebb into sobs and then into hiccupping whimpers. The quiet scrape of the mask against the window continues, but it is soft, almost rhythmic. Maybe that's just the wind. The squawk of crows is faint in the distance. I take a few deep breaths. They aren't breaking in, so maybe they've already left? My head is still buried in my hands, and I refuse to look at the window. John will be home soon. I will see my babies again. It will all be alright. Everything has to be alright.

With the AC out, the room gets hotter and hotter. The humidity steadily increases until the whole room feels like the air from a freshly run dishwasher. The crows continue to caw. Was I really that mean to Alison? How can she expect me to have candy when she comes back if she has the house surrounded by her minions?

The smell is the harbinger of the awfulness that is about to invade my bathroom. It's earthy and foul, mildewy and rotted, and fetid with hints of algae, and the sea, and a whole lot of shit. I stand up to see thick viscous mud and poo begin to bubble out of the toilet. I try the flusher, but nothing happens. The ooze continues to rise. Then, it starts bubbling out of the sink drain and the shower. As the bowl continues to fill, I stare horror-struck by something moving in the muck. Something is wriggling. A pink earthworm flails out the top of the rising sludge reaching for the safety of the rim. Soon the entire bowl is filled with a writhing tangle of worms trying to escape.

Worms, I cannot do worms. I can't stop my brain from imagining them on me, wriggling. Their horrid pink bodies inch across my skin, leaving their trails of filth and mud. They crawl into me, invading me, until I am covered with worms, inside and out. My body rots as rapidly as the food in the refrigerator. With super speed, the worms transform me from a living breathing woman to dark fragrant soil in a matter of seconds. Why the freak is my brain making this worse? I scream again and run from the room.

I need to get to my son's room. I can hide in his loft bed. There is no window there and no rising tide of mud and worms. I pass through the kitchen, trying not to look at the mask pressed against the glass. Bone white with worms crawling out of the eyes and nose. Could that be right? Was he the one in that window before?

There is a loud and long creak followed by an ear splitting crack. The wood floor splinters and splits, like a natural disaster movie of an earthquake, but the ground isn't shaking. The chasm opens wider, and there is a loud thud. I think I must have done something even worse than refuse a playdate and run out of candy. The faerie queen is out for blood.

One end of the kitchen island sinks into the hole. The empty candy bowl, the day's mail, and my wine glass tumble down the inclined plane of marble. A few seconds later, the other end falls and the whole island disappears under the house.

I'm afraid to get closer, but I can't stop myself. The curiosity of what's in the hole is too great. There is the rush of flowing water, and the house continues to creak and groan and crack. I move a little closer and crane my neck. I can see the top of the island and a rush of mud flowing around it. Then, comes the exodus, the proverbial rats scurrying from the sinking ship. But there is no ship, only a gaping hole in the floor of my kitchen, and thank God for small miracles, only one rat.

But then that lone rat is followed by a horde of beetles. Their shiny black bodies catch the light from my outdoor visitors, who vigilantly stay watching the scene unfold. Their multitude of tiny segmented legs clack and tap on the floor as they spread out into the house. I have a moment of relief. I don't know why worms send me into convulsions, but the beetles, while creepy, aren't terrifying. I take a few tentative steps closer to the yawning maw of the hole in my floor, too curious as to what might follow the beetle army.

When the snake slithers out of the hole, I freeze. Snakes are worm adjacent. In a Venn diagram of the two, their center overlapping ellipse is large: legless, disgusting, slithering, wriggling, awful, and in a perfect world, something that should never, ever, ever be in my house. The terrified part of my brain screams, *This is your cue to leave, bitch—RUN.* And then there is my body, buzzing and swimming with adrenaline, but it can't or won't move. Transfixed, I watch the snake slither towards me, its scales gleaming blue in the faint light. Its fork tongue darts in and out of its mouth. Its beady black eyes fix upon mine, black and glossy and wet, like crows, like masks, like the end of everything. The snake is only a few feet away before I get my body to cooperate. Too terrified to scream, I run for the loft bed and fly up the ladder.

Snakes cannot climb ladders. The men are staying outside. Worms cannot climb ladders. Maggots cannot open refrigerator doors. This has to be a dream. John and the kids will be home soon. John and the kids will be home soon. John and the kids will be home soon. I say it over and over again as I soak Xander's pillow with tears.

I don't know how long I cry, huddled in the fetal position, sobbing into the pillow. There is another ear splitting crack, groan, bang, boom, all rolled into one cacophonous sound. I cover my ears, and by the time I realize the sound has stopped, it's replaced with the loud cawing of crows. A light rain is falling, and I am getting wet. Why am I getting wet in my house? I roll over and see a gaping hole in the roof. Rain mixed with clumps of dust from the attic crawl space splat down on me in heavy, soggy clumps.

I sit up, and before I have a chance to stand up and climb out through the attic onto the roof, the house cracks and groans again. A beam falls, and the loft bed collapses. In a tumble of falling debris and dust and rain, my leg is pinned under something heavy. Pain erupts in my leg, radiating out from the impact into every nerve and cell. I barely have time to process the hurt or figure out how to extricate myself before there is a whoosh of wings and the sharp stab of a beak on my cheek. I flail my arms, trying to bat away the attack of crows. Between the rain and the feathers and the sharp stabs at my flesh, I lose all sense of time and place. I live in the moment of fending off the birds, unsure if it is only a few seconds or an entire lifetime.

"Caw, caw-andy, caw, caw-andy," the crows scream.

It's the last thing I remember before I move to a place that is not here. Not this earth, not this realm, not this dimension, and not this time. It is dark and quiet, and there is a knowing. A knowing that I have done wrong in the world, both intentionally and by my own ignorance. I have violated the old ways. The ways of my ancestors, my people. While it is quiet and dark, it is not reassuring. There is no peace here. There is a desperation in this place. The knowing is filled with time ticking away. A time in which I must make amends, and I will. I have learned my lesson. I am determined to make things right. If I don't, the knowing place will claim me, and I will never escape.

When I return back to my own dimension, it's still raining, but mercifully the crows are gone. There is a roar I can't identify, and a figure descending from the raining hot heavens. I don't know what is real anymore. How is he floating down to me?

I scream out to anyone who will listen, "I have to put out the candy."

My neck is immobilized in one of those braces you see on ER shows, and a helicopter roars overhead. Someone is strapping me to a board. He's attached to a rope and suspended above the roof.

"I have to put out the candy," I tell him, struggling to free myself from his strong arms.

"Ma'am, I need you to calm down. I need to secure you to the board so they can lift you up," he yells over the rain and the spinning helicopter blades.

"There's a snake, maybe more than one, and beetles and worms, so many worms. And my strawberries, they're gray and fuzzy, and I have to put out the candy. I have to put out the candy!"

"Ma'am, you've been injured. We need to get you to the hospital."

"You don't understand," I scream and beat on his chest. "I have to put out the candy. She said she'd swing by later."

"Ma'am, your house is being swallowed by a sinkhole. We have to go now," he says in an *I'm not going to take any more of your crap, you crazy lady who is making my job a living hell tone.*

"Please," I whine, but all the fight has gone out of me. My leg hurts like hell, and all I want is to wake up from this nightmare. I blink through the tears and rain and look into his clover green eyes as the helicopter pulls us away from the collapsing house.

I only realize I have been slowly coming back into consciousness for a long time when my eyes finally blink open. I remember the shuffle of footsteps and the muffled voices and the cawing of crows. I remember the pain in my leg and the pressure on my chest and wrists. The hospital room is dim, lit only by a small fluorescent tube shining over a white board scribbled with patient information. My information. I try to sit up but am held firmly in place by a strap across my chest, another binding my head to the bed, and more holding my wrists in place. I struggle against the restraints, my heart racing. I have to get out of here.

It all comes rushing back. I scream for someone to let me out. My house, my precious family, the masks, the candy. I need to put out the bowl of candy. I don't know why, but it's important. I have to do it before it is too late.

"I have to put out the candy," I scream.

My eyes dart wildly around the room. I barely make out a dark figure sitting on the windowsill. It taps its beak on the glass.

Tap. Tap. Tap.

"Caw, caw-andy," it shrieks.

Desperate to escape, I struggle, but I can't get free. In my peripheral vision, I can just make out a red button near my finger. I push my hand forward, straining against the rough leather holding my wrist in place, and barely manage to press the button.

"I have to put out the candy," I call out.

The door creaks open. I strain my eyes, furious I can't turn my head. It's a nurse in pink scrubs, her ID badge hanging from a lanyard around her neck.

"Please help me," I whimper. "I need to put out the candy."

"Caw, caw-andy," the crow echos.

"You've run out of time, love. Samhain is already over."

The Irish brogue.

It has to be a coincidence. It has to be. Pink scrubs, no faerie queen costume. She has a lanyard, a lanyard for fucks' sake. But there is the cawing, and it smells like bad things, rotted things, things from deep inside the earth. It smells of that knowing place. I struggle against the leather, fighting hard to escape.

Her feet squeak as she makes her way across the polished vinyl floor. She is at my bedside now, but I can't turn my head to see her face. She leans closer, the smell of rot burning my nostrils. She moves into my field of vision and smiles, the pointed teeth glisten wet with saliva.

A crow, dark and oily, sits on her shoulder and screams, "Caw-andy!"

Her face inches closer, her breath moist and foul. Her clover green eyes bore into me. "You should never run out of candy, love."

About the Author

While buried under a mountain of yarn and fabric, Sara realized she needed a creative outlet that didn't take up so much space. Now she can craft entire worlds that fit on your Kindle. She loves writing in almost every genre, but is currently working on an epic sci-fi romance series that explores the collision between two very different worlds. You can find her first published story, GALS Gone Wild, in the anthology Professor Feiff's Compleat Pocket Guide to Xenobiology for the Galactic Traveller on the Move. Sara is obsessed with birdwatching and sometimes finds the time to work on her yarn stash. She lives in Los Angeles with her husband and 13 year old twins.

You can find out more about upcoming projects, and where to follow Sara at saraclementina.com

Thanks for reading Twisted Tales of Halloween Horror!

Please consider leaving a review on <u>Goodreads</u> or <u>Amazon</u>. Every review helps bring more visibility for new books. Keep reading for details about the other anthology available!

Did you enjoy Twisted Tales of Halloween Horror? Keep an eye out for a special second edition of our holiday horror anthology, Twisted Tales of Holiday Horror, *releasing just in time for the Christmas season. We Ho-Ho-Hope to scare you twice as badly this time.*

Like our art? Check out the limited first edition of Twisted Tales of Holiday Horror, *featuring an illustrated cover with easter eggs planted throughout. Can you find the corresponding item for each story?*

Find that first edition on Amazon here *and see the blurb on the next page!*

Twisted Tales of Holiday Horror

For those who like a little scary in their merry, Twisted Tales of Holiday Horror *is an anthology of short stories released by masters of horror, The Sisterhood of the Black Pen. Featuring 10 original works, this festive fright fest is filled with delightful twists on holiday favorites that are sure to make your hot chocolate turn cold.*

Where does the Christmas train really go?

Is Santa filled with good intentions?

What could go wrong when a Christmas wish comes true?

Avoid the mistletoe and beware of carolers. This isn't a book of bedtime stories... Follow us on a twisted adventure if you dare. We'll make sure you never look at the holidays the same way again.

About the Sisterhood of the Black Pen

The Sisterhood of the Black Pen is an organization started by two female authors determined to lead a group built for indie authors by indie authors. They have made it their mission to be a foundation for women and nonbinary people to utilize in order to gain some exposure in the publishing industry and hopefully begin to gather a readership following. Self-publishing can seem like an overwhelming thing for some, but taking a small first step can lead to a monumental journey.

What is the Sisterhood of the Black Pen?

The Sisterhood of the Black Pen strives to produce quality horror content from the greatest new female and nonbinary voices in indie horror. It is their goal to be a platform for new voices to be heard over the din by providing them with an incredible team of indie authors, editors, and designers who have collective years of experience and want to use what they've learned to help them be heard.

Who is the Sisterhood of the Black Pen?

Faye Knightly and Laurae Knight co-founded this group in 2021 when they became frustrated with the amazing talent in the indie publishing world going largely unpublished and unnoticed. It was time to do something unique. Something empowering. Something twisted. Far too often in the publishing industry, new authors—especially those who identify as women—hesitate to make the leap into the self-publishing world. They decided that they would be a foundation to reduce that leap to a casual skip—one that can easily be made with trusted friends and professionals at your side. Although there is an emphasis on helping new authors, the Sisterhood is proud to say their group also includes seasoned authors who are always happy to share their knowledge and experience. Follow the Sisterhood on Instagram, Facebook, and TikTok (@TheSisterhoodoftheBlackPen) where they make calls for submissions and strive to connect with new talented authors to guide through the publishing world.